War
and Peach

SUSAN FURLONG

BERKLEY PRIME CRIME
New York

BERKLEY PRIME CRIME
Published by Berkley
An imprint of Penguin Random House LLC
375 Hudson Street, New York, New York 10014

ISBN: 9780425278963

First Edition: February 2017

Printed in the United States of America
1 3 5 7 9 10 8 6 4 2

Cover art by Erika LeBarre
Cover design by Sarah Oberrender
Book design by Laura K. Corless
Map copyright © by Nurul Akmal Markani

This is a work of fiction. Names, characters, places, and incidents either are the product
of the author's imagination or are used fictitiously, and any resemblance to actual persons,
living or dead, business establishments, events, or locales is entirely coincidental.

PUBLISHER'S NOTE: The recipes contained in this book are to be followed exactly as
written. The publisher is not responsible for your specific health or allergy needs that may
require medical supervision. The publisher is not responsible for any adverse reactions to
the recipes contained in this book.

Praise for

Peaches and Scream

"Cozy readers will savor every word of this peach of a mystery. Ms. Furlong's turn of phrase is delightful, her characters are endearing and the mystery will keep readers guessing until the very end. The Georgia Peach Mysteries are loaded with Southern charm, sassy characters and tantalizing recipes—a pure delight!"
—Ellery Adams, *New York Times* bestselling author of the Charmed Pie Shoppe Mysteries

"Georgia belles can handle anything—including murder—as Susan Furlong proves in this sweet and juicy series debut."
—Sheila Connolly, *New York Times* bestselling author of the County Cork Mysteries

"This wonderful series is going to have you humming 'Georgia on My Mind' and have your mouth watering to try the five peach-inspired recipes included in the back of the book! This series has everything a cozy mystery lover could want: loyal family, fantastic friends, wonderful juicy story line and a dog called Roscoe."
—A Cup of Tea and a Cozy Mystery

"Susan Furlong really captures the heart of Southern traditions in her characters . . . [A] fantastic start to a new cozy mystery series . . . From the yummy-sounding recipes to the wonderful ambiance of Cays Mill, *Peaches and Scream* has it all!"
—Fresh Fiction

"Furlong kicks off this new series with a great mystery . . . Very entertaining."
—*RT Book Reviews*

Berkley Prime Crime titles by Susan Furlong

PEACHES AND SCREAM
REST IN PEACH
WAR AND PEACH

To Patrick Nyle Bolliger

My Southern mother's life is bound by rules. Rules she believes are key to raising strong, confident children who cherish tradition, know hard work, have good manners and, above all else, treasure family. For as long as I can remember, she's been doling out these regulations in hopes of turning me into not only a proper, polite and oh so polished woman, but a woman who's independent, strong and indestructible.

Over the years, depending on the situation, she's called these rules different things: Southern Belle Facts, Debutante Rules and even Southern Girl Secrets. Most of these little gems of advice are the same bits of advice mothers everywhere have handed down to their daughters. Of course, my mama always adds her own peculiar slant, but nonetheless, I've come to treasure her quirky tenets. I've also learned that no matter how far I travel from home, if I remember my mama's rules, I'll be okay. Because simply put, I've been blessed to be raised by a woman whose well-maintained exterior is only exceeded by her dogged determination and unsurpassable inner strength. And by passing on her special codes of living, she's taught me how to tackle life with just the right blend of toughness and kindness.

Mama has always told me that one day I'd thank her . . . and I do—every single day.

—NOLA MAE HARPER

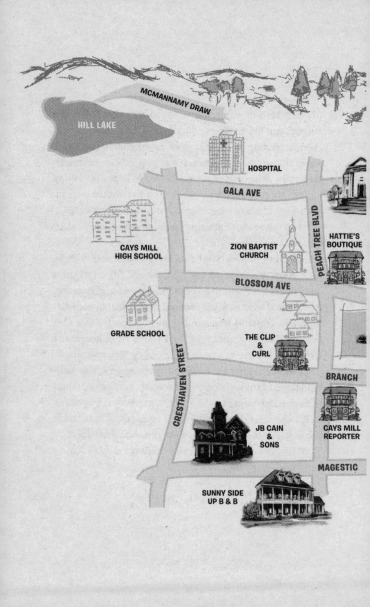

CAYS MILL, GEORGIA

HONKY TONK

TO THE HIGHWAY

CAYS MILL BANK & TRUST

WAKEFIELD LUMBER

PISTIL PETE'S FLOWER SHOP

SUGAR'S BAKERY

SHERIFF'S OFFICE

TOWN SQUARE

MERCANTILE

EARL'S BARBER SHOP

ORCHARD LANE

O'HENRY AVE

STREET

PEACHY KEEN

RED'S DINER

CHURCH

BLVD

JOE PUCKETT'S CABIN

HARPER PEACH FARM

Chapter 1

Southern Girl Secret #045: A Southern gal never starts a fight, but she sure the heck knows how to finish one.

"I do say, this election business has folks as divided as the states during Mr. Lincoln's war," one of the Crawford sisters was saying. I glanced from one gray-haired sibling to the other and stifled a chuckle. The Crawford sisters were old, but not *that* old. Although, I had to agree with them. Our little Georgia town was definitely divided.

"And did y'all read the latest issue of the *Cays Mill Reporter*?" her sister asked. "Seems the paper's predictin' an excitin' debate. You're going, aren't ya, Nola Mae?"

"Of course," I replied, putting on my best shopkeeper's smile as I passed their bag of peach preserves across the counter. "Wouldn't miss it for the world." When our esteemed mayor, Wade Marshall, announced his plans to leave his political office to launch a back-road bar tour with his blue-grass band the Peach Pickers, the political scene in Cays Mill exploded. In the aftermath, two candidates emerged: Clem Rogers, a local peach farmer who quickly won the support of the agricultural community, and Margie Price, owner of Sunny Side Up Bed & Breakfast, and the favorite contender of local business owners.

The sisters exchanged a sly glance before narrowing their eyes on me. "Town folks are wondering just which side you're on," said the older sister. "Sister here says that since you own this new shop and all, you'd be for Ms. Price. But I'm bettin' you're going to stand by your peach farmin' roots and cast your vote for Clem Rogers."

"Uh . . . well. I'm still undecided."

"Undecided?" they asked in unison. The younger sister clucked her tongue and shook her head. "What would your daddy say, if he heard you talkin' that way?"

Oh, I already knew what he'd say. I'd been hearing it all week. The election had been a point of controversy at our house. Daddy, of course, was all about supporting Clem Rogers, one of our own. Clem had rallied support among most of the local farmers by promising tax cuts for local peach producers. Unfortunately, he planned to engineer those cuts by raising municipal retail taxes. A prospect that business owners, like myself, worried might send shoppers to nearby Perry or down to Hawkinsville, maybe even up to Macon, to save a few bucks. Still, I was surprised by Daddy's vehement support of Clem Rogers. The two of them had a contentious history that went way back when. I'd never quite known what started their rivalry, but whatever it was, Clem Rogers had been a thorn in Daddy's side ever since. Still, Daddy was backing his candidacy and expected all the Harpers to follow suit. I just wasn't entirely convinced yet that Clem was the man for the job.

It was one thing to run a successful farm; another altogether to handle the politics of even a small town like Cays Mill.

The older sister tugged at her sweater and shook her head. "How anyone can vote for an outsider is beyond me. I'm castin' my vote for Clem. He may be ornery as an old bulldog, but least we know what we're gettin' with him."

"That's right, sister," the other agreed. "Ms. Price isn't one of us. How's she supposed to know our ways?"

A few years back, Margie Price, owner of the Sunny Side Up Bed & Breakfast, had moved from somewhere up North and bought a neglected, dilapidated antebellum home over on Majestic Boulevard. She'd spent over a year painstakingly restoring every inch of the three-story home to its original glory and was now running a successful inn. To me, she'd more than proven herself an asset to the community, but to many she'd always be considered an outsider— or, worse yet, a Yankee.

"Well, maybe someone with a fresh perspective would be a good thing for our town," I offered, struggling to maintain my smile. I knew what it was like to feel like an outsider. After more than a few youthful indiscretions, I had fled Cays Mill and embarked on a career as a humanitarian aid worker. My job took me to some of the most remote areas of the world and immersed me in cultures so different from my own southern roots that I often felt like an outsider. I'd felt that way again, more recently, upon my return to Cays Mill, as I struggled to reinsert myself into this tight little community. Sure, Cays Mill was a wonderful place to grow up, but the people here, my own family included, were so rooted in culture and tradition, they were sometimes slow to be accepting of others.

"What on earth are you talkin' about, Nola Mae?" the older sister asked. "Fresh ideas? Why, everything's been just fine the way it is. There's nothing around here that needs changin'."

"Could be," the other sister jumped in, "that all that traveling Nola's done has made her forget her roots and what's important."

I shook my head. "Now both of you know that's not true. I've always been grateful for my raising. I came back, didn't I?" I waved my hand through the air, taking in the expanse of my shop with its rustic country charm and displays of peachy products. "And I opened this place to help my family."

The sisters exchanged glances and nodded. "That's true, dear. But you've always been one of us. You understand how it is 'round here. Just like Clem Rogers does. Why, that boy's been livin' here his whole life."

"That's right. Livin' here his whole life," her sister echoed. "I was good friends with his grandmama, rest her soul. She made the best peach pie. Always said it's best to use yellow peaches. Not white peaches. The white ones are too sweet. Did you know that, Nola?"

I breathed a sigh of relief, glad the conversation had shifted from politics and my apparently inflammatory, too-worldly concept of "fresh perspectives" back to something neutral—peaches. "Yellow peaches, for sure," I nodded, recognizing a sales opportunity. "Which is why, being that it's November and all and since there aren't any fresh peaches available for pie, I put up some of the best canned spiced yellow peaches you'd ever want to taste." I came out from around the counter and directed their attention toward the far wall of shelves, which held several straight rows of bright yellow peaches in sparkling jars. "We always heat them and serve with a dollop of vanilla ice cream. My nana's recipe," I added in a conspiratorial whisper, which garnered an appreciative smile from the women.

"Then they must be good," the older sister said, reaching back into her bag for her pocketbook. "We'll take a couple of those, too. Then we better get going. We want to have time to get some supper before the town hall meeting tonight."

My focus quickly shifted out the front windows and across the street to the courthouse lawn, where I noticed a man unloading folding chairs from the Baptist church's minibus. They must have needed to borrow extra seating for the meeting. "Looks like it's going to be a big crowd," I said, ringing up and packaging their additional purchase. "Hopefully, people will remain civil tonight." I was referring to the last debate, held in conjunction with the Chamber of Commerce's monthly luncheon. After several rounds of heated bantering about who should carry the tax burden, the farmers or the business owners, Doris Whortlebe, the owner of the Clip & Curl Salon, got so mad she stood up and chucked a chicken leg across the room at Harley Corbin, who in retaliation slung a spoonful of potato salad her way, and on and on until a full-fledged food fight was underway. What a mess!

The oldest Crawford sister leaned across the counter, an unmistakably mischievous glimmer in her blue eyes. "Don't bet on it, Nola. Rumor has it that Clem Rogers is going to drop a bombshell tonight. Something that's goin' to change everyone's opinion about Ms. Price."

"Really?" *What could that be?* Margie was an honest businesswoman and always willing to lend a helping hand to those in need. I couldn't imagine what Clem would have to say that could possibly change everyone's opinion of such a wonderful person. "Who told you about this?" I asked.

The older sister dipped her chin my way. "Why, everyone in town is talking about it, dear. Supposedly it's something that has to do with Margie's past. She's from up North, ya know."

"And," the other sister added, "haven't you ever wondered what brought Ms. Price all the way down here in the first place? She doesn't have any kin in the area."

I shrugged. "I just assumed she'd stumbled upon a good business opportunity with the bed-and-breakfast."

The sisters harrumphed in unison. "Not likely," one of them said. "There's more to that woman than just business. And whatever this bombshell is, it's going to be big. Why, even Frances Simms said she thinks it's going to be big news. She's plannin' a special edition this week."

Now I did roll my eyes. Frances Simms was the editor of the *Cays Mill Reporter*, our town's one and only source for breaking gossip—oops, I mean news. Normally, the paper released every Tuesday and Saturday, but something really big might spur the printing of a special edition. Although, I only remember it happening one time before, and that was when Bobby Tindale picked the winning numbers for the Georgia Powerball lottery. Thanks to the *Cays Mill Reporter*, the news of his eleven-million-dollar win spread so fast the poor guy couldn't walk down the street without someone holding their palm out. Finally, he ended up packing it in and leaving town. I certainly hoped Frances would exercise more prudence this time around. Of course, Frances wasn't known for her prudence, a fact I'd learned the hard way: once when she published a series of innuendos that almost resulted in a lifelong prison term for my brother-in-law, and another time when she published a completely biased story that turned my good friend Ginny into an overnight social outcast. "You certainly don't believe everything you read in the newspaper, do you?" I countered. Especially not the *Cays Mill Reporter*.

The sisters exchanged a glance. "Well, of course we do," one of them said, giving me an incredulous stare. "It's the newspaper, after all." Then she turned to her sister. "Come along, sister. If we don't get home and get supper fixed, we'll miss that meetin'. And it's supposed to be the biggest barn burner this town's ever seen."

The enticing smell of Mama's cooking wafted through the screen door and greeted me as I mounted the steps of our front porch. As I did every evening, I paused and leaned against one of the posts, letting my eyes wander over our farm. Autumn was one of my favorite times of year. Summer was behind us, along with the hard labor and pressures of the harvest season, the fruit long ago packed and shipped. Then, late summer brought the Peach Harvest Festival, where we celebrated our successes, and oftentimes placated our losses, in the company of good neighbors and family. Now, in November things had finally settled down, the cooler night air bringing relief to the burdensome heat of summer and the heavy workload of the previous seasons. Of course, there was still a lot to be done: mowing, pruning and fertilizing, planting new trees, record keeping and strategizing for the next season, but for the most part, life on the farm had slowed to a manageable pace. A time to catch our breath and count our blessings.

Blessings were something I'd had plenty of lately. We'd enjoyed a bountiful harvest, punctuated by a surge in peach prices that resulted in enough to cover our operating costs, plus some to sock away for harder times. And my new shop, Peachy Keen, was experiencing success beyond my imagination. Not only had foot traffic picked up in the storefront, but online orders had almost doubled. With Christmas quickly approaching, I was hoping to see even more sales, especially with the addition of a new line of peachy gift baskets.

And to top it all off, my personal life was on the upswing. Just recently, my friend Hattie had asked me to be the maid of honor for her upcoming wedding to Pete Sanchez, love of her life and owner of Pistil Pete's Flower Shop. They were perfectly suited for each other and I was so happy for them! Best of all, my relationship with Hattie's brother, Cade, was blossoming. After working through a few minor hitches last spring, we had started seeing each other on a regular basis. With all the excitement over Hattie's wedding lately, I couldn't help but dream a little about the day Cade and I might . . . well, maybe I wasn't ready for all that. But I was happy. In fact, the past year or so since my return to Cays Mill had proven to be one of the best times in my life. Except for the murders, that is. I shuddered, squeezed my eyes shut, inhaled the smell of woodsmoke, probably a neighbor burning off his recent pruning, and exhaled the unpleasant memories of the murders that had occurred over the past year, one right here on Harper land.

"Nola Mae? Is that you?" The sound of my mama's southern drawl cut through my thoughts. "Come on inside. We're waitin' supper for you."

"Coming, Mama!" Inside I found my parents sitting at the table, three red-and-white-checked place mats already set with plates and silverware. In the center of the table rested a large platter of chicken fried steak, flanked on either side by a bowl of greens and a nearly overflowing gravy boat. Mama was pouring from a sweating pitcher of iced tea. I leaned in and gave Daddy a quick peck on the cheek, inhaling his familiar scent of spent cigars and perhaps a touch of Peach Jack whiskey, before settling into my spot. "Looks good, Mama." Of course, if Mama made it, it was good. For as long as I could remember, people had been talking about my mother's skill as a cook. In fact, it was her famous peach preserve recipe that inspired and made Peachy Keen the success it was today.

"How'd things go at the shop, hon?" she asked.

"Busy. I'm going to need to make a few more batches of preserves if I'm going to cover my online orders and the extra business in the shop. Chutney's selling well, too."

"It's the cooler weather," Mama commented. "Ladies are making more pork roasts. Y'all know how well peach chutney goes with pork."

I nodded, casting a glance toward my father. "You're quiet this evening, Daddy. Everything going okay?"

He grumbled, but didn't bother looking up from his plate.

"Never mind him," Mama said, reaching again for the tea pitcher and topping off her glass. "He's had a bad day."

I put down my fork. "What happened? Something with the orchards?"

"No, nothing like that," Daddy said, pushing his own food around his plate. "A problem with Snyder's."

"Snyder's Fruit Stand? I don't understand. What's going

on?" The Snyders ran one of the largest produce stands in the county. A couple seasons back, Daddy negotiated a sweet deal with Jack Snyder—he gave Daddy a higher percent of profit than we'd normally get at other stands on all the bushels of fresh peaches we could provide. In exchange, the Snyders' stand got the best of our crop. It was an exclusive deal and we were his only supplier, which meant a sure-thing market for our highest quality peaches, plus we didn't have to pack and ship. Which saved even more money. Rumor had it that Jack hoped to open other stands in nearby counties as well, though so far it was just a rumor.

From across the table, Mama let out a long sigh. "Raymond, is it really necessary to talk business at the dinner table?"

Daddy waved her off. "Seems Clem Rogers stole the contract out from under our noses. Snyder said Clem offered a better deal—ten percent less retail than we've been getting. I'm not even sure how Clem can afford to do business that way."

"I don't either. Sounds like he deliberately undercut you."

Daddy shoved his plate away and leaned back in his chair. "Wouldn't surprise me. Clem Rogers bears a grudge."

"For what? What ever happened between the two of you anyway?" I asked.

Mama and Daddy exchanged a quick look, but offered no explanation. I sighed. For as long as I could remember there had been contention between Clem Rogers and my father. And most of it coming from Clem, in my opinion. Once, he cut off our water supply by diverting the small branch of the Ocmulgee River that ran through our property and provided our irrigation water. Thank goodness my brother, Ray, a local attorney, was able to talk some sense into the man, but not before some of our trees were damaged. Then there was the time Clem ousted Daddy for the coveted role of General Lee in the local Civil War reenactment. Didn't think Daddy would ever survive that disappointment! He did so love to ride into battle on Traveller, the horse, and scream the rebel yell. Now this thing with Snyder's Fruit Stand. Just one more of Clem's dirty deeds.

"Did you try talking to Snyder again? To change his mind?" Mama was asking.

"Yes, but he wasn't around by then. But I couldn't let it rest, so I stopped in at Clem's. Just got back from his place a while ago. We had a few words. None of them good, I'm afraid."

She shook her head. "I just can't figure that man. So bitter. And to think you've been supporting him in his race for mayor."

Daddy shrugged. "Who should I support? Some city slicker with big ideas?"

"You're not being very nice, Raymond," Mama admonished. "Margie Price may not be from this area, but she's a very nice woman. Why, I was just at her place yesterday for afternoon tea and it was quite pleasant."

Daddy placed his elbows up on the table and waved his fork as he spoke. "All I'm saying, Della, is that Clem's a farmer, like us. We want someone in office who'll protect farmers' interests. I don't think your friend Margie is the best man . . . *woman* for the job."

"Yeah, but what about *our* interests?" I wanted to know. "Clem's definitely not supporting us. Sounds like he wants to put us out of business."

"It's just one small fraction of our distribution list, Nola. It's not like it's going to hurt us all that much. Besides, there's other fresh fruit markets out there. I'll get another deal going with one of them." He sighed and started pushing his chair back from the table.

"Where are you going?" Mama demanded. "Sit back down and eat something." She glanced over our plates. "Both of you need to eat. All this good food's going to waste."

Daddy stood and looked back. "Sorry, dear. 'Fraid I don't have much of an appetite right now. I'm going to look over some paperwork in my den for a while. Call me when it's time to leave for the meeting." I watched as he retreated to the safe haven of his den—a place where he stored his worries, right along with a full box of cigars and a bottle of Peach Jack. I imagined he was going in there now to relieve some of this latest stress with a quick tip of a shot glass.

I turned back to my own plate, speared a piece of meat and slid it through a smudge of gravy before popping it into my mouth. Guess we all have our special ways to mollify stress. Daddy's was partaking in liberations, while I preferred to drown my worries with gravy, grits or any other southern delish Mama cooked up. "The gravy is perfect tonight, Mama. And there's a little kick to the chicken fried steak. Did you do something different?"

She smiled with pleasure at the compliment. "Added a little Cajun spice to the flour."

"Well, I love it." I was about to spear another piece when we heard the sound of sirens coming down the road.

"What in the . . ." Mama popped out of her seat and ran out to the porch. I followed on her heels, the screen door slapping shut behind us. "Sounds like fire trucks," she said, scanning the horizon. We couldn't see the main road from our house, so there was no telling which direction the trucks were heading. "I don't see any smoke, do you?"

The screen door screeched open again as Daddy joined us. "See anything?"

The early-evening sun was quickly setting, making it difficult to see much of anything. "No," I answered, still searching. Then I spotted it. A small plume of black smoke rising above the peach orchards. "There! I see it," I cried, pointing north.

For a few seconds, we all stood frozen, staring at the cloud of smoke in silence, before Daddy jumped into action. "Looks like it's coming from Clem Rogers's land. Come on, let's go."

I held on tight as our farm truck roared down the gravel drive and turned out onto the main road, dust and pebbles flying out from under the wheels. "You don't suppose it's Clem's house, do you?" Mama asked, her brows furrowed with worry. The Rogers had settled in this area even before the Harpers, and their home, built in the early 1800s, had survived the Civil War. "What a shame if that beautiful, old home caught fire."

"Let's just hope no one's hurt," Daddy said, taking a wild turn off the main road onto the country lane that ran between our properties.

"Maybe he's just burning off some old wood scraps, cleaning up the place," I said, hopefully. But as we neared Clem's land, those hopes were dashed by the bright red and orange flames licking the air like a hungry lizard. Thankfully, they weren't coming from Clem's house, but his barn.

Mama's hand flew to her mouth. "Oh no! What a shame. Looks like the whole barn will be lost."

We got out of the truck and squinted through the smoky air. I watched the water from the firefighters' hoses as it arched across the sky in a seemingly futile effort to quell the angry flames engulfing the structure. Next to me, Mama was pointing and saying something, but her soft voice was drowned out by the popping and crackling of burning wood and the roar of the oxygen-hungry fire. Not that it mattered. Because the only thing I could hear were the words playing over and over in my own mind. The very words I'd heard one of the Crawford sisters say earlier that day when she referred to tonight's debate—*a real barn burner.*

Chapter 2

Southern Girl Secret #060: There are only two reasons someone new comes into your life: They're either gonna be a blessin' or a lesson.

"Where's Clem?" I asked, my eyes wandering to the front of the house, where Clem's truck was parked next to the small crowd of onlookers who were starting to gather in the front yard. The local law, Sheriff Maudy Payne and her deputy, Travis Hines, were busy keeping the order. Frances Simms was also there, buzzing around, snapping pictures and interviewing bystanders. My eyes darted back to the parked truck, but I didn't see Clem anywhere, and a horrible thought occurred. "Clem's truck is here. You don't suppose—"

"Naw," Daddy said. "When I left him this afternoon, he said he was heading into town. He wanted to get to the court-house early to check on things before the big meeting."

I breathed a sigh of relief. "That's good. He must have taken his car." Like most farmers in the area, Clem drove a half-ton, four-wheel-drive pickup truck. But he'd also

recently purchased some type of fancy new car. Not that
I'd seen him driving it. But I'd heard enough talk around
town to know it was something expensive. Really expensive. That's the thing about Cays Mill. Stuff like that gets
noticed. Heck, just a couple months ago, Mama had a new
couch delivered from the furniture store over in Perry.
Before the delivery guys could even plunk it in the front
room, there was a knock on the door. It was Betty Lou Nix
from the church. Just passing by, of course. Mama, who's
ever so house proud and never put off by unexpected visi-
tors, kindly invited her in and served her iced tea right
there in the front room on her new davenport. By that very
afternoon, word was out that the Harpers had bought a
new piece of furniture. As crazy as it sounds, that new
couch of ours quickly became talk of the town.

"I'm sure that's it," Mama said. "He probably wanted
to impress everyone with that new car of his." She turned
her palm up and glanced at the watch she always wore
turned to the inside of her wrist. "It's already close to six.
Poor man. He probably has no idea that he's even lost his
barn. At least we know he doesn't have any animals that
might be trapped inside."

Next to her, Daddy and I nodded. That was true. Clem
had never kept animals—not even an old barn cat to keep
him company. Which was kind of odd, considering most
of the farms I knew included a cat or two, a dog or even a
few chickens. Suddenly, the sound of spitting gravel caused
us to look over our shoulders. A shiny new black sedan
was speeding down the drive. "There's Clem now," my
father said, but stopped short when the car screeched to a
halt and a young woman jumped out and started running
for the house.

"That's not Clem," Mama said. "It's his niece, Tessa." We watched as a young man climbed out of the passenger side of the car and ran into the house after the girl. Mama stood a little straighter. "Something's wrong. Come with me, Nola."

We started across the yard, but just as we were about to reach the house, the young couple came outside, wide-eyed and frantic looking. "What is it, Tessa?" Mama asked as soon as we reached their side. "Where's your uncle?"

"I don't know, Mrs. Harper. He's not in the house." Her lips trembled as she wrapped her arms around her midsection, her eyes wandering toward the burning barn. I followed her gaze, noticing the firemen had abandoned their efforts and turned off the hoses. A couple of loud popping noises sounded as pieces of the roof fell to the ground, sending bursts of red embers high into the air.

"He never showed up at the courthouse," the young man said.

"And we were expecting him over an hour ago," Tessa added.

We were still trying to digest this bit of news when Daddy caught up to us. "What's going on? Where's Clem?"

Mama reached over and grasped his arm. Her voice, barely a whisper, was hard to hear over the crackling of the fire. "No one knows. He's not in the house. And these kids are saying that he didn't show up at the courthouse, either."

I could see the muscles in Daddy's jaw stiffen. He looked directly at the young girl. "He didn't show up for the meeting?"

She shook her head and swallowed hard; a small tear escaped the edge of her eye before she broke into a full sob. The young man stepped forward and placed a comforting arm around her shoulder as we turned our gazes toward the fire just as the last bit of roof gave way. With one final *whoosh*, the whole structure collapsed.

"I'm telling ya, Ginny, it was horrible. Just horrible." I shook my head, my cold hands tightening around a steaming mug of morning coffee. Though the chill I felt had nothing to do with the cooler November weather and everything to do with the turmoil I felt inside. "It's the not knowing that's so difficult," I told her. It was late and well after dark by the time the fire chief declared the burned-out barn safe enough for a search. But the lack of light, and lingering smoke and ash, made the search nearly impossible. Sometime around midnight, the chief sent the men home with orders to continue at daybreak.

"At least they didn't find him last night. That's a positive sign, right?" Ginny remarked as she hovered nearby, wiping invisible stains from the counter. "Maybe Clem wasn't even in the barn," she said, tossing aside her rag and reaching under the counter for another coffee mug. "Could be that there's some other explanation for his disappearance." She filled her cup with black coffee and tipped the pot my way.

"No, thanks," I muttered, briefly moving my hand over the cup's rim. I continued, "It just seems strange that he didn't show up for the town hall meeting last night."

Ginny pulled a couple packets of sugar out of her pocket and emptied them into her coffee. "It is strange. Especially since that town meeting was all he talked about yesterday."

"He was in here yesterday?"

She stirred and nodded. "Yeah. Came in for coffee yesterday morning. Sat right over there with that bunch." She thumbed toward a couple tables in the back of the diner where a group of older fellows sat, their heads bent in conversation. Speculating about Clem, I supposed. Ginny continued, "They're local farmers. Come in nearly every mornin' in the off season." She leaned in and whispered, "Moochers is what they are. They take up two of my best tables and all they ever order is coffee."

As if on cue, one of them held his mug up in the air. "Can we get some refills over here, Ginny?"

"In a minute, fellas. I'm takin' a break. Anyway," she continued, still leaning forward, "Clem's been a regular lately. Trying to earn votes, probably. Yesterday he was really on fire about something. Had the boys all riled up. Supposedly he found out something about Margie. Something that was going to sway votes. He planned to bring it up during their debate."

"Do you know what it was?" I'd already heard the same thing from the Crawford sisters the day before, but I was wondering if Ginny might have heard something more.

"Nope." She shook her head, red curls bouncing off her full cheeks. "He wouldn't say anything more. It was like he wanted to build up suspense. It worked, too. Half the town was talkin' about it all afternoon."

"How much longer ya gonna be on break, Ginny?" one of the guys yelled out as he tipped his cup upside down. "We're dry as dust over here."

"Oh, for Pete's sake," Ginny muttered under her breath, snatching the pot from under the coffeemaker and stomping over to their table. "Here y'all go. Help yourselves, why don't you?" she said, plopping the pot down in the middle of the table. A little sloshed out the spout, but she didn't bother to wipe it up.

As she started back to the counter, the diner door opened and a middle-aged man wearing a nylon jogging suit and white sneakers walked into the diner. First thing I noticed about him was his wavy, dark hair. Unlike some men his age, he had a lot of it. A lot. But its fullness served to balance his strong jaw and wide shoulders. "Well, hello there, Mr. Whitaker," Ginny beamed.

"John, please," he said, heading for one of the booths along the far side of the diner.

"Certainly . . . uh, John." Ginny's cheeks brightened. "You're not eating breakfast at the inn this morning?" she asked, patting down the back of her hair.

The man settled into the booth and cleared his throat. "Afraid not. Ms. Price is busy this morning."

"Oh, I see." She removed an order pad from her apron and snatched the ballpoint pen from behind her ear. "Well, what can I get for you?"

"Hey, why's he getting special treatment?" one of the guys ribbed.

Ginny shot him a murderous look. "Hush up, Randy." Turning back to John, she smiled. "We're runnin' a breakfast special this mornin': two eggs, bacon, toast, orange juice and coffee. Grits, too, of course."

"Sounds perfect. But no coffee. Tea if you have it."

That stumped her. "Tea? Like iced tea?"

"No. Hot tea. Earl Grey, perhaps."

Ginny faltered for a second, looking over her shoulder toward the kitchen. From across the room, one of the farmers sniggered. She turned back to the table and made a few scribbles on her notepad. "Uh . . . sure. I'll see what we have. Be right back."

"Did ya hear that?" she hissed in my ear on her way back to the kitchen. "Earl Grey. Now that's class."

"Who is he?" I asked, keeping my voice low. I dared another peek his way and saw that he'd brought yesterday's copy of the *Cays Mill Reporter* and was reading it with interest.

"John Whitaker. I'm surprised you haven't heard about him. He's caused quite the stir around town."

"He has? Why?"

Her eyes slid back toward the booth. "Seriously, Nola. Do you really have to ask?"

I shrugged. "Is he new to town?"

"Yep. He's been staying over at the Sunny Side Up for almost a week now. Keeps to himself, I guess." She sighed. "Mysterious and handsome." Her eyes caught on something over my shoulder. "Speaking of handsome, here comes your guy."

I wheeled around on my stool, spied Cade and waved him over. And Ginny was right. Cade was handsome in his rough-hewn way, but hardly mysterious. *Trusty, reliable Cade,* I thought as he moved across the room, his work boots leaving a small trail of dirt. Nothing mysterious about Cade. Just a hardworking, honest guy. And that's the way I liked him. Loved him, actually. Although I hadn't told him that. Cade, Hattie and I had grown up as neighbors, spending every summer together and getting into all sorts of mischief. Sometime during the teen years, I developed a crush on Cade, but the feeling was never reciprocated.

Then, that summer after graduation, I drifted a bit. Caught a wild hare, as my mama would say. Made more than my share of mistakes, too. Rather than ruin my family's good name, I took a job with Helping Hands International, left town and spent the next fifteen years or so traveling the world and helping folks in need. I loved my job, too. But it lost its appeal when I was reallocated to a desk job up in Atlanta. So I returned to my roots, so to say. And in the process I'd discovered just how much I'd really missed my family, this town, the farm and surprisingly enough, Cade McKenna.

He bent down and planted a peck on my cheek. "Hey there." I caught a familiar whiff of fresh soap.

"Hi. How's it going? Heard anything?" Before bed the night before, I'd called Cade and told him everything that had happened. Although, he'd already heard most of it from the local gossip mill.

"Nothing yet." He took the stool next to me, lustfully eyeing my coffee before glancing around for Ginny. "Where'd she go?"

I looked around, spying her at John Whitaker's booth, serving up a little flirtation with his tea. She was twirling a curl with her finger and tittering like a schoolgirl. I turned back around and told Cade, "Looks like she's busy with the new guy in town, John Whitaker. Have you met him yet?"

"Nope. But I've been busy with the house, so I really haven't been in town much."

"How's it going out there?" Cade had started his own contracting company a few years back, but since the economy hadn't been all that great, he mostly took on remodeling work. He'd even had to take a construction stint up in Macon for a while, just to pay the bills. So he'd been thrilled when he'd received a contract to build a new house just a few miles out of town.

"Good, but . . ."

"But what? Has something gone wrong?"

"No. I mean, maybe." He shrugged. "I don't know, actually. It's just yesterday when I was out at the construction site, I discovered we were short a spool of copper wiring."

"Copper wiring?"

"Yeah. We're getting ready to wire the house, so I just had it delivered along with a bunch of other supplies. Afraid I didn't check the order all that carefully. I called the supplier, but they're insisting they sent everything. So now, I'm out some money. Can't afford too many more mistakes like that."

I blew out my breath. "I'm so sorry, Cade. Maybe it'll turn up."

He shrugged again. "Maybe."

Ginny appeared, grabbed a cup from under the counter and filled it for Cade. "Mornin', sugar. How are ya?"

"Hey, Ginny. Hungry. Think I'll have your special."

"Sure thing." She set the coffeepot on the counter and took out her pad and scribbled down his order. Then she tore it off the pad and clipped it to the silver spindle behind her. Giving it a spin, she yelled out, "Another special, Sam."

A loud clanking noise sounded, and then Sam appeared at the window that separated the kitchen from the dining area. "Got it," he said, shooting Cade and me a friendly wave. "Hey, all. Any news?"

Cade slowly shook his head. "Not yet, buddy."

Sam nodded grimly and went to work on Cade's order, while Ginny busied herself wiping down the counter around the coffeemakers. As I looked on, I caught her glance briefly through the window at Sam, who looked up, caught her gaze and shot her a lopsided grin. She quickly glanced down, then back up with her own smile, cheeks glowing happily. A warm feeling came over me. Despite Ginny's good-natured flirting with the new guy in town, I knew she was madly in love with her husband. And love like theirs wasn't easily found these days. Especially considering the hard times they'd been through together. They'd been high school sweethearts, Sam being a star football player and Ginny part of the cheer squad. Then, they jumped the gun, so to speak, and ended up having to get married right after graduation. Sam worked several odd jobs, but when Ginny's parents decided to retire and move down to Florida, he and Ginny took over Red's Diner. Now, two kids and twenty years later, they were still working together and still happily married.

Suddenly the front door swung open again. This time several men from the Cays Mill volunteer fire crew plodded into the diner, their steel-toed boots clomping loudly on the tile floor. Even though they'd shed their heavy uniforms, their matted hair and soot-smudged faces indicated they'd come straight from searching the fire scene.

"Sam," Ginny said, "get me four specials right away. And make them heavy on the bacon." Then she quickly filled a tray with glasses of ice water and coffee mugs and hustled over to their table. "Hello, boys. Breakfast is on the house this morning," she said, filling their mugs.

"Thanks, darlin'. It's been a rough night."

"Even rougher morning," one of the other guys threw out. The whole room seemed to suck in its breath, waiting for him to continue. "We found Clem's body."

Ginny's put down the coffeepot and shook her head. "Oh no. He got caught in the fire? How horrible."

The fireman shook his head. "I'm afraid Clem wasn't simply caught in a random fire. It was arson. And whoever did it stabbed Clem with a pitchfork first and left him there to burn."

Chapter 3

Southern Girl Secrets #107: If someone's tryin'
to bring you down, it's just 'cause they know
you're above them.

I was a little late opening my shop that morning. After
hearing the news about poor Clem, the diner turned into
a fiery—excuse the pun—forum of heated accusations.
Margie Price rose to the top of those allegations. Many of
the folks, especially the rowdy group of persnickety peach
farmers, were sure that Margie had killed Clem to protect
the secret he threatened to expose. But I didn't agree with
their reasoning. After all, what secret could sweet, hardworking Margie possibly have that would be worth killing for?

I pondered that question as I worked to restock Peachy
Keen's shelves. The influx of customers yesterday had
about cleaned out my jars of preserves and chutney. Luckily I had a couple cases in reserve, tucked away in the
storage closet behind the counter. I'd need to schedule
some time with Ginny to make a few more batches, though.

Especially since I planned to be open during that week's Founder's Day Parade, which was sure to bring a lot of foot traffic into the shop.

Every year, during the second week of November, Cays Mill celebrated Founder's Day to commemorate our little village's birthday and pay homage to our first settler and grist mill owner, Malcolm Cay. We'd always celebrated the day with a small parade and a street dance. This year, since Founder's Day coincided with the mayoral election, the council had decided to ramp up the festivities with an inaugural dance following the announcement of the new mayor. The whole town was looking forward to the event, including me. I'd even picked out a new dress at Hattie's Boutique just for the occasion. It had thrilled Hattie, our little town's fashion expert, to see me expand my all-too-meager wardrobe, especially in the dressy category. I guess my years in the humanitarian outbacks of the world made me see clothing as just one more hard-to-acquire necessity for most people. I remained happy in jeans and T-shirts for the most part. But for Founder's Day I'd chosen a simple red dress, because Cade said it was his favorite color. My short-cropped, dark hair helped make the red dress seem a tad bit more sporty, which I rather preferred than stand-out glamorous. And besides, I figured red could also do double duty for any sort of holiday parties coming my way in the next month or so.

The bells over the front door jingled just as I returned to the closet for another box of preserves. I peeked out and saw my part-time helper, Carla Fini, breezing into the shop. I breathed a little sigh of relief when I noticed she'd paired her usual baggie black jeans with our newly designed, brightly colored Peachy Keen T-shirt. Not that I minded

durable work clothes for daily attire—that was my prefer-
ence as well. But her usual outfit choice—black on black
with more black—had some of my customers wondering
if they should start baking a casserole for the deceased's
family.

"Back here," I called out. She smiled and rounded the
counter to give me a hand. That's the thing about Carla.
Despite her somewhat dark and tough outward appearance,
inside she was one of the biggest-hearted people I knew.
I'd witnessed the depth of her kindness and compassion
last spring when a mutual friend faced a near-death situation. Despite her own problems at the time, Carla devoutly
stood by her friend's bedside until the threat of danger
passed. "Grab some jars of chutney, would you, Carla?" I
said as I made my way up front with the preserves. "We're
running low on about everything out here."

"Sure thing, boss." Carla tucked her bag under the counter and jumped in to give me a hand. "I've got all morning
to help. Ezra doesn't need me at the bakery until later this
afternoon."

I'd been sharing Carla with Ezra Sugar, owner of Sugar's Bakery and best peach scone maker in the world.
"Good. We'll work on gift baskets. Orders have already
started to come in."

She sat a box of jars on the floor next to me and retreated
back behind the counter, where she opened one of the
cabinets and pulled out the shop's laptop computer. "By
the way," she said, booting up the computer to check on
our orders, "what's going on next door? Seems to be a big
crowd in the diner. Is Mrs. Wiggins running one of her
breakfast specials again?"

"Yes, but I'm afraid that's not what's drawing the crowd

this morning." I reluctantly filled her in on the fire and
Clem's murder. "I'm surprised you didn't know about the
fire yesterday." In a town our size, something like a fire
was hard to miss.

She shrugged. "No, I had the whole day off yesterday,
so I headed up to Macon with some friends. We did some
shopping and then checked out a band playing at one of
the bars up there."

"Was your aunt okay with that?" Carla had moved here
last year during her senior year of high school and was
living with her aunt.

She shrugged. "I guess so."

Which probably meant that Carla hadn't told her about
the bar. I sighed. I'd never known the full story, but it
seemed Carla had become mixed up with the wrong crowd
in Chicago and her mother was hoping to give her a fresh
start by sending her to live with her aunt in Cays Mill. At
first Carla hated it here, but after being offered a job at
both my shop and Sugar's Bakery, she decided to stick
around for a while and try to save some money for college.
Which was great, except I had an inkling she'd found
another questionable group of friends to run with down
here.

"Anyway," she continued, "that's horrible about Tessa's
uncle. They were close."

"You know Tessa?"

"Yeah. I met her at a party a while back. We've become
friends."

What type of party? I wondered, but didn't ask. "I'm
sure she's heartbroken," I said instead. "And the shock of
knowing how he died must be very difficult."

Carla shifted uncomfortably and refocused on the

computer screen, biting her lower lip and squeezing her eyes shut briefly, apparently to avoid displaying tears. She wasn't big on expressing her emotions—she had that too-cool teenage attitude to keep up—but I could see the death of her friend's uncle was definitely bothering her. I decided to change the topic. "Did you find those orders yet?"

She nodded. "Yup. It looks like we'll need two of the Hot Jam! baskets and one Son of a Peach!" We both giggled. The names for the baskets had been Hattie's idea. She suggested I do something to stand out in the market, so she brainstormed—with the aid of a little Peach Jack, I'm sure—a few memorable names for the baskets. Hot Jam! featured my spicier recipes, the ones with the extra punch that made you say "Hot damn!" and reach for something cold to drink. Products like peach salsa, peach pepper jelly, hot cinnamon peach preserves and one of my newest creations, peach hot sauce. Son of a Peach! was exactly what the name suggested: small samples of bigger-sized products. This basket was proving to be quite popular with folks who wanted to try a little of everything before committing to full-sized merchandise.

"I'll get these packaged," Carla said, moving from the counter to a small worktable I'd set up in the corner of the shop. My shop was originally a storage room for Red's Diner, which was right next door. When I decided to get into the peach product business, Ginny offered to rent me this space. She also made me a deal I couldn't refuse: For a reasonable percentage of profits, I'd get full use of their industrial-sized, fully licensed kitchen after the diner closed each day, plus a couple hours daily of Ginny's time and expertise in cooking. Since the diner was only open for breakfast and lunch, we could easily be in the kitchen and cooking by late afternoon, allowing Ginny enough time to be home for supper with her family. So far the deal had worked great for both of us. I needed the extra help and Ginny needed the extra money. Especially with both of her kids in college now.

I'd just finished stocking my shelves and was about to join Carla at the worktable when the bells above the door announced a visitor. I looked over my shoulder, expecting a customer, but was surprised to see Mama.

She hovered near the door with a pained, watery expression. I went directly to her and snatched up her hands. They were icy-cold. "Mama? What is it? Has something happened?"

"It's your father, Nola. I'm afraid he's in trouble."

"In trouble? Daddy?"

Mama's head bobbed up and down. "The sheriff came by asking all sorts of questions about his visit with Clem yesterday. She's got him now at the sheriff's office. I already called Ray. He's on his way."

"Ray?" My brother, Ray, worked as an attorney in nearby Perry. "But, Mama, Maudy would just want to get some facts, you know, about . . ." And I couldn't even finish. Sheriff Payne would surely ask what they talked about, and Daddy was honest as could be, not one to skirt the truth—that he and Clem had argued. Well, no wonder Mama was upset and called my brother. We knew Maudy all too well. She was a bulldog of a sheriff who'd bite into an early conclusion and hold on forever. Especially if Harpers were involved. "This is ridiculous. No one in their right mind would think that Daddy could have anything to do with murder! That Maudy Payne is just out to get this family." It was true. There was absolutely no love lost between

the Harpers and Sheriff Maudy Payne. It stemmed back
to our high school days, when my sister, Ida Jean, beat
Maudy up behind the school bleachers. I'd never really
known what prompted my normally very proper sister to
get into a brawl with Maudy, but she did. And she won.
And Maudy had never forgiven her for it.

Carla stopped working and stepped out from behind the
table. "I can handle things here. You go help your family.
I'll lock up before I head to the bakery."

I quickly retrieved my bag from under the counter,
thanked her and grabbed my mother by the arm. "Come
on, Mama. Let's go get to the bottom of this."

Our sheriff's office, a small satellite of the county's main
department, was located in a freestanding building on the
corner of Blossom Avenue and Orchard Lane. At one time,
it was housed inside the old courthouse, but sometime during the late 1960s it was decided that the office needed to
expand to include several holding cells, something that
wasn't possible in the already overly crowded municipal
building. So, the village planners decided to relocate the
sheriff across the street in the old Texaco gas station. The
place was completely overhauled with fresh paint and
the addition of a small front porch deep enough to fit two
chairs, which were often occupied by Maudy and Deputy
Travis. The main part of the building held desks for various
workers, like the office's secretary and other part-time
volunteer deputies who were brought in from time to time,
depending on the need. On the south side of the building,
the attached former mechanics garage had been converted
into three holding cells. A committee from the Baptist

Ladies' Altar Society kept the bedding clean and brought in meals for the poor wayward souls who found themselves there. My brother-in-law, Hollis, claimed the ladies made some of the finest fried chicken he'd ever eaten.

One of the best things, though, about having the sheriff's office separate from the courthouse, was its secluded back entrance. The building backed up to an alley and had a small parking pad for the police vehicles with a direct path to the back door. Which worked great, because the back entrance was partially obscured by an overgrown evergreen hedge. An obscurity that many errant townsfolk appreciated if they were being hauled in by our oftentimes overzealous sheriff.

Today, I decided to use the secluded back entrance myself. Why give the town gossips any extra fodder? So, I guided Mama down the street toward Sugar's Bakery and then doubled back and slipped through the alley quietly and hopefully unseen.

Inside the sheriff's office, we found Daddy sitting across from Maudy at her desk. She was leaning forward, her bushy brows angrily furrowed as she pummeled him with questions. Even from across the room, I could detect the grayish pallor of Daddy's skin and the sheen of sweat glazing his forehead.

"Raymond!" Mama said, scurrying across the room to be at his side. "Why are you answering more questions? Bud said to wait until he could be here." My brother was a man of many names. My parents always called him Bud—a nickname that had carried over from his younger years. Other folks called him Ray Jr., and his colleagues at the law firm called him Raymond Harper II. To me, he was just plain old Ray.

"Calling in your son, the lawyer, huh?" Maudy's eyes flashed between Mama and me before homing back in on my father. "Is there a reason you might be needin' a lawyer, Mr. Harper?"

Daddy shook his head and sighed. "No, I don't need a lawyer. Like I told you, Clem was alive when I left him."

Maudy looked down at her notes. "Which was around four thirty, you said."

"Raymond, honey, let's wait until Bud gets here," Mama said, but Daddy held up his hand to stop her pleas.

"It's okay, darlin'. I don't have anything to hide." Then, turning back to the sheriff, he said, "No, I said it must have been just a little before five, because Clem's place is only about ten minutes from our farm and Della had supper on the table when I got back to the house." He reached over and patted Mama's arm. "Della always serves supper at five o'clock. A person could set their clock to it."

Daddy's time estimate made sense to me. I usually locked my shop door around four each day and, after counting out my register and locking up, would get home around five o'clock. Daddy was already there by that time.

"What made you go out to Clem's in the first place?" Maudy was asking.

"I explained already that we had business to discuss."

Maudy narrowed her eyes. "What type of business?"

"Peach business," Daddy answered with an incredulous tone. After all, what other business was there?

"I figured that," Maudy said with a smirk. "I meant, what *about* the peach business were you discussing?"

When he hesitated, I took it as an opportunity to try to jump in and do some explaining of my own. "They were just discussing peaches. Is that so hard to understand? After all, Daddy and Clem are both peach farm—" I stopped short, however, when my father shot me a look that about made my toes to curl.

"I can speak for myself, Nola Mae," he snapped. Mama handed him a hanky and he began wiping down his forehead. "Clem underbid me on a deal with Jack Snyder. I was angry and I went out to his farm to have a few words with him. But I didn't kill him."

Maudy licked her fingertip and flipped open a manila file in front of her. "Says here in my report that the fire was called in at five minutes past five. By the time the trucks arrived on the scene, the barn was almost completely lost."

Daddy shrugged. "I'm tellin' ya the truth, Maudy. When I left Clem's place, he was alive. He was getting ready to head into town for the meeting."

Maudy narrowed her eyes. "Did you see anyone else while you were at his place? Any other vehicles?"

"Nope."

"Pass anybody on the road back to your place?"

Daddy shook his head. "No. Sure didn't."

Maudy's chair let out a loud squeak as she shifted her weight. "So, what you're sayin' is that you went out to Clem's place, you two argued, you left and someone else snuck onto his property within the next fifteen minutes, killed him and set the barn on fire. Can you see how that might be kinda hard to believe?" She smirked. "Besides, I've been asking around 'bout you, Raymond. Some of the folks seem to think that you might have another reason for wantin' Clem Rogers dead. An old score to settle, they're tellin' me."

Daddy leaned forward and shook his head. "You shouldn't put stock into any rumors you've been hearing, Maudy. All that happened a long time ago. I was just a hotheaded kid back then."

"Lawdy," Mama said, sinking into the empty chair next to Daddy. "Do we really need to bring all that up?" She reached into her pocketbook and took out a tissue, dabbing at her flushed face. "It was all just a misunderstanding. You know how people around here twist and turn things to fill their own depraved appetite for ugliness."

"Mama," I said, moving next to her. "Are you feeling okay?"

"I think we're about done here," Daddy said, glaring at Maudy. It was one thing for him to be badgered with questions but another altogether to see his Della upset. "I'm going to take Della home now."

I stood by, speechless. *What's going on here? What does Maudy mean by "an old score to settle"? And why is Mama so upset?*

Daddy rose, taking Mama's elbow. Mama inhaled deeply and stood from the chair. "I'm fine, Raymond." She gave him a soft and appreciative nod. Then she turned a steely gaze on the sheriff. "Obviously, our sheriff doesn't have anything better to do than listen to idle gossipers. And speaking of old scores to settle, *Maudy*"—she said "Maudy" in a tone so sweet it hurt your teeth—"everyone knows you have it out for the Harpers because my daughter Ida Jean whipped your butt behind the school bleachers way back when. So if you think you're going to go and pin this murder on Raymond, just to settle *your* old score, well, you'll have another think coming." She turned for the door, then turned back again and added, "All these years, I'd been wondering what would have made Ida do something so uncouth. A catfight behind the bleachers of all things!

But you know what?" She leaned in real close, her nose just inches from Maudy's. "Now I understand what might have motivated her."

Just then, Ray burst through the front door, his tie undone and hair disheveled. "Sorry it took me so long to get here." He walked over and plunked his briefcase on Maudy's desk. "Until I have a chance to confer with my client, no one will be answering any questions."

Maudy let out a little chuckle. "Oh, you're a little late for all that, lawyer boy. Your parents have been talkin' plenty." Her lips curled into a cruel little sneer. "Both of them."

Chapter 4

Southern Girl Secret #061: Every family has a skeleton or two in their closet. Don't be tellin' anyone about ours, or you'll find yourself in there with them.

"Think I'll make a couple of my peach cakes to take over to Tessa tomorrow," Ginny was saying. "That poor girl! I feel so awful for her." It was late afternoon and we were in the kitchen at Red's Diner finishing a batch of peach preserves and starting on the newest addition to the Harper Peach Products line—peach hot sauce.

"I do, too," I agreed. Although, inwardly, I was finding it difficult to feel much of anything except anxiety over the latest turn of events, which I had promised Mama I wouldn't mention to anyone. *Let's not stir up the past,* she'd said. *We don't want to cause any more trouble for your father.* I wasn't exactly sure what had happened between Daddy and Clem Rogers all those years ago, but it must've been a doozy. I sighed. Just one more skeleton in the Harper family closet. If we kept this up, we'd soon have an entire graveyard in there. "Mind if I go with you? Just to offer my condolences?"

Ginny seemed pleased with the idea. "Sure. Maybe if we get enough cookin' done this afternoon, we can head over to the Rogers farm after close tomorrow." She looked up from the pot she was stirring and added in a low voice, "Clem was all she had, ya know. They don't know who the father was and her mother ran off when she was just an itty-bitty thing. Clem's raised her all these years. Couldn't have been easy for a man living alone."

"No, I suppose not." I dipped a clean spoon into my bubbling hot sauce, blew on it and took a taste test. Whew! I'd better hold off on adding any more peppers; this batch had a kick. I reached for a napkin and dabbed at the corners of my eyes. "Wonder if she'll stay in this area now that he's gone?" I asked.

Ginny was placing sterilized jars on a tray, preparing to fill them with the hot peach preserve liquid. She paused and glanced over with a shrug. "Dunno. Guess I hadn't given it much thought. I hope she stays around here. If you ask me, we don't have enough young people sticking around these days. They all seem to leave us for the city. Like we're not good enough for . . ." She let her words trail off, biting her lip and shooting me an apologetic smile. "I don't mean you, Nola. You left for good reason. All those people you cared for in those countries around the world. Well, that was *important* work."

I just smiled and let her go on. Despite my *important* work, as she called it, I'd left town all those years ago for a less than honorable reason. Besides, I knew what was really bothering my friend, and it had nothing to do with Tessa Rogers and everything to do with the fact that her own daughter, Emily, was off to the "big city" of Atlanta for college and Ginny missed her something awful. Adding to the wound, her son, Jake, would soon be finishing his undergraduate degree at the University of Georgia and was talking about taking an internship at a company down in Jacksonville. "So Tessa doesn't really have any family left in the area, does she?" I asked.

Ginny sighed. "No, guess not. But she's got a good job over at the Pack and Carry. She's a manager. Actually, I believe that's where she met Lucas."

"That's her boyfriend?" My mind flashed back to the young man at the fire.

"Yes. Lucas Graham. He is a good kid. He was in the same class as my Jake, you know. They used to hang out together, before Jake went to college."

"Lucas didn't go to college?"

Ginny stopped ladling and looked my way. "Now that you mention it, I can't really recall. He was a pretty good basketball player in high school. Everyone thought he would go on a scholarship." She scrunched her face as if trying to remember. "Must not have worked out for him. Anyway, he's here in town and working a couple jobs: the one at the grocery store and part-time for Clem. Too bad. Wonder what he'll do now that Clem's gone."

"What was he doing for Clem?"

"Helping at the farm. Guess the kid pretty much managed this year's harvest. What with Clem so wrapped up in politics and all."

I'd set my hot sauce aside to let it cool before transferring it to the fridge. It was best if it rested for a couple days before being packed into jars and processed for the final time. That way, all the flavors would have a chance to mellow and blend together. The final result being a wonderful blend of peachy sweetness with just the right amount of peppery punch.

I moved over to help her finish the preserves, following behind her ladle with a clean cloth to swipe away any excess liquid from the rims of the jars. They needed to be absolutely clean for the lids to seal properly. "Do you suppose Tessa inherits the farm?" I asked.

"I'm sure she does. Why?" Her hand jerked to a stop, peachy liquid slopping over the edge of the ladle and hitting the hot stove burner, sending an acrid puff of burned peach into the air. She turned and narrowed her eyes at me. "I know what you're thinking, Nola Mae, and you're wrong. There's no way that sweet little girl could stab her uncle with a pitchfork and set him afire."

The door swung open and Hattie breezed in, a stack of bridal magazines in her hands. "Hey, all." She stopped and fanned in front of her nose. "Ick. What's burning?"

I cringed. "We were just discussing Clem's death."

"Terrible, isn't it? It's all I heard about at the shop today." She tossed the magazines down and leaned up against the counter, folding her arms across her chest. "Everyone's speculating about who the killer might be. They're throwing around all sorts of scenarios."

"Like what?" I asked, hoping one of those scenarios didn't include my father. All of a sudden, my fingers stiffened, making it difficult to place the lids on the jars.

"Here, let me do that." Ginny snatched a lid from my trembling hands. "What's wrong with you, Nola? You're all shaky." She gave me a concerned once-over. "Bet you didn't get any lunch today, did ya?" She tipped her head toward one of the refrigerators. "There's some pecan pie left over in there. Help yourself."

"No, thanks." My stomach was so full of nerves there wasn't room for anything else. "So, who do the townsfolk suspect?" I asked Hattie, who was heading to the fridge with a little extra bounce in her step.

"Well, Margie Price of course," Hattie replied, leaning over and peering into the fridge. "Where'd you say that pie was?"

"Second shelf." Ginny started putting the jars into the canner. "The same thing was going around the diner today. Everyone thinks Margie killed him over that secret he was about to expose."

"But you two don't believe that, do you? Margie's our friend."

"Of course not!" Ginny snapped back. "I feel bad for her. I know how it feels to be gossiped about. Remember all that debutante stuff last spring? Why, people were talking so much about me, I learned stuff about myself that I didn't even know."

That was true. The past spring, Ginny had been the object of vicious gossipmongers. And while she stayed strong through the whole demeaning ordeal, I knew it still hurt her that so many of her longtime acquaintances had turned against her.

"For what it's worth, I don't think Margie did it, either," Hattie added. "But we're about the only ones who don't." She took a quick bite of pie, licking the sticky sweetness off her lips before continuing. "Oh, except a few people who think it might be that new fellow in town. The one who's staying over at Margie's inn."

Ginny gasped. "Not Mr. Whitaker!"

Hattie shot a wry smile my way. "'Not Mr. Whitaker,'" she mimicked, thumping her free hand on her heart with a teasing laugh. "Nola, I do believe our dear redheaded friend has a crush on Mr. Whitaker."

"I do not!" Ginny protested, but the blush of her cheeks betrayed her true feelings. "Y'all know I'm madly in love with my husband. It's just that I think Mr. Whitaker is so . . ."

"Mysterious," Hattie finished for her. "So does everyone else in town. Seems they can't figure out why he's stuck around here for so long. He doesn't seem to have any business. Just hangs around. Only leaves his room a couple times a day, and that's to go for a long walk or head over to the library."

"Resting. Reading. Long walks." I rolled my eyes. "Sounds like a killer to me." It never ceased to amaze me what our local gossip mill could churn out about a person. Poor guy. If he knew what was good for him, he'd pack up and get the heck out of town.

Hattie pushed aside her pie and grabbed one of the magazines. "Well, something good did happen today. I finally found the perfect dress."

Ginny and I exchanged a look and took a few tentative steps forward. Lately, every time Hattie brought up her wedding dress—or anything about her upcoming nuptials, for that matter—she worked herself into a blubbering mess. Ginny and I were at a loss. Hattie was by far the most fashion-confident one out of the three of us. Dresses were her livelihood, after all. One would think choosing a wedding dress would be easy for her.

"It's lovely," Ginny said with a tentative smile.

I peered at the elegant, off-the-shoulder gown with its pearled bodice and intricate stitching and put on a smile of my own. "Yes, just lovely," I echoed, following up with some enthusiastic nodding. "I think that's the one, don't you, Ginny?"

"Sure do, Nola. That's the one. It's perfect."

Hattie looked between the two of us and pursed her lips, something unrecognizable flashing in her blue gray eyes. I held my breath. Next to me, Ginny took a step backward. "You two are just yanking my chain, I know you are," Hattie started. She slapped the magazine shut and pushed away from the counter. "You hate this dress. I can tell." She huffed a couple times, but didn't say anything else as she gathered the rest of her magazines and stormed out of the kitchen.

"Goodness gracious," Ginny said, after she left. "Something's wrong with that girl these days."

"Wedding jitters?" I suggested.

"I don't think so. It's still so far off. No, it's something else. I'm just not sure what. Maybe I should make an extra peach cake for her. She seems to need a little consoling herself."

I smiled. Ginny firmly believed that most of life's problems could be solved with food. And I sort of agreed with her. After all, I had started Harper Peach Products to help ease some of the family farm's financial problems. And it was working fairly well. "That would be real nice of you," I told her. Although, I had a good idea of what might be bothering our friend, and unfortunately, it was one problem that couldn't be solved with cake.

. . .

Early Thursday morning, I swung by my shop and picked up a dozen jars of peach preserves to deliver to Sunny Side Up Bed & Breakfast. When I'd first started selling Harper Peach Products, Margie had shown her support by placing a standing monthly order for peach preserves, claiming they provided just the right amount of down-home taste for her customers. Technically, her monthly order wasn't due until next week, but I was hoping to ask her a few discreet questions and maybe even get an up-close look at her mysterious guest, John Whitaker.

I maneuvered our old farm truck off the square and turned onto Majestic Boulevard, driving slowly and taking in the scenery. I loved this part of town, with its deep front yards and mature trees. The fall colors had already peaked, the last of the bright rust and reds fading a few weeks ago. All that was left was the dull yellow and brown leaves that still stubbornly clung to almost bare branches. But it was such a clear, crisp day that even these muted colors seemed to pop out against the bright blue sky.

Parking the truck in the alley behind the inn, I carried my box of preserves through the garden gate and along the path leading to the home's back entrance. While Sunny Side Up boasted a lovely formal front entrance with a deep pillared porch and three stories of true southern antebellum architecture, I found the back entrance to be all the more charming with its informal gardens and white picket fence.

I was just ascending the wooden steps leading to the screened back porch when Margie called out my name. She waved me over to the corner of the yard, where she was tending to a perennial bed.

"Hey, Margie. Just making a delivery," I said, joining her by the small garden. I slid the box onto a nearby bench.

"My goodness," she said, removing her garden gloves and tucking a loose strand of silver-blond hair under her wide-brimmed hat. "Is it that time already?"

"I'm a week early, actually." I glanced around. Margie, an avid gardener, had managed to turn her once-ordinary backyard into a relaxing oasis of private gardens and intimate seating areas, all connected by a meandering stone path. "I haven't been back here for a while. You've done a great job with your gardens."

"I can't take all the credit. I hired Pete Sanchez to help. He's got quite the eye for landscape design." Then she cocked her head at me. "But surely you didn't come here a week early with my delivery just to discuss gardens." She lowered her chin and shot me a pointed look. "Did you?"

This seemed like such a good idea when I started out this morning, but now I found myself tongue-tied and unsure how to broach the subject of Clem's murder. "I just thought you might need . . . I mean, want . . . a little company now with. . . ." *With what?* Obviously I hadn't thought this through well enough.

"With Clem's murder, you mean? That's what's brought you over here today." She tossed her gloves onto the bench. "You can't possibly think I might have had something to do with it."

"No. Of course not! That's why I came by. I thought you might, you know, want some company."

"Because that's what people are saying, aren't they? That I killed Clem over the secret he was about to expose?"

I nodded.

She wiped some dirt from the front of her shirt and

sighed. "You might as well come in and sit for a while," she said, motioning toward the back porch. "I didn't sleep well last night. I could go for some coffee. Care to join me?"

That sounded good to me. I hadn't slept all that well, either. Visions of my father, pasty-skinned and sweating it out in Maudy's hot seat, had caused me to toss and turn all night. "That would be great," I said, scooping up the box. I followed her down the path and up the porch steps. Once inside, she removed her hat and placed it on a peg inside the door. "There's a nice breeze coming through this morning." She took the preserves and indicated toward a cozy seating area. "Why don't you make yourself comfortable and I'll get us some coffee. Cream?"

"Just black. Thanks." I used to be a cream-and-sugar person, but I'd lost my taste for it while working abroad. Such luxuries, let alone the basic necessities like food and water, weren't readily available in most of the remote regions I'd worked.

I sat down in a pretty pinstriped rattan chair and admired my surroundings. Margie was right—a refreshing breeze was coming through the screens, ruffling the leaves of several potted ferns. In front of me, a rustic table held a large photo album. I picked it up and leaned back into the cushion. The pictures showed the different phases of Sunny Side Up's remodeling: from the complete kitchen redo to the addition of two bathrooms upstairs. It was amazing how Margie had managed to make so many changes to the house, yet maintain its historical character.

"Here you go," she said, returning a few minutes later with a full tray. I returned the album to its spot on the coffee table and eyed the contents of the tray. My stomach rumbled its approval at the sight of a plate of Ezra Sugar's peach scones. I struggled to remember my manners and not take one until it was offered. "I see you found my album," she said.

"It's amazing, everything you've been able to accomplish in such a short time. You only bought this place, what, three, four years ago?"

"That's right. I've been here almost four years already. Still a newcomer by most folks' standards." She chuckled, reached for the carafe and filled my cup then filled hers. "But to some, I'll always be a newcomer, no matter how long I live here."

"Just how it is in small towns," I offered.

"Guess so," she conceded, holding out the plate of scones. I took one with a grateful smile. "But despite all the small-town gossip, I love it here."

I understood how she felt. I'd come to think that living in a small town was like being part of an oversized, dysfunctional family—you had your share of squabbles and petty jealousies, and a few crazies, of course, but somehow you all stayed together and made it work.

"And this old house," Margie was saying. "Well, it's always been a dream of mine to own a place like this. Be my own boss . . ."

"Yes, but it must be a lot of work to keep this place up." I popped a piece of scone into my mouth and savored the salty, buttery softness and little sweet peachy pieces. Delicious!

"Oh, believe me. It's a lot of work." She dumped a spoonful of sugar into her coffee and stirred. "In a house like this, there's always something that needs fixing."

"I can imagine." I took a quick sip of coffee before continuing, "Weren't you worried about throwing the responsibilities of being mayor into your busy schedule?"

She shrugged. "A little. But I feel very strongly about this town and want to see it succeed." She set her cup down and leaned forward. "Truthfully, I think Wade Marshall did a good job while he was in office, especially considering the economic slump that's hit this area. But there's still quite a few empty businesses on the square, and I know with my business savvy I could bolster our downtown area. Bring in some new stores." She raised her chin defiantly. "Oh, I know the farmers are worried that I'm going to achieve all this on their hardworking backs, but that's simply not true. Peaches are the heart of this town. I believe if we could get more businesses, perk up the town a bit, we might be able to bring in more tourists during peach season. Maybe even create some sort of agritourism venues: peach farm tours and such. It'd be a win-win for everyone." She let out a long sigh. "But I'm not sure what's going to happen now. With Clem gone and me as the primary suspect, there may not even be an election next week."

"Did the sheriff say you were her primary suspect?" Part of me hoped she had—only to get Maudy off Daddy's back—but I knew Margie couldn't be guilty, either.

"Not yet, but she might as well have. Maudy always worries me just a bit. She's sort of a loose cannon, don't you think?"

I swallowed and nodded. "Oh yes! She's possibly the narrowest-minded person I know. Not a good quality for a sheriff, if you ask me."

She lifted her mug to take a sip, but paused and

scrunched her brow. "That's right. Maudy went after your brother-in-law a while back."

Yes, and once again, Maudy has set her sights on a Harper. "Do you happen to have an alibi?" Realizing how crass that sounded, I hurried to backtrack. "I mean, an alibi would prove your innocence to her. Not that you have anything to prove to me."

"Unfortunately, no. I was here at the house preparing for the debate when Clem was supposedly murdered. No one else was here."

"Not your houseguest?"

"Mr. Whitaker?" She shook her head. "No, he'd gone out that afternoon."

That piqued my interest. "Do you know where?"

"Probably for a walk. Or maybe for a drive. He often goes out for a couple hours at a time. I don't really know what he does."

"I bet Maudy asked you the same questions."

She shook her head. "No. She didn't bring him up at all. I couldn't have told her much anyway. I don't know anything about him really except that he's a good guest. Quiet. Keeps to himself."

My gaze slid toward the double French doors that led to the kitchen and the rest of the house beyond. "Is he here now?"

"No, he's out for a run. Left about a half hour ago. Goes every morning at this time, like clockwork. Then he comes back and locks himself in his room until early afternoon."

"Interesting." I glanced at my watch. It was a little after eight o'clock.

"Are you thinking that he might have something to do

with the murder?" She sat back. "That's a scary thought. Considering I'm alone in this house with him."

"You don't have any other guests right now?"

"Nope. But one should be coming in tonight." She set her cup down and sighed. "I know this sounds silly, but I've got too much to lose to just sit back and let this accusation stand. I intend to be proactive about this. That's why I've called on a past guest for a favor."

I closed my eyes for a second and took a deep breath. "Let me guess. A private investigator."

"Yes. Dane Hawkins." A spark of realization crossed her face. "Oh, that's right. You already know him, don't you?"

Oh yes, I thought. *Do I ever.* I nodded and offered a little smile, but didn't comment. "Margie, I hate to ask, but is there any truth to the rumor that Clem knew something that could ruin your chances at becoming elected for mayor?"

She focused her gaze on the gardens beyond the porch screen, the corners of her mouth drooping as she spoke. "I'm afraid so, Nola. But please don't ask me to tell you what it is. I couldn't bear to think of you knowing about . . ." She reached for the fringe of a nearby throw pillow, absently rubbing the yarnlike material between her fingers, letting out a labored sigh. "I hope you can understand. I'm not exactly proud of everything in my past."

I leaned forward and touched her hand. "I do understand, Margie. Really I do." *Besides, who am I to judge? Especially since my own sordid past is due to roll into town any time now.*

Chapter 5

Southern Girl Secret #065: The key to a happy life is to let the good times roll and the bad times go.

And roll in he did. Just twenty minutes later, as I was opening the door to my shop, a loud rumbling noise drew my attention upward and to a tight-jean-wearing, leather-clad Dane Hawkins cruising down the street on his Harley with his canine buddy safely tucked behind him in a custom-designed dog carrier. I stood there, hands on hips, shaking my head as he rounded the corner and parked his bike in front of the Clip & Curl. Stopping in to see his sweetie, no doubt. When Dane first reappeared in Cays Mill last year, he took up with Laney Burns, a local nail tech with a penchant for red nail lacquer and hair as big as Dane's ego. As far as I was concerned, they perfectly suited each other. Still, as much as the sight of Dane Hawkins got on my nerves, the one good thing about him being back in town was the thought of spending time with his adorable hound, Roscoe. Since Margie adhered to a strict no-pets rule at Sunny Side Up and Laney was highly allergic to dogs, Roscoe usually ended up at our place. Not that we minded. Actually, we'd grown quite fond of the little fellow. Especially Mama, who spoiled him as much as one of her grandbabies.

The idea of seeing Roscoe again made me smile as I continued into my shop, turning on the lights and flipping the sign in the door to "Open." But no sooner had I stashed my bag under the counter than the bells above my door jingled. I glanced up to see my sister, Ida, with my little nephew in her arms. Glancing at the clock above the door, I realized Ida must have just dropped his twin sisters at school.

"Hey, sis!" I came out from behind the counter to give her a hug and snatch my nephew from her grip. "And how's my little buddy today?" I nuzzled his chubby cheeks and planted tiny kisses all over his face. In return, he let out a hearty little laugh and clutched a handful of my hair in his tiny fist. "Ouch!" I cried, trying to hand him back, only to find he had a death grip on my hair. "Help," I pleaded.

Ida grabbed his hand and shook. "Stop that, Junior!" she admonished. Only the harder she shook, the tighter he gripped. I stepped forward and craned my neck in an effort to lessen the tension, but Junior pulled harder.

"Oh for cryin' out loud, let go of Aunt Nola's hair," Ida said with one final jerk.

"Eeeouch!" I yelped as a few of my hairs were ripped from their follicles. I straightened up and eyed the little monster suspiciously. Was that a devilish gleam in his eye? If you asked me, Junior had a lot of his daddy's mischievousness in him. And to think he hadn't even hit those "terrible twos" yet!

"Sorry about that," Ida said, pulling a few of my dark hairs from between his fingers and releasing them to the floor. "I'm surprised he was able to get such a firm grip, being that your hair's so short and all." My eyes were immediately drawn to her shoulder-length, honey brown tresses. Both Ida and I were natural brunettes, but her frequent trips to the Clip & Curl resulted in a bouncy, carefree, sun-kissed look, while I'd kept my flat brown shade. I'd long ago traded my long tresses during my stint as an aid worker for a more practical, no-fuss, cropped style. And I'd kept it that way upon my return to Cays Mill over a year ago, much to the dismay of my Southern girlfriends, mother and sister.

"He's been a handful lately," Ida continued. "Gettin' into everything, makin' messes . . . his shenanigans have 'bout worn me out. Like I need any more stress, what with everything goin' on with Daddy and all."

"You mean this stuff with Clem Rogers?" I asked, still rubbing my sore head.

She nodded. "Yes. It's just awful. Poor Daddy. And with his bad heart. Why, this is the last thing he needs!"

A while back, Daddy had been diagnosed with heart palpitations and the doctor had recommended he cut back on strenuous activity and stress. Problem was, running a peach farm had plenty of both. And now all this stuff with Clem . . . "I agree. But I'm not sure what we can do about it. Maudy has her sights set on Daddy. She won't just give it up."

"Yes, she has it out for us Harpers. And it's all my fault. Had I known all those years ago what trouble it would cause, I never would have laid into her behind the bleachers that day. She's been set on vengeance ever since." She set

Junior down and immediately he toddled toward a shelf of my neatly stacked glass jars of spiced peaches.

"Speaking of past grievances, do you know whatever happened between Daddy and Clem Rogers?" I asked, quickly grabbing my nephew and redirecting him back toward Ida. "Because whatever it was has Mama all upset."

Ida paused, a strange look crossing her face. She quickly recovered and waved her hand through the air. "I wouldn't worry about all that." She shifted her weight and started rummaging through the diaper bag hanging from her shoulder. "Did I just see that detective friend of yours riding into town?" She pulled out an oversized set of plastic keys, which Junior quickly tossed aside. This time he headed straight for my corner cabinet, where I kept my handmade soap display.

I intercepted him midtoddle and returned him to Ida. "Yeah. Dane Hawkins is back in town."

"Well, I know at least one person who's probably over-joyed to see that man."

A vision flashed through my mind—Hawk and Laney reuniting, right at this moment, in a passionate embrace, Laney gripping his taut muscles with those red claws of hers, while he ran his fingers through her teased-out tresses. I tried not to gag. "He's here to investigate Clem's murder. Margie Price hired him."

Ida rolled her eyes. "Suppose he'll be taking that mutt of his out to the house again." Ida didn't feel as kindly toward Roscoe as Mama and me.

"Suppose so," I replied, making another dive for wandering Junior and plunking him back at Ida's feet.

"Lawd help us," she said. "First Maudy and now that

private investigator. They're both about as dumb as a box of rocks. We can't trust Daddy's well-being to either one of them."

I nodded. She was right. "Good thing Ray's working on things."

"Ray?" Ida's looked at me like I was crazy. "Ray's a lawyer—a darn good lawyer—but he's no investigator. That's why I stopped by to talk to you this morning. What Daddy needs is someone resourceful. Someone who understands people and what motivates them. Someone with a little experience with these types of things. Someone like you."

Me? Experience? If she meant my little forays into crime solving, that wasn't experience. It was dumb luck. With an emphasis on "dumb." And both times I'd gotten involved, I'd almost found myself defunct and departed. Still, this was Daddy we were talking about. And while I didn't relish getting involved, there was no way I was going to allow my own father to go down for a crime he didn't commit. And besides, I'd already been thinking about who might have had the motive and opportunity to kill Clem Rogers. I'd even done a little poking around myself, hence my visit to Sunny Side Up that morning. Still, it wouldn't do to have Ida think I was on board with her crazy suggestions.

But before I could think through a reply, a loud crash came from the other side of the room. We turned to find Junior reaching out for an overturned basket of peach soap. "No, Junior!" Ida cried, running over to yank away a bar of soap making its way to his mouth. Thwarted, he balled his little hands into fists and let out an ear-piercing scream.

In return, Ida let out an exasperated sigh. "I best get him home for his morning nap," she said, swinging him up to her hip. "But you'll think about what I said, won't you? I just couldn't bear the thought of anything bad happening to Daddy."

"Me either," I said, leaning in for a quick good-bye hug, keeping my hand up to block Junior's probing fingers. "Me either."

After Ida and the toddling terror left, I busied myself catching up on work around the shop. But while I packaged baskets for shipping, my mind kept wandering to our family's current dilemma. Ida was right about one thing: all this stress couldn't be good for either of our parents. I thought back to the day before at the sheriff's office. Daddy had looked pale and drawn, and Mama was so upset . . . I tried to shake off the image, preferring instead to think of my parents as I'd always seen them: invincible, young and vibrant. Oh, I knew they had stress with the farm and raising a family. But they'd always been able to overcome that stress and persevere through the hard times. Lately, though, something had changed. Slowly at first, and just little things. Things like my father's bad back and now his heart palpitations and Mama needing her reading glasses for even the large print. It was a little disorienting to admit that they were getting older, to think that one day they might . . . I squeezed my eyes shut, unable to bear the thought.

The bells above my door jingled again, pulling me from my pessimistic thoughts. A couple ladies breezed in, carrying small foam leftover containers from the diner next door. I blinked a couple times and put on my best shop-keeper's smile. "Morning, ladies." I recognized these two from church, acquaintances of Mama's, but couldn't quite recall their names. "Just let me know if there's something I can help you with."

The door opened again, and this time, unfortunately, I definitely knew the visitor—Frances Simms. I immediately bristled. "Good morning, Frances. Are you here about a monthly ad?" About once a week, Frances stopped into my shop to pester me about taking out a monthly line ad in the *Cays Mill Reporter*. So far, I'd held off, not wanting to give my financial support to her gossip-spreading tab-loid. "Because, I'm really not interest—"

"Nope. I'm not here about the ad," she said, a tiny smirk playing on her normally pinched lips as she sauntered about. "Looks like you've expanded your inventory."

I nodded and glanced toward the ladies, who were busy sniffing the soap. "Those are all natural and handcrafted locally," I threw out, trying to entice a sale and sort of hoping they'd hurry up and finish their shopping. Because I recognized that hungry look in Frances's eyes—she was hot on the trail of a story. And that story, undoubtedly, was Clem Roger's murder. And if she was here, that could only mean one thing: she'd found out that Daddy was a suspect.

"Did you happen to see the special edition of the *Cays Mill Reporter* this week?" she asked.

I shook my head. "No, sorry. I must've missed it."

"Well, I was going to put out a special edition to cover the mayoral debate, but as it turned out there was a much bigger story."

I nodded and smiled tightly. "Sure was." I looked back over at the ladies, who were still sniffing, and said, "Special sale on soaps this morning. Twenty percent off." There was no such thing, but I hoped to get them moving along. "Would you ladies like me to wrap up a couple bars for you?"

Frances stepped in my line of sight. "I was just over at the diner, having a cup of coffee. Heard something interesting about Clem Rogers's murder."

I craned my neck and saw that the ladies had stopped sniffing and started listening. *Oh boy.*

Frances leaned against the counter, casually folding her arms across her chest as if she was staying for a while. "Heard your daddy had been talking to the sheriff and apparently needed that lawyer brother of yours at his side. Then I also found out your daddy was out at Clem's place just minutes before the fire started." I saw the women exchange surprised looks, grab a few bars of soap and scurry to the cash register.

My heart started pounding in my throat. I swallowed hard as one of the ladies placed soap on the counter. "These are just lovely," she said with a sappy smile. "I've decided on these three, but could you bag them individually? I'm giving them as gifts."

"Certainly," I said, ringing up her purchase.

"Funny thing that he'd be out visiting Clem," Frances went on. "I didn't think he and your daddy were on friendly terms."

The women exchanged a knowing look, their eyes gleaming with excitement. Anticipating, no doubt, a piece of juicy gossip. I quickly made change and pulled out tissue and three small, handled bags and started wrapping the soaps.

"Of course," Frances continued, "maybe your daddy wasn't paying Clem a friendly visit."

A piece of tissue stuck to my suddenly moist palm. "I don't know what you mean by that. Clem just lives up the road from our place. You know how it is in the country. We're all"—I searched for the right word—"neighborly with each other."

"That's true, Frances," one of the ladies said. "Country folks can be right friendly with their neighbors."

I nodded and sent an appreciative smile her way, narrowing my eyes instead when I noticed the little smirk that played on her lips.

"Yes, ma'am. I've heard that about country folk." Frances chuckled.

Personally, I didn't get what was amusing. But who cared, as long as Frances didn't know the real reason Daddy had gone to Clem's that day when they fought over the peach deal. Of course, I knew all that had absolutely nothing to do with Clem's death, but Frances could stretch the truth six ways to Sunday.

The sound of the door opening drew everyone's attention. This time Ginny burst inside, an oversized bag in her hand. "Sorry I couldn't get away 'til now," she said.

I scrunched my face. "Huh?"

She pointed to the bag slung over her wrist and raised a brow. "That errand you promised to help me with." She crossed the room. "Hello, ladies. Sorry to interrupt your shopping, but I need to borrow Nola for a little while."

I had no idea what she was talking about, but the flushed

look on her face told me something was up. I handed over the neatly packaged soaps and smiled at the ladies. "Please come back soon."

As they headed for the door, Ginny turned to Frances and said, "And I'm sure you'll be wantin' to get out to the high school to cover the breaking news."

Frances's squinty eyes popped with surprise. "Breaking news?"

Ginny touched her cheek dramatically. "Oh, I'm surprised you haven't heard. There's an entire set of bleachers missin' from the football field. It's caused quite the ruckus. Guess the principal's fit to be tied."

Frances was already on her way to the door. "I'll catch up with you later, Nola," she said over her shoulder.

As soon as the door shut, I turned to Ginny. "What's all this about?"

"Oh, probably just some kids playing a prank."

"Not the bleachers. This errand you said I promised to run with you. I don't remember—"

"To take these peach cakes out to Tessa." She pointed to the bag in her arms. "I figured, due to the circumstances"—she dipped her head toward the door—"we'd best alter our schedule a bit. Go now, before the lunch crowd shows for the diner."

"I don't understand."

She let out a long sigh. "Those two old biddies who just left?"

"'Old biddies'? That's not very nice."

She pursed her lips. "Well, it's a heck of a lot nicer than what I really want to call them." She blew out a long stream of air, lifting a few red curls off her forehead. "They were in the diner this morning, talking about your mama."

"Mama?" I could feel my muscles tensing. "What were they saying about my mother?"

Ginny glanced about uneasily. "Easy now, Nola. Why don't you take a break and come with me to drop off these cakes? We can talk all about it on the road."

Chapter 6

Southern Girl Secret #078: You know your family roots are strong when other peoples' hot wind can't knock you down.

We decided to take my truck out to the Rogers farm. No sooner had we left the square than I turned to Ginny and demanded to know what people were saying. "And don't hold anything back, either. I want to know every single lie the local gossip-slinging snips are making up about my mama."

Ginny seemed to shrivel in her seat. "Well, no one came right out and said anything nasty, if that's what you're thinking. Mostly just innuendos."

I took the turn onto a local access road a little sharper than intended. Ginny reached out and grasped the inside door handle to steady herself. "Innuendos about what?" I asked.

She took a deep breath. "About your mama and Clem Rogers. Being . . . friendly."

I cranked the wheel and came to a screeching halt on

the side of the road and turned to face her. "What? Clem Rogers and my mother? You've got to be kidding me! My family and Clem don't even get along well as neighbors! These people around here can be such—"

"I know." She held up her hand. "But it seems this was a long time ago. Before you were even born."

"I don't understand. What exactly are we talking about? Did they date, or something?" I tried to estimate Clem's age. It could have been that they were in school together. "What's the big deal about that?"

Ginny shrugged. "Beats me. I just caught bits and pieces of the talk. You know how it is at the diner. Next to the Clip and Curl, it's the town's hub of gossip."

That was true. If a person sat in the diner long enough, they'd hear just about everything going on in the county. Still, this didn't sound as bad as she'd first made it out to be. My heart rate had calmed enough for me to continue driving, so I put the truck back in gear and continued toward the Rogers farm. "It's weird Mama never mentioned anything to me about her and Clem having any sort of past relationship," I said, watching the road for my next turn. "She's told me about some of her other high school boy-friends. You know, stories about her first date, first dance and all that type of stuff."

"Well, from what I gathered, this happened when your Daddy was away in the service."

"'This'? What do you mean by 'this'? 'This' what?"

"Their dating, I suppose. Heck if I know, Nola. I didn't know your father was even in the army."

"He went right after high school. I think." I shrugged my shoulders. "Guess I'm not really sure. We never discuss it. Still, what's the big deal? That was a long time ago." A really long time ago. At least fifty years, because my parents had just celebrated their golden anniversary last year. Still, in this town, people were known to twist and turn things until they came up with their own version of the truth. And around here, rumors never really died. They just went dormant until something happened to spark a new tongue-wagging frenzy. Which is exactly what Clem's murder was. The spark that ignited the fire and brought old gossip boiling to the surface. A foreboding feeling crept over me, settling in the pit of my stomach. With his health being the way it was, this was the last thing my father needed.

"Nola? You okay?"

"Yeah, why?"

"Because you've got a horrible look on your face."

"Yup. I'm fine." I forced a tight smile, keeping my eyes on the road. "So who all was talking about this today?" I wanted to get to the bottom of this, quash it before it got out of hand.

"Well, about everybody in the diner was talking about Clem's murder."

"Yes, but what about the talk about my family?"

"Well, don't ask me who, because I can't remember, but someone said they saw your brother and father coming out of the sheriff's office yesterday. That's when Frances got involved. She was sitting at her usual booth in front of the window."

"Uh-huh."

"Well, Frances asked if Clem and your daddy did business together or something, and one of the men spoke up and said it was about the opposite, that they'd been competing with each other. That Clem stole some peach deal right out from under your daddy."

"Was it Jack Snyder who said that?"

"Yep. Believe so."

"Yeah, well, that's what happened. Daddy had been doing business with Jack, and Clem butted in with some ridiculous bid. Stole the contract from him."

"I see."

"But that's not something to murder someone over!"

"Of course not."

I'd reached the turnoff to Clem's farm, so I slowed down a bit, wanting to make sure I got the whole story before we got there. "So, what was said then?" I prompted.

She kept her gaze focused out the window. "Just what I said. Then those ladies brought up about how Clem and your mama must've dated when they were kids. They seemed to know your mama from way back when. Classmates probably."

"I got that. But what were their *exact* words?" I pulled up in front of the farmhouse and took the truck out of gear. When she didn't respond, I asked again, "Ginny?"

She turned my way, her eyes full of concern. "They said it wouldn't be the first time Clem attempted to steal something from your daddy. Meaning your mama, I guess. And that it wouldn't be the first time your daddy tried to kill him over it. Right after that, Frances hightailed it out of the diner, heading toward the sheriff's office."

While I knew it was the right thing to do, visiting the bereft always made me nervous. Even more so today, since what Ginny had just told me about Mama and Clem had left me completely unsettled. So, I trudged across the lawn, my legs heavy with dread as I followed Ginny to the farmhouse door. Truth be known, what I really wanted to do was turn tail and run home to find my parents and get to the bottom of all this nonsense about Mama and Clem Rogers. Because certainly, I was letting my imagination get away from me, spurred by trumped-up rumors spread by malicious gossipers. What was it Mama had said at the sheriff's office? People in this town twisted things to fill their own decrepit appetite for ugliness? I thought back to those ladies in my shop, their double-talking innuendos becoming clear now. That's all those women were—ugly, backstabbing witches, eager to bring others down to elevate their own sense of importance. Because there's just no way my mama would ever be involved in something unseemly. Poor Mama. How hard it must be to know false rumors from the past were resurfacing, rearing their hideousness and, even worse, perhaps providing Maudy with yet more reason to pin this murder on Daddy. And as for Daddy trying to kill Clem way back when, well, if that was even true, I knew Daddy, and he'd have had good reason. First thing this evening, I'd have a sit-down with Mama. Reassure her, like she had me so many times, that the family was completely behind her. That we'd fight through this latest dilemma in true Harper fashion—together, united as one team.

When we reached the house, I was surprised to find it wasn't Tessa, but her boyfriend, Lucas, who answered our knock. His puffy eyes blinked a few times as he ran a hand through dark, wavy hair that was smashed flat above one ear. Sleep lines etched his cheeks and an odor of staleness drifted around him. "Tessa's not up to seeing anyone right now," he said, standing in the frame of the open door with his arms folded across his wrinkled T-shirt. "She's still pretty upset."

Ginny pointed at her bag. "We understand. Just wanted to bring these by and say how sorry we are for her loss."

But before Ginny could hand over the goodies, Tessa appeared in the doorframe, her face pale and puffy and a throw blanket pulled around her shoulders like a shawl. "Mrs. Wiggins. Ms. Harper. It's good of y'all to stop by. Come in, please."

Lucas sighed and stepped aside, motioning for us to follow them down a short hallway to a room that at one time must have been a parlor but had been revamped as a family room. It was decked out with a large-screen television, leather furniture and a modern glass coffee table. All great stuff, but a bit out of character for the flower-print wallpaper and wide farmhouse moldings. Or maybe that was just my perception. Except for the new davenport Mama bought last year, we really hadn't updated for a few decades.

"Sorry for the mess," Tessa said, clearing a stack of magazines from an adjacent chair and inviting us to sit down. Ginny took the chair, while I settled into one corner of the davenport and Tessa sank heavily into the other. Lover boy hovered above us, a broody look on his face.

Tessa peered up at him. "Would you mind clearing out some of these things, sweetie?" She nodded toward a row of empty beer bottles lining the coffee table. I counted at least seven before Lucas scooped them up and sauntered off, clinking like a Saturday night barmaid at the Honky Tonk. Not that I'd heard that sound for a while. I tried my best to avoid the Honky Tonk—too many unpleasant memories.

"We're very sorry for your loss, Tessa," I said, my eyes glazing across the pile of magazines she'd tossed to the floor. I recognized one of them as the same magazine Hattie had showed us the day before. Was Tessa planning a wedding? I stole a glance at her ring finger. Bare. Probably just adolescent dreaming. It'd never been my thing, but I remembered Ida spending half of her teen years poring over bridal magazines and dreaming of her future wedding. I'd always been more of the *National Geographic* type. "How are you holding up?" I asked.

She seemed to shrink farther into the sofa. "I'm getting by, I guess. I really miss him."

"Bless your heart. Of course you do, sweetie," Ginny said. "What can we do to help you?"

Tessa let out a shaky breath and shrugged. "There's nothing really that anyone can do. I'm just praying that the sheriff finds out who did this. I'll feel much better knowing that the murderer is behind bars for good."

"Did the sheriff mention any suspects?" I asked.

Again, she shook her head. "No. She didn't say." She pulled the blanket tighter around her shoulders, shivering as if she'd just caught a chill. "The way he was killed . . . I can't imagine anybody doing such a horrible thing."

"Are these questions upsetting you, Tess?" Lucas asked. He'd returned from his task and was hovering again.

"Actually, it helps to talk about it," she told him. Then she managed a small smile and said, "Lucas has been such a comfort to me. I don't know what I'd do without him."

I'm sure. Ginny had spoken highly of this young man, but so far I didn't have the best impression. I took another long look at Lucas, wondering how well he got along with Clem. Maybe Clem wasn't thrilled about the hired help dating his niece.

Tessa continued, "I know my uncle wasn't always the easiest man to deal with. He had run-ins at one time or another with half the people in town."

I could feel my cheeks grow hot, knowing that my daddy was one of those people.

"And not everyone in town agreed with his political ideas," she added.

"Yeah." Lucas spoke up. "Like Margie Price." He'd moved to a recliner in the corner and was sitting sideways with his legs thrown over the arm of the chair. "Or maybe one of her supporters. Those people are nuts. They'd been calling here, harassing Clem about this and that. Some of them were getting nasty, too."

"You're right about that," Ginny agreed. "Everyone's gone a little nuts about this mayoral race. Arguments start up almost every day at the diner. And you should have been at the last Chamber of Commerce meeting. After Clem and Margie finished talking, people started getting into it over the issues. It got out of hand real fast. Finally ended in a food fight, if you can believe it. The craziest thing I've ever seen. Grown people throwing food at each other."

Food was one thing, but I couldn't see driving a pitchfork through someone because of a difference in political positions. No, this seemed more personal than politics. "Right before he was murdered, your uncle mentioned that he knew something personal about Margie. Something that might prove detrimental to her chances of winning the election."

"Her secret, you mean?" Tessa said, looking away. Her eyes seemed to wander absently around the room. "I'm almost embarrassed to talk about this. My uncle was obsessed with winning the election. It's all he talked about. It took over his life, our lives. But there was more to it than just wanting to win the election." She shifted and took a deep breath. "I really hate to say this, but my uncle didn't think a woman should be mayor. Especially not a woman 'like Margie,' as he said."

Ginny's head bobbed up and down. "An outsider? Lots of folks feel that way, since she's not from around here. An up-North Yankee, actually."

"You'd have thought people would have given up those type of notions years ago," Tessa said.

Lucas snorted. "Not around here."

We all nodded our agreement. Sad, but true. I'd heard those very sentiments from the Crawford sisters; heck, even from my own father. Truth being that a lot of folks in town distrusted outsiders, especially ones from up North. That type of sentiment, though, mostly rang true among the older folks. I'd like to think that prejudices like those weren't as pronounced in my generation. Thanks in part to an increase in mobility, or perhaps a broader perspective spurred by the Internet and even social media. Who knew? But, what Lucas said was true: Clem wasn't the only person in town who didn't take to the notion of a Yankee for mayor.

"Anyway," Tessa was saying, "I never knew what it was he'd found out about Margie. I didn't have a chance to find out."

"He didn't tell me, either," Lucas said. "I think he didn't want anything to leak out until he could reveal it at the town meeting. More impact that way."

"How'd he find this information in the first place?" I wanted to know.

I caught a fleeting emotion pass between Tessa and Lucas before she finally replied, "I don't know for sure."

Lucas swung his legs around to the floor and stood.

"We'd better get ready to go." He looked our way and explained, "We have an appointment at J. B. Cain and Sons funeral parlor pretty soon. I'm going along to help Tessa."

"Of course," Ginny said, standing. We said our good-byes to Tessa and followed Lucas back through the house to the front door. Out on the stoop, Ginny turned back and reached out to touch Lucas's arm. "You've grown into such a fine young man. Tessa is so lucky to have you."

Lucky? Was Tessa lucky to have Lucas on her side? I glanced again at the young man, thinking how neatly this whole deal had worked for him. He'd just gone from being the hired hand to, if those wedding magazines were any indication, soon marrying the girl who inherited the entire farm. Did luck actually have anything to do with it? Or was it a contrived outcome?

It was just a little before eleven when we made it back to town. Ginny scurried back to the diner, while I was greeted at the front of my shop by a disgruntled Mrs. Purvis. She was tapping her finger against the door. "This note says you'd be back at ten thirty."

"Sorry, Mrs. Purvis." Henrietta Purvis, our town librarian, was a spry little woman who favored pencil skirts and sensible blouses buttoned to the collar and secured with a cameo broach. Her only other adornment, unless you counted the chain from which her readers dangled around her neck, was a reliable wristwatch with humongous numbers, which she was currently peering at with squinty eyes.

"It's almost eleven. You're nearly a half hour late."

I fumbled with my key, trying to open the door. Henrietta Purvis was a stickler for punctuality. I knew this for a fact. I couldn't even recall how many times she'd busted my chops over late returned books. "I'm very sorry," I reiterated. "Ginny and I were just paying our respects to Tessa Rogers. I didn't expect our visit to take so long."

"Oh, dear. In that case, your lack of punctuality is completely forgivable. It was good of you to drop by on that poor girl." She shook her head and made a *tsk, tsk* sound. "So dreadful the way her uncle died."

I finally managed to open the door and motioned for her to step ahead of me. "Did you know Clem well?"

"Known him since he was a kid. Of course, at my age, I've known about everyone since they were kids." That was true. But not only did Mrs. Purvis know everyone—she remembered all their names. Oh, at first glance, the arthritic joints, sparse gray hair and slightly stooped shoulders indicated that she was every bit of her eighty-plus years, but the intelligent sparkle in her eyes and her quick-witted humor indicated the astuteness and vibrancy of a much younger woman. *Must be all that reading.*

She continued, "It pains me to know how he died. So very sad. How's Tessa doing? Maybe while I'm here, I'll pick up a couple extra jars of preserves to take out to her. I could make her some of my peach drop cookies."

Another thing Mrs. Purvis could still do well, despite her years or perhaps because of them, was bake. In fact, those peach drop cookies she'd mentioned were well-known in these parts. She always brought at least a couple dozen to the church picnics and they were always the first to get eaten. "That'd be nice. I know she'd appreciate that." I removed a jar of preserves from the shelf and looked her way. "How many then?"

"Three. No, make that four." Two bright circles of pink

appeared on her cheeks. "I'm giving a couple jars to Joe as a surprise." Joe Puckett lived in a small cabin on a few acres of wooded land adjacent to our farm. He was known in these parts for his special recipe of moonshine, made from peaches he pilfered from our trees. Not that any one of us Harpers minded, especially Daddy. As far as he was concerned, Joe could help himself to as many peaches as he needed, just as long as he kept distilling his special brew. And slipping a bit Daddy's way.

"How nice!" I said. "A special occasion?"

"No. Just because he loves them so much." I noted the blush still on her cheeks and wondered if Joe's visits to the library had to do with his newfound love for reading or some other newfound love.

I smiled as I carried the jars back to the cash register. Joe did love peach preserves, especially my mama's recipe. I thought back to the time Joe took a couple dozen jars of Mama's preserves in exchange for mowing the farm's orchards. A huge job, but he seemed to think it was a fair deal. "And how have things been at the library?"

"Just fine. Been having some trouble with some of the local teens. A bunch of them like to come over after school lets out every day. They use my back tables to work on homework. Usually they behave themselves. Lately, though, a few of the boys have been acting up. Disturbing the other patrons and such, at first. Nothing I couldn't handle."

I'm sure of that.

"But, now they're turning into vandals."

"Vandals?" A slow heat crept over my cheeks as I remembered a time back in high school when Hattie and I carved our initials under one of the library tables. I wondered if Mrs. Purvis knew about it. "That *is* horrible," I finally said.

"I don't believe you know the full extent of it, Nola Mae." She lowered her chin and looked at me with raised brows. "The type of vandalism I'm speaking of is much more serious than marring library tables."

Yep. She knows. Nothing gets by Mrs. Purvis. "What type of vandalism are you talking about?" The missing school bleachers came to mind, and I suddenly wondered how serious this breach of etiquette might be.

She harrumphed. "Destruction by dismantlement, that's what. Why, those hooligans stole the downspouts right off the library's gutters!"

"Downspouts? Really?" I shook my head and opened the cash drawer to make change. *Better than missing bleachers.* "Probably their idea of a practical joke. Kids are hard to figure nowadays. Hopefully, once they've finished having a good laugh, they'll put them back." I handed over her change and started wrapping the jars in tissue. Wanting to change the subject, I recalled what I'd heard about John Whitaker going for long walks and doing a lot of reading. "There's a new fellow in town. Mr. Whitaker? Hear he spends a lot of time reading."

"Oh yes. He's been in a few times."

"Checking out books?"

"No. Of course not. He's not a cardholder."

"Oh. What's he doing then?"

"Mostly researching."

"Researching?" For its size, our little library had a wonderful selection of books. Many provided by the tireless fund-raising projects orchestrated by the Friends of the Library group. Still, unless you were researching root-eating nematodes or the effects of brown rot fungus—because believe it or not, the entirety of one of our seven bookcases was devoted to various peach infestations—you were out of luck. "What type of research?"

Mrs. Purvis clamped her lips tight and shook her head. "Now, Nola. You know I never divulge such information." Mrs. Purvis ran library business like the back room of a law firm, concealed and confidential. "But I will tell you this: He's a nice man. Respectful of his elders, too. He even gave Joe a ride home Tuesday. Joe always comes in on Tuesday afternoon to read the library's copies of the Tuesday edition of the *Cays Mill Reporter*."

I blinked a few times.

Tuesday was also the day Clem was murdered. And Joe's cabin was just south of our land. Although there was no direct access to Joe's place, there was a well-worn path that led from his cabin out to the main road. When he caught a ride from townsfolk, they often dropped him at the head of that trail. Just a mile down from there was the turnoff to Clem's farm. "You wouldn't happen to remember what time Mr. Whitaker and Joe left the library, would you?"

"As a matter of fact, I do. They left the library just before my dinner break."

"And what time do you usually break for dinner?"

"I break for an early dinner every day at precisely four thirty," she answered with a curt nod of her head.

I smiled and held up her purchase. "Thank you, Mrs. Purvis. I hope Joe enjoys his preserves." The bag felt a little heavy, so before handing it over, I said, "Why don't you let me carry this out to your car for you?"

"Oh no, dear. I can manage just fine. I'm not that old, you know."

I knew she was going to say that.

"By the way," she added, "the library's going to be closed next Monday and Tuesday."

"Oh?"

"Yes. I plan to take some time to go up to Macon and visit my older sister." She leaned over the counter and lowered her voice. "I'd like her to meet Joe. So we're heading up on Saturday and won't be back until late Tuesday." I must have had a funny look on my face, because Mrs. Purvis quickly added, "Of course, we'll be back in time to vote on Tuesday. We wouldn't want to neglect our civic duty."

"Of course not," I said, biting back a grin. It hadn't been the idea they might miss voting that had struck me at all, but knowing that Mrs. Purvis and Joe would be, well, traveling together. Overnight. If it had been any other woman of any age in town I wouldn't have been so surprised, but Mrs. Purvis was, well, Mrs. Purvis! I turned my gaze to this spunky and surprising woman and had to smile. How little we know of people. And how lovely that Joe and Mrs. Purvis had found each other. "I hope you have a wonderful trip."

She smiled, turned and shuffled back out the door. I watched her leave, hoping that when I reached her age, I would be as capable and independent as the plucky Mrs. Purvis. All those books she read must keep her mentally alert. One thing for sure, she undoubtedly had her facts straight regarding the time that John Whitaker left the library on the day of the murder. Which meant that John Whitaker was in the right place at the right time for murder.

I'd be paying Mr. Whitaker a visit, real soon.

Chapter 7

Southern Girl Secret #081: One of the reasons we Southern women deal so well with our mistakes is because we know one day they'll make good stories to tell our children.

The rest of the afternoon passed by uneventfully, with only a few customers trickling in here and there. Finally, at around four, I turned my sign to "Closed" and hurried through my task list of chores. I was anxious to get home and talk to Mama.

I found her out on the porch swing.

"Mama? What are you doing out here? Thought you and Daddy would be sitting down for supper right about now."

She touched the toe of her shoe on the porch floorboards, slowing the swing and motioning for me to hop on with her. "I'll probably just heat up some leftovers. Don't feel much like cookin' tonight."

"That's fine. Or if you want, I could fix something for us."

She shook her head and we continued to rock back and

forth in silence for a few minutes, my jumbled thoughts and questions calming with each movement. The creak of the swing's rusty chains made a rhythmic click like it was the heartbeat of our family's home. I took a deep breath and looked out over the yard, noticing that the crickets seemed to chirp in unison, their noise reaching a crescendo like a well-orchestrated concert. Time slowed. I breathed easier. Then, somewhere off in the distance, the yip of a fox reminded me of another small animal. "Thought we might have some company this week," I said, looking around for any telltale sign that Roscoe was on the premises.

Mama looked my way, her face brightening. "You mean Roscoe? He's here. Dane brought him by earlier. He's coming back a little later with some food and other supplies."

I squinted back out toward the yard, looking for the dog. "I don't see him."

"He's inside. Your father has him in the den with him."

"Really?" I chuckled. "Daddy must be warming up to him then. Usually he just complains and grumbles when Roscoe's around."

"Oh, your father likes to put on a good act. He's quite fond of the dog, actually. And tonight he seems to need the extra comfort."

I knew what she meant. All this stuff with Clem's murder was weighing heavily on him. He was probably in his den right now, soothing his worries with a glass of Peach Jack. Which might be for the best, since I wanted to talk to Mama alone. But before I could figure out a good way to bring up the topic of her and Clem, she started with her own explanation. "Suppose you're wondering what folks are talking about. The gossip about Clem and me?" she said.

I cocked one knee and turned to face her. "I have been wondering, Mama. But I don't want to upset you by talking about something so personal."

She looked down, picking at the frayed cuff of her old cotton sweater. "It's something that happened years ago, Nola. I was just a kid. Both your daddy and I were. It was one of those stupid things kids do, you know?"

My heart started beating faster. *Yes, I know about the stupid things kids do. I've done more than my fair share.* But Mama? Certainly she never would have made the same types of mistakes I had.

"Your daddy and I met for the first time at the Peach Harvest Festival," she went on. "Oh, I'd seen him around school, but never dared speak a word to him. He was a couple years ahead of me and so handsome. Half the girls in school had a crush on him."

I smiled at the idea of my father as young and handsome, with girls swooning all around.

"Anyway," she continued. "The night we met, a bunch of my friends had talked me into going to the Peach Festival Dance. Somehow your father and I ended up dancing together, and . . ." She shrugged. "I just knew. Silly, huh? Being that I was so young and all."

"No. It's not silly, Mama." After all, I was just a kid when Cade McKenna first caught my eye. Unfortunately, life got in the way and it wasn't until much more recently that we'd finally found each other again.

"We dated for a couple years," Mama was saying. "Then when it came time for him to graduate, he decided to join the army. Wanted a chance to see some things before coming back here and settling into his daddy's peach farm. Sort of like you, I suppose." Her eyes slid my way with a smile. "Anyway, your father was anxious to get out and prove himself in the world. As much as I hated to see him go, I knew it was something he had to do. So I promised to wait for him and we got engaged. Probably sounds crazy to you that I got engaged so young, but girls back then did." She sighed. "He asked his best friend to watch over me while he was gone."

"Clem?"

Mama nodded. "Only, soon after your daddy left, Clem started to change. Just little things at first—compliments, sly looks—"

"He wanted you for himself."

"Yes. Only, I didn't realize it at the time. Or maybe I didn't care. I was lonely. Clem was handy to have around for dances and such. I was always just careful not to let things get out of hand. But looking back on it, I realize I led him on."

"So, what happened?" I was teetering between wanting to know everything and being afraid of knowing too much.

Her shoulders sagged. "I'd gone to a dance with a group of friends and Clem was there. He started right in asking for dances. I obliged him, but was careful to dance with other young men, too." She paused for a second, wringing her hands in her lap. "Lawd, but it was hot that evening. I still remember how hot it was. Clem kept bringing me punch to drink. I thought it was so very kind of him. But . . ."

I reached over and placed my hand on hers. "But what, Mama?"

She slid her hands away and stood, moving over to lean against the porch post. "It must have been spiked. Next thing I knew, he was helping me out to his car. Offering to drive me home, but that's not where he took me."

"Oh, Mama." I reached out to her. Prickles of fear and worry stung my neck as I held my breath over anticipation of what might have happened next.

She stiffened with my touch. "He took me up to Hill Lake. There was a spot out there where kids used to go to make out. I tried to fight him off but he's a big guy, too strong . . ." She shut her eyes tight at the memory.

"Oh, Mama! Did he . . . ?"

"No, no. He didn't, not that he wouldn't have." Her eyes had popped open and she faced me with a sheepish look. "Between the heat and the spiked punch and struggling with him, well, my stomach couldn't handle it all." She shook her head. "I never thought getting sick would be a salvation for anyone, but it sure was that night. He took me home, opened the door and nearly pushed me out. Only that wasn't the end of it."

"He tried again?"

"No, thank goodness. But some kids saw us out there that night. By Monday morning, it was all over school. And Clem . . . well, he didn't bother to set the record straight. Actually, he went around bragging that something *did* happen between us. There were a few nasty girls in my class that believed him and took great delight in my downfall. One of them even sent a letter off to your daddy."

My hand went to my mouth. "Oh no."

She nodded. "Yup. His tour of duty was almost over by that time. I was due to graduate the next weekend and we were going to be married right after the peach harvest that year."

"Had you talked to him? Told him what Clem did?"

"It wasn't like it is nowadays with the Internet and e-mail. And calling Europe was so expensive." She pulled

her sweater tighter around her chest. "Besides, how could
I possibly write and explain something like that in a letter?
Clem was your daddy's best friend, after all. I figured it
best to explain it in person, somehow, when he got home."

"So what happened when you explained after he returned?"

"Well, I had no idea anyone else had written to him about
it. So by the time he got home, there was no talking to your
daddy. He was madder than anything. Went right out to
Clem's orchard, dragged him off a ladder and beat him to
a pulp. They said one of the farmhands had to pull him off
Clem. They were afraid your daddy was going to kill him."

I placed my hand on her shoulder. "And now those very
same women are talking again. Bringing it all back up and
spreading lies again." I could see why she was upset. Something like this could make things look bad for Daddy.

She shook her head. "Yes, and that's bad enough. But
I'm afraid that now something worse has happened. It's
the reason your daddy has locked himself up in his den."

"What? What's happened?"

She took a deep breath and exhaled in jagged little
bursts. "Deputy Travis drove out here just before you got
home. He asked for one of my monogrammed handkerchiefs, you know, the ones your great aunt made for me
before she passed on a few years back. She embroidered a
dozen of them. Gave them to me that year for Christmas.
I just treasure them."

I shook my head. "I don't understand. Why'd he want
one of your handkerchiefs?"

"To compare it to the one he already had. Seems they
went back over Clem's house from top to bottom this afternoon, searching for any sort of motive for his murder, and

they found a hankie with my initials. Travis showed it to me. He had it in his pocket, zipped up in a plastic bag. It was mine all right."

"You're kidding. Clem must've stolen it from you."

"A handkerchief? Why in the world would he do that?"

"Well, what other possible reason would there be for one of your handkerchiefs to be in his house?"

She wrapped her arms around her midsection, her shoulders sagging forward. "Especially tangled up in his bedsheets."

My mouth was still gaping open a couple seconds later when Dane Hawkins roared up the driveway on his motorcycle. After my intimate talk with Mama about how her past problems had invaded her present life, Dane's appearance felt more disconcerting than usual.

The porch light cast just enough light for me to see him dismount his bike and take off his helmet. A few seconds later he came up the steps carrying a small duffel bag. He nodded my way and offered his usual velvety greeting. "Hey, darlin'."

How does he make those two words sound so sexy? I smiled politely. "Hey, Dane . . . I mean, Hawk." Since turning to investigative work, Dane Hawkins had insisted on being called Hawk. Better for his image, he'd claimed. "We're glad to have Roscoe visiting," I said, trying to sound casual despite the sick feeling in my stomach. Eager to get him moving along, I reached out for his bag of supplies and lifted my chin toward his parked bike. "Thanks for bringing these by. We'll be sure to take good care of Roscoe for you."

I hoped he'd take the hint and scurry off to do whatever he planned to do for the night. Of course Mama, always the polite one, invited him into the house. "Have you eaten yet? We'd be pleased to have you stay for supper. Just leftovers tonight, but there's plenty," she offered, leading him into the house and back toward the kitchen. Roscoe must have detected his master, because from behind the closed door of Daddy's den, he let out a series of excited yips.

"Thank you, ma'am, but I've already had supper. Actually, if you don't mind, I'd like to talk to your husband."

I narrowed my eyes. "What exactly do you want to talk to him about?"

He shifted, jamming his hands into the pockets of his jeans. "Someone in town hired me to look into Clem Roger's murder. I need to ask your daddy a few questions."

I gritted my teeth. "What type of questions? And why my daddy?"

Hawk's blue eyes darted between Mama and me, finally settling on Mama. He must have thought she was easier than me. "I'm sorry to have to do this, being that we're friends and all, Mrs. Harper, but your husband and my client are both suspects in the murder. You can see how that puts me in an uncomfortable position."

"Margie Price is his client," I explained to Mama.

Mama smiled tightly. My brother, Ray, had hired Hawk a year ago to help out in a case involving my brother-in-law. Hawk had been an ally then; suddenly the tables were turned. Tension bit the air as Mama answered politely, "Well . . . he's in his den, working on some paperwork. But I don't know if he's up to talkin' or not. He's not feelin' very well this evening."

"If it's okay, ma'am," Dane said, starting down the hall,

"I know where the den is. I'll just go ask him if he has a few minutes to spare."

The audacity! I started after him, but he was at an advantage with his long-legged stride. "Mr. Harper," he called out, rapping on the outside of the den door. "It's Dane Hawkins." At the sound of his master's voice, Roscoe went crazy, barking and pawing at the door.

"Come in," Daddy hollered.

Hawk opened the door a crack and turned to me. "I think your father and I should talk in private."

I ignored him, pushing in ahead of him and plopping down in one of the guest chairs in front of Daddy's desk.

Hawk mumbled something under his breath as he crossed the room to shake hands with my father. "It's good to see you again, Mr. Harper," he said, before settling into the other guest chair, Roscoe snuggling at his feet.

"Likewise, Hawk." Daddy smiled. He pushed back in his chair and reached forward to open one of the desk drawers, pulling out a couple shot glasses and a bottle of Peach Jack. "Care for a drink?" His face looked drained and tired, but his eyes seemed relieved that his dark mood had been interrupted by what he no doubt considered to be a friendly visit.

"Sounds good to me."

There was a bit of awkwardness as Daddy looked my way. "Pardon me, darlin'. Did you care for a glass?"

Not really, but then again, I hate to be excluded. "Yes. I think I will."

Hawk quirked a smile, but the last laugh was going to be on him. I knew the stuff Daddy kept in his desk looked like a store-bought bottle of Peach Jack, but the bottle was really filled with Joe Puckett's special brew. I'd had a little practice with the stuff. And while I wasn't fond of it, I could put it away with a straight face.

Daddy pulled out another glass and filled all three to the brim. I took mine, raised it in a mock salute, steeled myself and took a drink. I pressed my lips tightly together as the fluid burned its way down my throat. In turn, Daddy slammed his back, exhaled and smacked his lips together with satisfaction. Out of the corner of my eye, I saw Hawk raise his own glass and take a healthy sip. Immediately, he started sputtering and coughing. "What the . . . what is this stuff?" he asked, placing his glass on the edge of the desk. I shrugged and took another sip, reveling in the moment. Over the rim of my glass, I caught a quick wink coming from Daddy. Just a small gesture, but it spoke volumes. He was proud to have me on his team.

"Anyway," Hawk continued, his voice dry and raspy, "Margie Price hired me to help clear her name in Clem Roger's murder. So, I'm following up on a few leads."

Daddy's face darkened, any look of relief from a friendly visit long gone. "And I'm one of your leads," Daddy said, his voice flat.

Hawk nodded. "Other than my Ms. Price, you're the only suspect. To be honest, I think the sheriff's leaning more toward you than my client."

"Is that so?" Daddy filled his glass again and tipped the bottle my way. I declined with a little shake of my head.

Hawk cleared his throat. "I hear you had both means and motive." He glanced quickly my way and shifted uncomfortably.

"Don't worry about me," I said. "I already know about it all."

Daddy's expression remained neutral. If he was surprised that I knew the story of Clem and Mama, he didn't let on. "I didn't kill the man," he said, tipping back another glass of moonshine before capping the bottle and returning it to the drawer.

"For what it's worth, I believe you," Hawk said. I did a double take, not sure of what to believe from this man; after all, he was hired to clear *his* Ms. Price, not Daddy. "But I also believe my client's innocent. So you see, I'm in a bit of a tough position."

"That's easy, boy. Just find the real killer. Then both *your* Ms. Price and I will be off the hook."

"I intend to do that, sir, but it would be easier if I knew where to start. The sheriff's not offering any insight, and I didn't know enough about the man to know who his enemies might be. And there seems to be a lot of talk going around town about Clem and . . ." He rolled his neck a few times and exhaled. "Clem and Mrs. Harper."

I looked over at Daddy. In the split second our gazes connected, I saw a flash of fear in his eyes. This latest twist with the handkerchief worried him more than he was letting on. But certainly, other folks didn't know about it already? Did they? I mean, the sheriff had just found it this afternoon.

"What exactly are they sayin'?" Daddy wanted to know.

Hawk hesitated, glancing my way before continuing. "That Clem and Della had a thing going while you were away in the army. That you about killed him over it."

"That's not completely true—" I started, but Daddy held up a hand, silencing me.

"Is that all they're sayin'?"

My mouth hung open. Why wasn't he correcting Hawk?

Telling him the whole story? That Clem pretty much got Mama drunk and tried to take advantage of her. Then I snapped my mouth shut—realizing that saying that would make Daddy's dislike of Clem even stronger, wouldn't it? Give him even more motive?

"That's all I've heard," Hawk said. "Why, is there something more?"

Daddy seemed to breathe a little easier but didn't answer Hawk. "It's true that I did go after Clem. It was a long time ago and he deserved it. I don't regret my actions. But I didn't kill him. And I didn't burn down his barn."

I swallowed back an impatient huff over this irritating man. All Hawk had accomplished so far was bumbling around town and stirring up more gossip when it was quite possible the real killer was right under his nose. "Maybe you ought to be looking into John Whitaker," I said.

That garnered a blank look.

"The fellow staying at the inn with you?" I worked real hard not to roll my eyes.

Hawk sat a little straighter. "Yeah. What about him?"

"I found out today that he was in the vicinity of the crime at the time Clem was murdered. He was giving Joe Puckett a ride home just before the murder was supposed to have occurred."

Hawk paused for a second, taking in this latest news. "Did he know Clem?"

I shrugged.

"What's he doing in town?"

"No one really seems to know. Something maybe an investigator should be, you know, looking into?"

"Okay. I'll check into him."

Hawk turned his attention back to Daddy, but I'd have

no part of that. "There's someone else," I said, jumping in again. "The niece's boyfriend. His name is Lucas Graham. He's been working for Clem on the farm." I thought back to those wedding magazines I'd seen. "He had a lot to gain from Clem's death, especially since it seems the two of them might be getting married soon."

"Good job, darlin'," Daddy said, looking on with pride from behind his desk.

"Yeah, good job," Hawk echoed. "Anything else?" he asked. I shook my head and stood, my gaze fixed on him. He took the hint and stood himself, bending down to rub Roscoe between the ears. "Did y'all hear they've called an emergency town meeting Saturday evening?"

"No, what for?" Daddy asked. He let out a little grimace as he stood, his hand moving to his upper stomach.

"You okay, Daddy?"

"Just a little indigestion, that's all. Now what's this about a town meetin'?"

Hawk went on, "Ms. Price was telling me that they're planning to go on with the election."

"How's that?" Daddy asked. "She's the only one runnin' for the position."

"Not any more. Guess someone came forward. Another fellow by the name of Jack Snyder. Do y'all know him?"

Daddy and I exchanged a look. "Yeah, we know him," I answered. It sure seemed strange that all of a sudden he'd decided to run for mayor. Or was it something he had planned all along?

Chapter 8

Southern Girl Secret #070: There are certain secrets that should almost never slip through a Southern girl's lips.

Despite the fact that Roscoe's incessant barking kept me awake through the wee hours of the morning, I dragged myself out of bed and was out on the walk in front of Sunny Side Up by seven o'clock. I was exhausted, but was determined to accidentally "run into" John Whitaker during his morning jog. My goal was to strike up a friendly conversation and find out a little more about the guy. The only thing anyone seemed to know about the man was that he had dark, wavy hair, was a good houseguest and was an avid jogger. There had to be more. Much, much more. Because no one comes to a small town like Cays Mill, in the middle of nowhere, Georgia, and just hangs out for couple weeks without a reason. I intended to figure out that reason.

I situated myself so I was partially secluded by the neighbor's hedge and then started raising my knees and shaking my arms as if I were warming up for a long morning jog. But after a couple minutes, I started to fatigue, and a twinge in my hip reminded me it'd been a while since I'd done any real exercise. Where was that man, anyway? Hadn't Margie said that he leaves every morning at about this time? Then, a sudden movement from the house caught my attention, but instead of Whitaker, it was Margie exiting the side entrance under the carport with her purse slung over her shoulder and a handful of reusable fabric grocery bags. It looked like she was off to the Pack & Carry for an early-morning grocery run. I ducked farther behind the hedge as she maneuvered down the drive and turned onto the road. Peeking out from behind the hedge again, I took note of the absence of Hawk's motorcycle. Either he was out for some early-morning detecting or he hadn't actually spent the night at the inn. I mulled that over for a second or two before deciding that I really didn't care.

Then, I spotted Whitaker coming out the front door. Only, instead of starting on his morning walk, he walked over to the carport, looked around and ducked through the fence gate leading to the backyard. *What's he up to?* I came around the hedge and glanced nervously about before scurrying across Margie's front lawn, stopping short of the fence that separated the front yard from the back. Not hearing anything, I quietly slipped through the gate and inched my way toward a group of bushes, crouched down and peered through the branches. I held my breath and watched as Whitaker made his way toward Margie's storage shed. Then he did something totally unexpected. He pulled out a set of keys and inserted one into the door's padlock and, in a flash, was inside the little building.

I waited and watched until the sound of Hawk's motorcycle announced his pending arrival. Whitaker must have heard it, too, because all of a sudden, he darted out of the little building, replacing the lock and pocketing the keys before leaping over the back portion of the fence and taking off down the alley.

I stood upright and made my way to the carport just as Hawk was dismounting his bike.

"Hey, darlin'. Didn't expect to see you this morning. Looking for me?"

"No. I was here looking for John Whitaker."

He bristled. "Told you I'd check into him."

I shrugged, my eyes sliding toward his bike.

"I was just at the diner," he said, as if reading my thoughts. "Chatting it up with the local farmers over coffee. Talked to Jack Snyder and had an interesting chat with that young deputy the sheriff's got."

"Really?" I was all ears. "What'd you find out?"

"Not a whole lot, actually. Most of the farmers seem to think Clem was going a bit overboard on the election thing. Said he had it out for Margie and spent most of his time bad-mouthing her around town. As far as the 'secret'"—he made a double quote sign with his fingers—"a couple of the guys thought Clem hired a private investigator and got it from him. Others said he got his information from the sheriff."

"The sheriff? Why?"

Hawk shrugged. "Just some talk that's going around."

I mulled that over before asking, "So they think Margie's secret has to do with some sort of criminal activity?" I'd assumed the secret had personal implications, like maybe in a previous life Margie had worked as an exotic dancer or whatever. But never something that would have involved the law. "Do you know what her secret is? I mean, she's *your* client, right?"

He shook his head. "Afraid not. She won't say. I did a brief background search, something I do on all my clients just because I want to know who I'm working for. But I really couldn't find anything on Ms. Price. Thought I'd check around a little more, though. Not that I don't trust her. Just that whatever happened in her past might have some bearing on this case."

I agreed. "My guess is that Clem probably hired an investigator. I mean, I can't really see the sheriff giving that type of information to Clem. She could lose her job over something like that."

Hawk pressed his lips together and tilted his head. "Who knows? I'm not overly fond of your sheriff, but all that does seem a bit far-fetched. Even for her."

"And Jack Snyder. What's your take on him?"

"Talked to him for a while. Guess there's some sort of rule in your town charter about getting a specific number of petition signatures before running for mayor, but he's too late for that, so he's getting around that rule by running a write-in campaign. Seems to have quite a bit of support from the farmers. Of course, with all the suspicion surrounding Margie, he's probably a shoo-in for the position."

"Awfully convenient, don't you think?"

Hawk nodded. "Yup. You got that right."

"You said you talked to Travis. Did he give up any information?" Travis was probably the youngest deputy in the county. A homegrown boy who'd studied criminal justice at Central Georgia Tech up in Macon. Since he'd started with the department, Maudy had taken him under her wing, showing him the ropes and giving him a myriad of responsibilities. If I hadn't known better, I'd think she felt motherly toward him. Then again, this was Maudy we were talking about. She'd be the type of mother that ate her young.

"Unless you're interested in turbo diesel V8 engines and high-performance transmissions, I didn't learn a darn thing from the kid."

"Engines and transmissions. What are you talking about?"

Hawk chuckled. "He just recently bought himself a brand-new truck. You'd think the thing was some hot chick the way he talked about it."

Talk about the pot calling the kettle black. Hawk could barely keep his head screwed on straight when our local nail tech and hot chick, Laney Burns, was around. "Great," I said, letting out a disgusted sigh. *Hot chicks, big trucks . . . some men are so easily distracted.* "That means he won't be focused much on his job. Did you find out anything else?"

"Nope. That's about it."

I proceeded to tell him what I'd seen in the backyard. "It was the strangest thing," I concluded. "What reason would Whitaker possibly have for snooping around in Margie's potting shed? We should probably tell Margie right away, huh?"

"Let me talk to her. It could be that she knows all about it." He shrugged. "Who knows? Maybe he has her permission to store something out there?"

I furrowed my brows, thinking if that was the case, he wouldn't have waited until the house was empty and then run off when he heard someone arriving. But, I supposed Hawk had a point. We should check with Margie first.

Hawk went on, "I'm just saying we shouldn't just jump to conclusions. We need a little more information. And just because the guy's weird, or snoopy, it doesn't make him a killer. Does there seem to be any connection between him and Clem?"

"No, not that I've heard. But I'll keep checking around." I hesitated, wondering if I should tell Hawk about the handkerchief. Ever since finding out about it, I'd become filled with dread. Probably because I knew the town's blabbermouths would have a heyday spreading around the implication of Mama's handkerchief in Clem's sheets. I should probably wait to tell Hawk, too. The fewer people who knew, the better . . .

"Nola?"

"Hum? What?"

"What is it you're not telling me? And don't bother to say it's nothing. I can tell by the look on your face that you're hiding something. Care to tell me what it is?"

I shook my head. Mama always did say that I wore my emotions like a mask. "No. Maybe later. It's personal. And something that I need to figure out for myself first."

"Typical Nola."

"What do you mean?"

He shrugged. "Just seems you always have something you're hiding in that pretty little head of yours."

He winked and I bristled. *What does he mean by that? Could he know? No. No way.* I shook off the idea. Hawk probably didn't even remember that night we'd shared all those years ago. If he did, he only remembered it as a tiny blip in what was probably a long line of sexual conquests. And as far as the pregnancy and the unfortunate miscarriage soon after, I'd never breathed a word of it to him. The few people who did know—Hattie and, just recently, Ida and Cade—well, they'd never betray my trust. I breathed easier. Just my imagination running away from me.

Hawk blew out his breath and glanced at his watch. "Never mind. I'm sure you'd tell me if it was something important. I'd better get going now. I've got plans for this morning."

"Another lead?"

A slow grin broke over his face. "Laney's got the morning off and wants me to take her up to Macon to this bike dealer I know. She's thinking about getting her own bike and taking up riding."

I nodded politely, or perhaps I mumbled something, I can't remember. I was dumbfounded by the fact that he was taking time off from the case already, just when leads were coming through. Case in point: some men are easily distracted.

A little before ten, I met Carla in front of Peachy Keen. She was looking a little fuzzy around the edges. "Out late again?" I asked, opening the door and motioning for her to go in ahead of me. The frayed bottoms of her too-long jeans scraped the floor as she crossed the threshold, but I happily noticed she'd neglected to insert the long silver arrow that usually pierced the outer cartilage of her ear. On more than one occasion, I'd caught customers staring at it with a curiously disgusted look.

"Went with some friends to the Honky Tonk last night," she replied. "There was a new band playing." Before putting her bag under the counter, she pulled out an energy drink and popped the top. "They were great. Had the place rocking all night."

"How'd you get in the door? Don't you have to be twenty-one?"

She shook her head and took a swig. "Naw. The owner's cool about it."

Cool, huh? I wondered if he was also serving drinks to minors, but I didn't probe her about it. That was her aunt's job, after all. Still, I couldn't help but worry about the crowd Carla was hanging with these days.

"I'll check for orders," she said, pulling out the store's laptop while I ducked into the restroom for a quick change. I emerged a few minutes later wearing my usual cargo pants and Peachy Keen T-shirt and found her setting out supplies for baskets.

"Two Hot Jams! And three Son of a Peach! baskets," she said. "Baskets are really selling, don't you think?" I nodded, and she continued, "I'm wondering . . . with Christmas right around the corner, maybe we should try to come up with a few more themed baskets. Maybe a couple other things, too. Give the online customers more to choose from."

"Sure." She was right. I'd been meaning to expand my online order form, but just hadn't got around to it yet.

I busied myself counting bills into the cash register, having to backtrack a couple times after I lost count. My mind was reeling with unanswered questions and possible suspects, making it difficult to focus on my work.

"Well, I came up with a couple ideas," I heard her say a few minutes later. "Thought I'd run them by you, but maybe now's not a good time."

I shut the cash drawer and turned her way. "Why's that?"

"It seems you're in a bad mood or something."

I sighed and shook my head. "No, I've just got a lot on my mind with . . . with everything that's been going on."

She dipped her chin and softened her voice. "You mean the murder. Is the sheriff still after your father?"

"Afraid so." I quickly glanced over the shop, then back at her. "I hate to ask this of you, but do you suppose you could take over here? Just for a few hours. I have some things I need to do."

Her face lit up. "You bet! Just tell me what needs to be done."

I started filling her in on a few of the extra responsibilities. "First priority is the customers, of course. But if you have some free time, you could run an inventory count." I pulled out the clipboard with my inventory spreadsheet. "I already have an inventory of what's in the storage room; I just need a quick count of what's on the shelves. I'll need to know what we're running low on so I can make out a shopping list."

She smiled and took the clipboard. "No problem."

"Oh, and I noticed we're almost out of wrapping tissue and bags. There's extra in the storage closet; would you mind restocking under the counter?"

"Sure thing, boss. And don't worry about a thing. I can handle this." Any reservations I had about putting my responsibilities on her were squelched by the eager look on her face.

"I know you can," I told her. Carla was a whiz with numbers and handled even the crankiest customers with ease. Now she was showing some creative initiative, too.

I only wished she could believe in herself enough to stay away from the bad influences. "I'll be back just before closing. We'll talk about your ideas then. I'm anxious to hear what you've come up with."

Just before walking out the door, I glanced back to see her already busy assembling baskets, humming to herself as she worked. It was the happiest I'd seen her in days. Maybe a little extra responsibility was just what she needed.

My first stop had nothing to do with the case, but everything to do with my stomach. Certainly a little sugar and caffeine fortification was just the thing to get me started. So, I hoofed it down the street to Sugar's Bakery, swinging the door open and stopping short at the sight of Maudy Payne. Her back was to me as she bent over the pastry case, her khaki-clad bottom sticking out like an overblown chewing gum bubble.

Ezra's eyes met mine, but before he could call out a greeting, I held a finger to my lips and started backtracking. Maudy hadn't seen me yet. There was still time to escape.

Only right behind me came Candace from the bank. "Nola Mae! How are you, sweetie? What's wrong? You act like you don't know if you're comin' or goin'." Maudy wheeled around and glared at me. Behind her back, Ezra mouthed, *Sorry*.

I tried to ignore the look Maudy was giving me and instead turned to Candace. "Hello, Candace. How are things at the bank this morning?"

Notice I didn't ask how she was personally doing. You see, Candace works for my brother-in-law, Hollis, at the bank. And while she's a wonderful person and a terrific worker, she's a bit of a hypochondriac and loves nothing better than to talk about her various ailments, in detail. Lots of detail.

"Well, things at the bank are just fine. Wish I could say the same for myself, though." She gripped the back of her hip. "My bursitis has been actin' up somethin' awful. Why, Doc Harris sent me all the way over to Columbus to see a specialist the other day. But that man was no help. . . ." She paused and drew in a deep breath.

"I'm so sorry to hear that. I was, ahh . . ." I said, jumping in to steer the conversation to something else, only for the life of me, I couldn't think of what that would be.

Before I could get anything out, Candace started in again. "Oh, forgive me, Nola. Here I am going on about my troubles, when I hear y'all are having plenty of your own. I was just shocked to hear about . . ." She glanced up at the sheriff and bit her lip. Then, reaching over to pat my shoulder, she added, "Just know that I've added y'all to my prayer list."

I stiffened. The sheriff sniggered.

"Thank you, Candace," I said politely. Although I wasn't sure if she was praying for us because she thought we were all a bunch of sinners in need of the good Lord's redemption or because she thought Daddy needed divine intervention to get out from under Maudy Payne's dogged pursuit.

Ezra cleared his throat and tapped on his pastry case. "Scones just came out of the oven not more than twenty minutes ago. Who'd like one?" My best bet was to get my scones and get the heck out of there. "I'll take two, please," I said to Ezra.

"Same for me," the sheriff said. "And a cup of coffee.

Black." Her eyes homed in on me as she added, "Don't be running off, you hear? I've got a couple questions for you."

As I fished in my pocket and handed over a crumpled bill, I could feel little prickles of sweat forming on the back of my neck. Probably caused by Maudy's hot breath bearing down on me. "Sure," I replied, taking my change and thanking Ezra. "I'll meet you outside, then."

Candace shot me another sympathetic look as I bid her good-bye and headed out to the sidewalk to wait for Maudy. She came out a second later, already munching on a scone. "Evidence is stacking up against your daddy," she started, swiping the back of her hand across her lips.

"You said you had a question?"

"You're pretty familiar with the day-to-day operations out at your daddy's farm, right?"

"Right."

She wiped at her mouth again. "You use diesel fuel out there?"

"Yeah." It dawned on me what she was saying. Diesel must have been used as the accelerant to burn Clem's barn. "So do most of the farmers in the area," I quickly added.

"I guess you know my crime scene guys have been back out working the scene."

I shrugged.

"Thing is, they've found something interesting."

"I already know about the handkerchief, Maudy. I'm telling you, someone had to have planted that. There's no way my mama and Clem Rogers were . . ." I hesitated as Candace came out of Sugar's and passed by with a concerned look. I forced a smile and waited until she was out of earshot. "It's just not possible," I reiterated in a low voice.

"That's debatable, but that's not what I was talking about." She reached into her front shirt pocket and pulled out a snapshot. "One of my guys found this in the ditch not far from the turnoff to Clem's place. Look familiar?"

I glanced at the photo and swallowed hard. "It's just a gas can. Lots of people have those." Only it looked just like one of the gas cans we kept in our barn—a red metal five-gallon can with a lightning bolt. A vintage collectible to most people, but still serviceable by my daddy's standards, and frequently used. I squirmed under her watchful eye, my expression undoubtedly confirming her hunch that it was our gas can. I really did need to work on my poker face.

"Yeah, well, guess we'll know soon enough. Shouldn't take long to get the print results back from the lab." She lowered the brim of her Stetson and smirked. "Be seeing you soon, Nola Mae."

Chapter 9

Southern Girl Secret #114: A Southern gal never lets life break her; she makes her own breaks.

If stress burned calories, I'd be a supermodel by now. Unfortunately, stress just makes me hungry. So, I sat behind the wheel of my truck, scarfing down scones as my mind reeled with worries. Someone was definitely trying to frame my father for this murder. First Mama's handkerchief and now the gas can, which I was pretty sure would turn out to have Daddy's prints on it. Probably my prints and half our work crew's prints, too. But who would want to frame my father for Clem's murder? And why? Or perhaps even more important, how did someone get these items in the first place? The gas can could have been taken by any number of people—extra hands, delivery people . . . but something as personal as one of Mama's handkerchiefs? Either a stranger broke in to our home and stole these things, or they were taken by someone close to the family. Neither was a good option.

Then there was Margie. Was her secret past so horrible that she'd kill to protect it? And the mysterious John Whitaker? What was he looking for in Margie's storage shed? I couldn't discount Lucas Graham, either. As possibly Tessa's future husband, he stood to profit from her inheritance, as did Tessa, for that matter. And now, Jack Snyder. Thanks to Clem's timely demise, Jack had moved into the primo spot for mayor.

A lot to consider—that's for sure. But first things first. Ray needed to know about this latest development. I wasn't sure how long it would take, but I knew as soon as Maudy came up with enough evidence, she'd come after Daddy with an arrest warrant. I dialed Ray's number on my cell and finished off the last bite of scone while waiting for him to answer. Only he didn't. So instead, I left a detailed message and asked him to give me a call back.

Next, I was off to find my own answers. My first stop was the Cays Mill Library, where I met up with Joe Puckett. After spending some time talking to Joe, I found out he was pleased to get a free ride from town once in a while with John Whitaker, but that they never struck up any real conversations. He wasn't sure what the man was doing in this area, but knew that he must have been from up North, judging by what Joe called "the funny way he talked." That was hardly much help. Actually, the only real thing of interest Joe recalled was that Whitaker was reading a book titled *Cays Mill: An Antebellum History.* I located the book on the back shelves and flipped through it, finding a dog-eared corner on the section about the Underground Railroad. I remembered studying in high school about the secret network of routes that helped enslaved people escape to free states, but I'd forgotten that Sunny Side Up was one of the safe houses used along the way to freedom. Apparently the original owner of Sunny Side Up, a staunch Baptist and abolitionist, helped dozens of slaves by hiding them on his property until they could be transported to the next stop on the network. But while these neat facts about Sunny Side Up were interesting, they still gave me no clue as to why Whitaker had come to Cays Mill. Or why he was so interested in the history of the inn.

After the library, I sat in my truck debating my next move. I wanted to pop in on Margie and talk to her about seeing Whitaker nosing inside her storage shed earlier that morning, but I'd told Hawk I'd let him talk to her first. And who knew if he'd had time yet, considering his plans to spend the morning test driving Harleys with Laney. Sure hoped Margie wasn't paying Hawk by the hour. Or by the mile.

My cell rang. I looked at the display, expecting it to be Ray calling back. Instead, it was Cade calling to see if I'd meet him for lunch at the diner. I smiled into my phone, readily agreeing to the suggestion. Cade had been busy at the construction site, so I hadn't seen much of him the last couple days and, well . . . I missed him.

"By the way," he added, "I saw that Hawk's back in town."

Just like that, my smile faded. Although I knew honesty was the key to a successful relationship, I sort of regretted telling Cade everything about my past with Dane Hawkins. It made for a lot of awkwardness whenever Hawk was in town. "Yes, he's back. He's working for Margie Price."

"Speaking of Margie. Did you hear Jack Snyder's running against her now?"

"Yeah, I heard. Convenient, huh?"

"You bet," Cade said. "Especially since he lost the last time he ran."

"The last time? What do you mean?"

"Oh, didn't you know? Well, no, I guess you wouldn't. You weren't here at the time. Jack ran against Wade Marshall some years ago. It was a close race. Jack only lost by a handful of votes. He insisted on a recount. Two recounts, actually."

"I didn't know that." How come nobody had thought to tell me this before? Was Jack so bitter over his prior loss that he connived to even out the playing field this time? I quickly dismissed the idea. Certainly someone wouldn't commit murder just so they could become mayor of Cays Mill. Talk about a big fish in a small pond. And Cays Mill was a very small pond. Still, there was no overestimating how competitive people could become over such things. My thoughts flashed back to a recent scandal surrounding our local Peach Queen Pageant—sashes and sabotage, I'd dubbed it. I was shocked at some of the underhanded—dangerous, even—tactics employed by the contestants and their mothers, and all in the name of winning some silly crown.

"And," Cade added, "it'll also be very convenient for the sheriff to have Snyder as her boss."

"For the sheriff? How's that?"

"Maudy and Snyder are pretty close, you know."

"They're dating?" The idea of it made me want to gag. Snyder was my daddy's age. And Maudy was, well, Maudy.

"No!" I could hear Cade half gasp at the thought. "Not dating. They're kin. Cousins on the mothers' sides, I believe. Didn't you know that?"

I shrugged. "No, guess not." But I could see how it

might be a problem. With Snyder as mayor and in charge of the municipality, Maudy could get by with just about anything. Who knew what changes or additions she wanted to her department to further her little power trips. I let out a long sigh and shook my head. Kin, huh? It figured. Half the town was related somehow. That could also explain why some people thought Maudy might have been feeding Clem with disreputable information about Margie Price. To knock Margie out of the competition and make room for her own cousin. I took another deep breath and slowly exhaled. So much to consider.

Refocusing, I updated Cade on a few other things that had happened since we last talked. I purposely left out the more sordid details, such as Clem's assault on Mama all those years ago and her handkerchief being found in his bedsheets. It all seemed too complicated to discuss in a quick phone call. Instead I promised to fill him in on more details over lunch. After pinning down a time to meet at the diner, I hung up and started on my next quest—Snyder's Farm.

The Snyders used to grow pecans, with over a hundred acres of their land consisting of mature groves. However, during the seventies "go-natural" craze, Jack Snyder decided to convert some of the old groves into organic vegetable plots. A great move on his part. But Daddy always did say that Jack Snyder was a man who didn't let obstacles break him, but made his own breaks in life. Something my parents admired about the man and a virtue they'd always tried to instill in their own children. Anyway, Jack's idea to go natural caught on quickly, and the Snyder family soon made a fortune supplying in-season organic veggies to boutique restaurants up North. More recently, they opened a roadside produce stand, which quickly became the seasonal destination stop for health-conscious folks from all corners of the county.

I drove past the produce stand, located on the main road, and turned onto a small gravel drive leading back toward the farmhouse and outbuildings. As I neared the residence, I spotted Deputy Travis's cruiser parked outside one of the barns. Why was he here? Was he questioning Jack Snyder about Clem's murder? Or, had something else horrible happened? Heaven forbid! I slowed to a stop, contemplating whether or not I should continue forward or turn around and come back at a later time. Then, Travis came around the side of the barn and lifted his hand in a friendly wave, so I continued down the drive and parked next to his cruiser.

"Hey there, Nola," he greeted me, politely removing his hat to reveal a light brown crop of hair closely trimmed in the front with longer strands curling around his back collar. "What brings you out this way?"

"I came to talk over some business with Mr. Snyder," I said. The business of murder, but I left that part unsaid. Better to let Travis just think I'd come out to talk about peaches. "Is everything okay with Mr. Snyder?" I asked, glancing toward the barn. "Is he okay?"

"Yes. He's fine." Travis replaced his Stetson and nodded toward the barn. "He's around back."

I maneuvered in front of him before he reached his car door. "I was wondering if I could ask you something about Clem's murder?"

He hesitated, shifting his stance. "I don't know, Nola.

Sheriff probably wouldn't like me talking to you about it. Considering your daddy's a suspect and all."

"I understand, but this is just a general question. I was just wondering who called in the barn fire?" The logistics of that call were still niggling at my mind.

"Oh, well, there's nothing secret about that. I did. I was out that way on a call to Candace's place and saw the smoke. Dark smoke. I knew something was wrong, so I called it in right away."

My shoulders fell. "Oh. I see." I'd been hoping he was going to say someone else, or even better yet, that John Whitaker had made the call. "Thanks, Travis."

With a final tip of his hat, he was off. I made my way around to the back of the barn, finding Jack Snyder standing with his hands on his hips, looking down at a pile of cast-off wood, concrete and other bits of farming debris with a puzzled look on his face. "Mr. Snyder?"

He squinted my way. "Nola Mae Harper?"

I held out my hand. "Yes, sir."

"Good to see you," he said, the wiry muscles in his forearm popping into action as he gave my hand a firm shake. Everything about Jack Snyder was thin, including his white hair, which fell in stringy pieces around his chiseled face. "You know, I've been meaning to give your daddy a call."

"About the peach deal?" I asked.

"Why, yes. Isn't that why you're here?"

No, but it's as good an excuse as any. I nodded.

He lowered his gaze and shook his head. "Horrible thing about Clem."

"Were you two friends?"

He shrugged. "We did business together from time to

time. I feel bad for that niece of his. Of course, she and
Clem didn't always see eye to eye. But that's how it is with
kids that age, I suppose."

"What do you mean? I was under the impression that
they got along well." Ginny had told me that Clem cherished his niece.

"Oh, they did! I'm not saying they didn't. Just the typical
stuff." He folded his arms and leaned in a little. "Clem was
angry with that boyfriend of hers, what's his name?"

"Lucas?"

"That's right. Said he was upset about something the
boy had done. Tried to pin him down on it, but he clammed
up. But if you ask me, Clem just didn't like the idea of his
niece getting so serious about the kid."

Probably too late for that, I thought. Especially considering all the wedding magazines Tessa had been reading.

"In fact," Jack continued, "he asked if I could recommend any good farm managers."

"But that's what Lucas does. Was he planning on fir-
ing him?"

Jack shrugged. "Guess so. It'd be something Clem
would do. Fire the boy, just to keep him away from that
niece of his."

Or maybe because Clem had good reason to fire Lucas.
I thought this new information over for a second before
switching gears. "So you're running for mayor, I hear."

Jack broke into a grin. "Yes, that's right. Someone should
step in to represent the farmers, right? Oh, but then you're
a business owner these days, aren't you?"

I nodded.

He reached over and gave my shoulder a friendly pat.
"Well, don't you worry none. I plan to support both the

peach growers and the downtown businesses. You'd do
well to vote for me this Tuesday. And I'm sure your daddy
plans to support me, right?"

I didn't know what to say to that, so I simply nodded
again.

My response seemed to satisfy Jack. He answered with
a toothy grin. "Oh, good. In that case, you just go ahead
and let your daddy know that I'm more than happy to rein-
state our previous deal. Same terms and everything."

"I'll do that," I told him. "Is everything okay here? I
saw the deputy leaving as I pulled up."

He scratched his head. "Oh, sure. Everything's fine. Just
seems that some things have gone missing around here."

"What type of things?"

He waved his hand through the air. "Nothing important.
Probably shouldn't even have bothered the deputy with it."
He pointed down at the scrap pile, piled high with the farming castoffs. "Just some old pipes and stuff. Junk really. Not
worth a darn thing." He laughed. "Heck, I should probably
thank whoever it was that took it off my hands."

I looked down at the pile and something clicked in my
mind. Jack might be glad to be rid of some of his "junk,"
as he called it, but he was wrong about one thing. It wasn't
worthless. In fact, someone knew exactly what its value
was. And that someone had been awfully busy lately.

"So you think someone is stealing scrap metal?" Cade
asked. After stopping in to check on Carla, who was handling the shop like a pro, I'd popped over for my lunch date
with Cade. We were sitting across from each other in our
usual booth, enjoying today's special: deep-fried pork

chops with gravy and a side of Hoppin' John—a wonderful combination of rice and black-eyed peas.

I dabbed my napkin along the corner of my mouth and nodded. "Think about it. The copper wiring from your construction site, the bleachers from the school, downspouts from the library and now pipes from Jack Snyder's scrap pile. Little things, but after a while they add up."

"You're right. There's probably other things missing, too. Things that people haven't bothered to report. Guess we'll have to be more careful at the site. Usually, we keep things locked down at night, but there's always the chance they'll start ripping out our wiring. Guess I'm going to have to figure out some security measures."

"Wonder where they'd be taking all this stuff?" I ran a forkful of pork through my gravy and rice, popped it into my mouth and sighed. The salty crispness of the pork paired just right with the creamy gravy. And when mixed with the firm, spicy rice and black-eyed peas in the Hoppin' John . . . well, it was perfection.

Cade shrugged. "The nearest metal recycler I know of is over in Perry. But your theory makes sense. Especially with things being the way they are right now. Some people are really hurting for money."

I took a sip from my iced tea and nodded. Cade was right. The economy was on the upswing, but many people were still in dire straits.

He continued, "Sounds like the sheriff has her hands full with crime right now. Any more news on Clem's murder?"

"Yeah. A lot, actually. I've been wanting to tell you about it, but it's not really something I could talk about over the phone." I gave a look around the diner. It was after one o'clock, and the main lunch crowd had left, with no one seated near us now. "It's about Mama and Clem." He set his fork down and gave me his full attention. I went on to explain about Mama and Clem's past. "I can't even imagine how angry my father must have been when he found out what Clem had tried to do to Mama. And he and Clem were supposed to be friends."

Cade shook his head, his dark eyes blazing. "I don't blame your father for going after Clem the way he did back then. If it'd been me, I probably would have killed the guy."

Something about the way he said that gave me tiny pricks of fear, mixed with tingles of thrill. I sort of liked the idea of Cade coming to my rescue. Not that I couldn't take care of myself. I shook off my romantic notions and refocused on the topic at hand. "The problem is that there are people who still remember what happened all those years ago. And they're talking. Making it seem like Daddy had an old score to settle."

"That's stupid. After fifty years? If that were the case, why wait so long? He could have taken Clem out at any time."

I shrugged. "You're right, of course. But unfortunately that's not how the sheriff sees it. Plus, there's more." I filled him in on the most current twists: the handkerchief and now the gas can. "It looks like someone is really working hard to frame my father, but I can't figure out why."

"Maybe because he's made it easy."

"What do you mean 'he's made it easy'?"

"Think about it. It's probably not that someone purposely set out to frame your father. The killer set out to kill Clem that afternoon and probably saw your father there. Maybe even overheard them arguing. As soon as your father left, he killed Clem, started the fire and fled, knowing all along that the timing of the crime would cast suspicion on your father. The handkerchief and the gas can were just an afterthought. Maybe the killer didn't even know about that old feud until the town's gossip machine started churning out fat to fuel the blame. A couple more nails in the coffin, so to say."

I cringed. I never wanted to consider anything about coffins when it came to my daddy. Still, Cade made an excellent point. I'd been sidetracked by all this stuff between Mama and Clem. Trying to figure out who might have a personal reason to go after my family. But maybe it didn't have anything to do with a personal vendetta. It could be happenstance, plain and simple. I needed to get back to thinking about the crime, the timing, and who had the opportunity to get ahold of that gas can and handkerchief. "I'm leaning toward John Whitaker," I told Cade. "He was in the area, giving Joe Puckett a ride home, just before the time of the murder. And he's up to something." I filled him in on the incident that had occurred earlier that morning at Sunny Side Up. "Hawk says that there might be a good reason—"

"Hawk?"

"Yes. We were talking earlier. Sort of trying to work through a few points of the case."

"Oh, I see. Well, what did Hawk say?" He shifted away from the table, folding his arms across his chest.

I took note of his sudden shift in demeanor, took a deep breath and treaded carefully. "He said that there might have been a good reason for Whitaker to be snooping in the shed. Like maybe he has something stored out there. But I saw the guy. It definitely looked like he was snooping. And there are other things. Like the fact that he's been looking up stuff about Cays Mill's history at the library."

"That's not so weird. He could simply be interested in

the area." He motioned for Ginny before adding, "Could be he's a writer or something and is setting a book here."

A writer? That hadn't even crossed my mind. Maybe . . . "But who'd want to set a book here? I mean, nothing happens in Cays Mill."

Cade chuckled. "I know what you mean. Three murders in eighteen months is so boring. Oh, and arson." He rolled his eyes mockingly and sighed. "But you're right . . . nothing ever happens here."

I laughed along with his joke, but my mind was already jumping ahead to other possibilities. "Jack Snyder just told me that Clem was getting ready to fire Lucas."

"Oh yeah? Why?"

"He wasn't exactly sure. But that could be motive for murder. And Lucas could have easily planted Mama's handkerchief in those bedsheets. But I'm not sure how he would have got ahold of it in the first place."

"Maybe the killer isn't one person but two," Cade suggested, as he glanced about. "Where'd Ginny go?"

Two people? That's a really good point.

"Hey, what can I do ya for?" Ginny asked, sidling up to our booth.

"Hey, Ginny," Cade said. "Can I get a slice of lemon meringue and a coffee to go?"

"Sure thing, sweetie." She tapped her knuckle on the top of our table. "You want the same, Nola?"

I shook my head. "No, thanks. But I've been meaning to talk to you. Is it okay if we skip our cooking session tonight?" We'd planned earlier to meet that night to make a couple more batches of peach hot sauce. "With everything going on, I'm behind. I don't even have my grocery list together. And tomorrow's that big meeting, and—"

"Fine by me. My feet are killin' me anyway. Haven't had a second to sit down yet. Let's just plan on Monday evening. Will that work? Oh, by the way, Hattie was in a while ago. She's planning to close down early for tomorrow's meeting. And Sam and I will be there. We'll try to save you a seat." With that, she scurried off to fill a few more cups and grab Cade's coffee and pie.

I'd just turned back to Cade when my cell phone rang. It was Ray. He said that he'd received my message and was wrapping up a few things at the firm so he could come home for the weekend. On one hand, I felt relieved that Ray was coming home. On the flip side, it worried me. Ray, a bit of a workaholic, rarely took time from his work. I wondered if he anticipated a downturn in events for Daddy. A sense of dread settled in my stomach.

But I didn't have much time to think about it, because I'd just disconnected with Ray when Margie Price showed up at our booth. Cade politely raised up out of his seat. "Ms. Price."

"I'm so sorry to interrupt," she said, answering Cade's polite gesture with a slight nod before turning to me. "I went by your shop looking for you, Nola, and your assistant said I could find you here."

"Please join us." I scooted over and patted the vinyl cushion.

She settled in, folding her hands together on top of the table. I couldn't help but notice how elegant they were. Long fingers and pretty nails. Margie was one of those women who always looked polished and put together. Which fascinated me, since most of the time it was all I could do to run a comb through my hair. Still, under all that put-togetherness, Margie seemed to be falling apart emotionally. "What's going on?"

I asked, even though I figured she was probably upset about her sneaky houseguest.

"Hawk told me what you saw this morning."

I blew out a stream of air. "I take it Mr. Whitaker didn't have your permission to be inside the shed?"

"No, he did not," she bit out. "I don't even know how he got my keys." She started wringing her hands. "And now I'm just sure that he's probably been sneaking around other places, too."

"What makes you say that?" Cade asked.

"Just little things, you know. Like the other day I was vacuuming the hall runners on the second floor and I noticed the attic door was slightly ajar. I hardly ever go up there. I just assumed a draft had caused it to open, but now I'm not so sure."

"Did Hawk confront Mr. Whitaker about it?" I asked.

She shook her head. "No. That's the problem. He suggested that we keep it to ourselves and watch to see what he's up to. He doesn't think the man's a threat to me."

"I agree," Cade said. "If Whitaker meant to harm you, he would have done so by now. Any idea why he would have been looking in your shed?"

"No idea. There's nothing but gardening equipment out there."

"Did you go through it? It could be that we're looking at this the wrong way. Maybe he wasn't searching for something. Maybe he was hiding something in there." Something small enough to fit into his pocket, I thought. Because I hadn't seen him carrying anything.

Margie's eyes grew wide. "Like what? Drugs or a weapon?" She let out a little gasp. "Do you think he's somehow involved in Clem's murder?" She raised both hands to her face. "Oh, thank goodness I'm having company tonight. I won't feel so . . . so vulnerable. Then first thing tomorrow I'll have Mr. Hawkins ask him to leave." She shook her head. "No, I'll do it. I'll just politely tell him that I have other guests coming. We never did discuss the length of his stay. He's been paying on a weekly basis."

I felt a stab of panic. If Whitaker left, I may not have a chance to discover the truth and clear my father. I glanced at Cade, unsure of how to proceed.

Maybe he sensed how I was feeling, because he held up his hand and said, "I think we're blowing all this out of proportion. We don't know the guy's a murderer. He's never acted violent. And there's no indication that he even knew Clem. I think we're jumping to conclusions just because he's . . ." He glanced sheepishly toward Margie. "Because he's an outsider."

Two pink spots appeared on Margie's cheeks. "You're absolutely right. I should know better! I've been fighting that type of prejudice my whole campaign. People distrust my motives because I haven't been born and raised here. And here I'm doing the same thing to Mr. Whitaker."

Cade smiled reassuringly. "It's understandable that you feel the way you do, Margie. He's staying in your house, after all. But, I really don't think you have too much to worry about with Hawk there."

"And you said you had a friend coming to stay, too?" I asked.

Margie nodded. "Well, yes. Just for tonight. She's helping me with some campaign strategies. We figured we'd be working late into the evening, so I invited her to stay the night."

One glance at Margie's fidgety hands told me that she

still felt nervous about the prospect of Whitaker staying at the inn. Who could blame her? Finding out about Whitaker's suspicious activities would make anyone feel a little threatened. Especially those times when she knew they'd be the only two people in the house. And considering that Hawk's honey was close by, that might be often.

Ginny came by and placed Cade's to-go order and the check on the table. While she said hello to Margie and took her order for salad and iced tea, I started formulating a plan. Perhaps if I played my cards right, there was a way for me to get a closer look at both Whitaker and Margie. After all, Margie, as much as I hated to admit it, still had the strongest motive for murder—her secret—and she had no alibi for the time Clem was murdered.

As Ginny hustled off to take care of another table full of waiting customers, I reached over and placed my hand on Margie's arm. "Would you feel better if I came to stay with you after your friend leaves? Because it would be no problem for me to come over for a few days."

"What?" Cade sat straighter. "Do you think that's necessary? I mean, Hawk's there. And he's a private investigator."

"Actually," Margie started. "Hawk isn't always around at . . . well, he has a girlfriend in town and—"

"That settles it," I said. "I'll just plan to stay for a few nights. I'll come over right after tomorrow night's meeting. Safety in numbers, right?"

Margie seemed relieved. Not Cade, though. "Don't you think it'll seem weird to Whitaker that you've suddenly showed up to stay? Especially since you live in town?"

"Not really. I'll just make up some excuse. Let's see . . . I could say that my parents are doing some remodeling and the dust is bothering me, or . . ." I shrugged. "I don't know.

I'll come up with something." I was trying to keep it light, but the look Cade was giving me was anything but light.

Margie seemed relieved, though. "Thank you, Nola. You don't know how much better I feel knowing you'll be around. And I won't say a thing to Mr. Whitaker about that shed incident." She turned her attention to Cade. "Like you said, all he's probably guilty of is being nosy. And I've certainly had my share of nosy guests."

Cade's chin jutted out. A sure sign that he was sulking over the fact that Hawk and I would be spending the next few nights in such close proximity. Actually, the idea didn't thrill me, either. But I was willing to do about anything to make sure my father wasn't implicated in a crime he didn't commit. I pulled out my cell and glanced at the time. "It's getting late. I'd better get back to my shop. Poor Carla's been on her own all morning. She could probably use a break."

Cade stood and grabbed his to-go order. "Me, too. I've got to get back out to the site. I'll walk you out, Nola. Good seeing you again, Margie."

I took a couple minutes to confirm plans with Margie while Cade paid the check. Before saying good-bye, she thanked me again for offering to stay with her. I could tell my suggestion must have relieved a lot of her stress, because as soon as we finished our conversation, she started for a nearby tableful of ladies and launched into her campaign pitch.

Outside the diner, Cade turned to me. "Do you really think it's a good idea to stay over at Sunny Side Up? What if Whitaker really is the killer? It could be dangerous." *Hmm.* Didn't he just tell Margie that he thought it was perfectly safe to be in the house with Whitaker?

"I understand." And I really did. "But I'm doing this to

help a friend . . ." I stopped and corrected myself. "Actually, that's not true. I'm doing this to help my father." I quickly explained why I wanted to check into both Margie and John Whitaker. "What better way to figure out what they might be up to than to observe them up close? And if my presence helps Margie feel more comfortable, then all the better. Besides, you heard Margie. Hawk's out most nights." I sighed. "I'm just saying that I can't fully trust my daddy's well-being to him. Not when his focus is so divided. Can't you understand?"

For a second, Cade simply stood there, staring down at me with concerned eyes. I shifted uncomfortably under his gaze, wondering if his concern was about me being in the same house with John Whitaker, a possible killer, or with Dane Hawkins, a past lover. Then, just like that, his expression changed again, this time to an emotion I couldn't quite read. To his credit, he didn't try to talk me out of my decision. Instead, he reached over and rested his hands along the sides of my arms and said, "I do understand that you need to help your family. In fact, I wouldn't expect anything less from you. I just want you to be careful, that's all." He pulled me close, leaning in for a kiss and mumbling, "I couldn't stand it if anything ever happened to you, Nola."

Chapter 10

Southern Girl Secret #104: Don't be one of those women who follows her heart and forgets to take her brains along with her.

After Cade's kiss, I practically floated back to my shop. But my feet hit the ground again when I opened the door and found Tessa Rogers leaning against the counter, deep in conversation with Carla. They both startled as I entered, Tessa quickly swiping her cheek with the sleeve of her sweatshirt. "Oh hello, Ms. Harper. I was just leaving."

"There's no need to rush off," I told her. "How are you doing?" As I crossed the room to stand next to her, I noticed that her eyes were red and puffy.

"It's been difficult," she said. "But I'm getting by okay. Things will be better once I get through the funeral. That's what I was just talking to Carla about. I was hoping she could be there. I'll feel better with my friends around."

"Of course." I glanced between the two of them. Carla was nervously fidgeting with a leather braided bracelet on her arm. I wondered if she'd ever attended a funeral before. I turned back to Tessa. "When is the service planned?"

"Monday morning at nine. I know it's a workday, but that's the only time I could get scheduled with the funeral home."

"I'm supposed to work at ten," Carla threw out. "But I was wondering if I could come in a little late that morning?"

"Of course. That's not a problem."

"The service probably won't be that long," Tessa added. "Since there's not a body to . . . well, we're not having a separate visitation or anything. Just a simple service at the funeral parlor."

I reached out and touched her arm. "I understand. Do you need help with anything? Is there something I can do?"

She shook her head. "No. I'm fine. Lucas has been just wonderful. He helped me pick out the music for the service and everything." I dropped my hand from her arm, lowering my gaze. Here Lucas was the one person who had been so supportive of her and I itched to ask if he might have killed her uncle! She pulled into herself, shivering a bit. "Ever since I got that awful call about the fire, Lucas has been right by my side. I just don't know what I would have done if he hadn't showed up when he did."

My head snapped up. "What do you mean? I thought he was at the courthouse with you, setting up for the debate?" I thought back to the fire, remembering that Lucas showed up in the same car with Tessa. I'd just assumed he was with her at the courthouse. If not, then where was he? At the farm, killing Clem?

"Oh no. He was working at the Pack and Carry that day until five. He'd planned to meet me at the courthouse right after his shift. He'd just arrived when I got the phone call about the fire." With another little shiver, she pulled her sweatshirt closed and zipped it up to her chin. "Anyway, as soon as I heard about the fire, I just knew something had happened to Uncle Clem. That debate was all he'd talked about that whole week. He wouldn't have been late for setting it up."

I steeled myself to scratch that itch to ask about Lucas's riff with her uncle. It was my daddy's neck on the line, after all. But I didn't want to upset Tessa or close her off from talking to me, either. "Your uncle's death must be difficult for Lucas, too," I said. "He'd been working for him for a while, hadn't he?"

"Yes, that's right. For a few seasons now. This summer he stepped up as crew manager, handling things for Uncle Clem since he was so busy with the election. Uncle Clem thought the world of Lucas. That's why he trusted him to run the farm. Lucas practically brought in last season's harvest by himself."

My thoughts whirled as I watched Tessa pull out a tissue from her pocket, give her nose a blow and seem to steady herself at the thought of her capable and trustworthy boyfriend running her uncle's—and soon to be her—farm. Had I misread something in Lucas? Or was I missing some alternative? If things were going so well, and Lucas was proving so capable . . . then it dawned on me: maybe Snyder had misinterpreted Clem's question. "So everything was going okay between your uncle and Lucas?"

She shrugged. "Yeah. Why?"

I lowered my voice and spoke softly. "Because I was talking to Jack Snyder today. Jack said that your uncle asked him to recommend a new farm manager. Could Lucas be thinking of getting another job?"

"No! He loves it at the farm. And now, well, I don't know what I'd do if . . ." she said, her voice becoming thin.

"Of course," I said, nodding. "I'm glad he's there for you. I just thought, you know, capable as he is and with what Jack said, well, maybe there had been some reason Lucas might have been thinking to leave. Like maybe there were harsh words between them? Misunderstandings happen, and mistakes, too. Especially on a farm." I knew this for a fact because I'd made my share of mistakes. I remember the first time I drove the tractor. Begged and begged my daddy to let me drive the thing. And what did I do? Plowed it right into a row of peach trees. Buggered up the whole front end of the tractor, not to mention the damage I caused to the trees. Oh man! Daddy was furious. If I wasn't his daughter, he would have fired me on the spot.

Now I had to reason that if Tessa didn't suspect Lucas of wanting to leave, maybe, as Jack assumed, it was Clem who had planned to fire Lucas for some reason. But Tessa shrugged the subject off, her eyes wandering across the floor, her mind suddenly far away. "It doesn't even matter at this point. Uncle Clem is gone." She let out a jagged breath. She shifted her stance, eyes darting toward the door. "I'd better be going. I've got to find a dress for the funeral." She made her way to the door, turning back at the last minute. "Thanks for talking, Carla."

"See you tonight," Carla answered.

"I'm sorry I upset her," I said as soon as the door shut behind Tessa.

"It's not you. Really. It's just everything else. I'm worried about her."

I reached over and patted her arm. "You're a good friend

to her, Carla. She's lucky to have you. You two have plans tonight?"

"Yeah, a bunch of us are getting together out at the Rogers Farm. We're having a party for Tessa. To cheer her up, you know?" I nodded and she continued excitedly, "It's supposed to be a surprise. I'm the decoy. I'm going to pick her up after work and take her to the Tasty Freeze for a while. While we're gone, the others are going to sneak into the house and set things up. We're hoping a little fun will take her mind off everything going on right now."

A party would be the last thing I'd want to do if I were in Tessa's situation, but what did I know? Carla and her friends probably considered me old and boring. Besides, I remember being that age; kids had a different way of looking at things. Which brought to mind something else: when I was Carla's age, a party meant one thing . . . booze, and lots of it. "A party, you say?"

Carla instantly caught my drift and shrugged. "Yeah, you know. Just a few friends." Her gaze shifted, avoiding my real question.

I had to bite my tongue not to lecture her about all the things that could happen at such a party. Booze and teens were a dangerous combination. Hypocritical of me, considering how wild I was that summer after my graduation. Hattie and I had attended our share of parties. Most held at a secluded spot on the west side of Hill Lake and most with plenty of beer to go around. Still, as much as I didn't want to assume that parental role with Carla, I had to say something. If anything, so I could have a clear conscious if something were to happen. "You know, if you get caught drinking, you could get into big trouble, Carla. Especially considering everything that happened last spring. You're probably still on the sheriff's watch list." During an especially difficult time last summer, Carla had made some poor choices and found herself in a little trouble with the law. Luckily, Ray was able to get her out of it, but I had a feeling the sheriff wouldn't be so lenient if she messed up again.

"It's not a problem," she said. "Really. Besides, I'm not drinking. And I don't think the sheriff really cares."

"What makes you say that?"

"Well, the guys were saying that a while back the cops busted a party up at the lake. They seemed to blow it off."

"Blow it off? Maudy Payne?"

She shrugged. "I don't know. I wasn't there. Lucas was telling me about it. Said the cops were cool about it. Kids will be kids; that type of thing. Said we don't need to worry about it. That nobody's going to bust us over a little beer."

I found that hard to believe. Hard-nosed Maudy Payne blowing off minors drinking? Of course, maybe it paled in comparison with murder, something we'd had our fair share of these past couple years. I was still mulling it over when Carla moved on to something else. "Anyway, remember when we were talking about coming up with some new baskets this morning?"

"I do." Wow, was that just this morning? So much had happened already today. It seemed like a week ago.

She continued, "I took a chance and put a couple samples together." She disappeared into our storage closet, emerging a second later with a couple baskets in hand and a grin on her face. She placed the first in front of me. It contained a jar each of peach pepper marinade, peach chutney, and peach

BBQ sauce. "This one's for meat. You know how meat is sometimes slowly cooked over a fire pit?"

"Uh-huh."

"And how we always take out the peach pit before we cook with peaches, right?"

"Yeah?" *Where is she going with this?*

She drew in her breath and tipped the basket my way. "Well, this one's called 'Scared Pitless!' It's a play on words. You know, like in 'fire pit' and peaches without their pits, and another phrase, which you probably wouldn't want me to repeat."

I started laughing so hard tears began running down my cheeks. "I absolutely love it, Carla!"

Encouraged by my reaction, she held up the other basket. "And I've dubbed this one 'Heaven Preserve Us!' It's full of our specialty blended preserves: peach pepper jelly, peach pecan preserves and peach cobbler jam."

I was still laughing, wiping my eyes double time.

Carla's smile faded, her expression suddenly turning serious. "Do you think the names are too funny? I just thought they'd fit in with our other baskets. You know, like be consistent."

"Like them?" I came across the room and gave her a hug. "They're perfect. You're a genius, Carla."

Her chest puffed out as she set the baskets on the counter and reached for a notebook. "There's more. I'm thinking we ought to expand our offerings to include candies. I got the idea the other day when I was working over at Sugar's. He carries a lot of great pastries and baked goods. And of course, you have all the jams, jellies and sauces a person could ever want. But nobody has candy. I'm just thinking it's a little niche we could fill. Nothing big. Maybe just start with peach-shaped chocolate candy at first." She paused and pulled out a couple folded sheets from the back of her notebook. "Here. I printed off some information."

I looked over the printouts. The first was for candy molds. She'd researched and found a couple cute examples of peach-shaped molds. The other was a printout of recipes. Both milk and white chocolate recipes. "I don't know what to say, Carla," I said, as I read over the recipes. They didn't seem all that complicated. *Could I do this?*

"I even found this packaging company out of Nashville," she added, her voice growing with enthusiasm. "They sell all types of candy boxes. Reasonable, too. But there might be better prices out there. I've only just started checking into it."

I was dumbstruck. How this young girl, who was so lost and troubled last year, had the foresight to come up with such a brilliant plan. Not only the baskets, but the candy, too. I looked up from the papers and met her enthusiastic expression with one of my own. "This is an amazing idea, Carla. I'll have to check into it further, but I think it might work. Let's order a couple of these chocolate molds and start experimenting with recipes."

Her hands formed into fists, which she lifted and waved about. "Yes! I was hoping you'd like my ideas."

"I love your ideas! All of them. Thank you."

In a rare display of emotion, she came around the counter and offered a quick hug. I happily reciprocated, hoping this young woman, who I'd grown so fond of, was making the right decisions in other aspects of her life, too. Because I didn't think I could bear the idea of her ending up in trouble.

. . .

The town was abuzz with excitement the next day, especially after the headline in the Saturday edition of the *Cays
Mill Reporter* promised a heated debate at the town hall
meeting. Note: heated, not "a barn burner," the term that
Frances Simms had used to predict the last debate, which
was unfortunately thwarted by a *real* barn burning. Not to
mention a brutal murder.

With everyone planning their day around the big event,
things were slow at the shop, so we closed down early in
order to make it to the meeting in time. As soon as I arrived,
I spied Hattie waving at me from across the crowded room.
I pushed through the standing crowd in the back and made
my way to the empty seat next to Hattie. "Thanks for saving
me a spot," I said, leaning forward and waving hello to
Ginny and Sam, who were seated on her other side.

"Is Cade coming?" Hattie wanted to know.

"No. He texted me a while ago. Guess he's tied up at
the construction site." I quickly scanned the room, noticing
that the farmers were grouped in a large section up front.
A few of the business owners, like Sally Jo from the Mercantile and Doris Whortlebe from the Clip & Curl, were
sitting in front of us. The people I didn't see yet were my
parents. I'd talked to Mama earlier and she said they were
going to be here.

"I have a feeling things could get heated tonight," I
whispered into Hattie's ear.

"No need for worries." She discreetly pointed to where
Sheriff Maudy and her deputy stood. "The local law is
standing ready."

Doris Whortlebe whipped around in her chair, her

cascading ringlets, emerging from the back of a poufy crown of hair, bobbing like fishing lures with her sudden movement. "The local law, my foot. Why, the sheriff is so wrapped up in this murder business, she can't focus on anything else. Do you know I was robbed today, and she didn't even bother to come investigate? Sent that young deputy over instead. Like that youngin's goin' to know how to solve the crime?"

I leaned forward. "Robbed? Are you okay?" I had visions of a gunman facing poor Doris, her ringlets quivering.

Her shoulders began waggling, her voice growing louder as she went on, "Okay? No, I'm not okay. Someone made off with my air-conditioning unit. Took the VFW's, too. Do y'all know how much that's going to cost to replace? Thanks goodness it isn't that hot out. Why, if this had happened a few months ago, I'd lose business. It gets hot as an oven in my salon during the summer."

Sally Jo had turned in her seat and was listening to our conversation. "Seems there's been a whole rash of crime lately. I just put up security cameras at the Mercantile. Cost a fortune, but I can't afford to be robbed, neither."

Doris agreed that maybe security cameras were a good idea and the two ladies veered off into their own conversation about the best camera models and how to install them for maximum coverage. I tuned out, looking up front to where Maudy and Deputy Travis stood, my thoughts wandering from the stolen air-conditioning unit—which most certainly was the work of our local scrap metal bandit—to the gas can Maudy had found out by Clem's place. I wondered if she'd been able to trace it to Daddy yet? If so, how long would it take her to issue an arrest warrant? I glanced around again—no sign of them. Perhaps that's why my

parents weren't here. Maybe they were trying to avoid
Maudy . . .

"You seem a thousand miles away," Hattie was saying.

My head snapped her way. "Sorry. I have a lot on my
mind."

"All this trouble with Clem's murder?"

I nodded. Usually there's not much I don't talk over with
Hattie, but she'd been so wrapped up in planning her wedding, and I hated to burden her with my own problems at
what should be such a happy time. I tried to redirect the
conversation. "I bet you have a lot on your mind, too. How
are the wedding plans going?"

She sank back in her chair and let out a little moan.
"Don't ask."

"Still having trouble choosing a dress?"

"I can't deal with it. It stresses me out." She pressed her
lips into a thin line and clasped her arms around her
midsection.

I touched her arm. "I understand. But I think I know
what's really upsetting you. And it's not the dress. Is it?"

She sighed and looked away. But before I could press
any more, a sharp squeal of the mic cut through the air.
All eyes looked to the front of the room, where Mayor
Wade Marshall stood at the center podium. Big and burly
with a handlebar mustache and a thin gray braid down his
back, Wade Marshal looked more like a member of a motorcycle gang than a small-town mayor. "Good evening, ladies
and gentlemen. And welcome to the Cays Mill Mayoral
Debate." He went on to introduce the candidates, both of
whom stood ramrod straight behind their own podiums.
Margie stole intermittent sips of bottled water and tugged
repeatedly on the hem of her conservative gray suit jacket.

Jack, on the other hand, looked calm and collected and quite dapper in crisply creased navy blue trousers paired with a light blue seersucker blazer.

"I'd like to allow each candidate to open with a brief introduction," Wade was saying. "After which I will begin presenting a series of predetermined questions. Each candidate will have two minutes to answer each question, blah, blah, blah . . ." As Wade droned on about the debate rules, I turned around in my seat and surveyed the standing crowd in the back of the room. I still didn't see my parents, but I did spot my brother-in-law, Hollis, who smiled and shot me a quick wave. Ida wasn't with him. But that wasn't surprising. After all, this was no place for Junior, their tiny terror, and it was difficult enough to find a babysitter for a fun evening out, let alone a mayoral debate when half the town wanted to attend.

"We'll begin with opening remarks from each candidate," I heard Wade say. I turned back around to see him lift his hand and indicate toward Margie. "Ladies first. Ms. Price?"

Margie cleared her throat as she shuffled a few note cards before leaning in and speaking into her mic. "Thank you, Mayor Marshall, and thank you, citizens of Cays Mill. It is my privilege to stand before you today and expound on my goals and dreams for our fine village . . ."

Already, at her use of "expound," I felt the farmers' side of the audience tense. After that I only half listened to Margie as she spoke. Instead, my thoughts wandered to Jack Snyder, who seemed cool and collected behind his own podium. For a man who just announced his mayoral intentions two days ago, as a write-in candidate nonetheless, he sure seemed well prepared. Not only did he have what looked to be a new suit, less formal and more appealing to our Cays Mills mind-set than Margie's tailored ensemble, but he'd already plastered professionally printed signs all over town. Just how did he get all that done so quickly? Or perhaps the signs were left over from his last attempt to run for mayor? Or—I narrowed my eyes and watched as he confidently began his opening statement—maybe he'd been prepared for this moment all along. What was it Daddy always said about Jack Snyder? That he was a man who didn't let life's obstacles break him. Maybe poor Clem was simply one of those obstacles that Jack felt he needed to eliminate to achieve his goal of becoming mayor.

"Unlike my opponent," Jack began, "I've lived in Cays Mill my whole life. Why, I know most of y'all personally. I understand the struggles you face. I've toiled in the same Georgia dirt and I've watched with you as many of our local businesses have closed or moved to the bigger cities. As one of you . . ."

"As one of you." Boy, not hard to figure out his game plan! Jack Snyder obviously intended to alienate Margie as much as possible. Make people think that she couldn't run the town because she was an outsider. Of course, a little part of me knew what Jack said made sense. Having lived here his whole life, he really did understand our town. But Margie brought with her fresh ideas and the possibility of change for the better. I let out a sigh. I guess, when it came down to it, I was still undecided about my own vote. Actually, I wished Wade Marshall would run again. Despite his less than mayoral appearance, Wade was a great town leader. He'd seen us through several bad harvests, managed to keep taxes low, and even succeeded in slowly bringing more businesses into town.

As Jack finished, Wade moved back to his podium, and after blinking away a couple blinding flashes from Frances's camera, he began reading the first debate question from a small notecard. "If elected as mayor of Cays Mill, do you plan to raise the municipal sales tax? Ms. Price, you have two minutes to respond."

The crowd started to stir. This was a hot topic. Margie drew in a deep breath and started, "There is no doubt that our town suffers from a lack of revenue. Revenue that is needed to maintain our fine school system, improve infrastructure and maintain necessary programs. However, I feel that raising sales taxes will discourage local shopping and therefore put an unfair burden on local business owners." A few heads bobbed up and down in agreement. "What I'm proposing instead," she continued, "is increasing the fee for business licensing renewal." That stopped those heads from bobbing. "As well as doing away with a percentage of property tax exemptions for local agricultural business. That way, both the business owners and local farmers will share in the increased burden of—"

"Do away with our property tax exemptions?" someone yelled from the crowd. "What are you trying to do, put us farmers out of business?"

Margie held up her hand. "Not all exemptions. Just a percentage of—"

But before she could get another word out, Jack interrupted. "What would y'all expect from an outsider? Like I was saying, I'm a farmer, like most of you. I also have the unique advantage of being a small business owner. I understand your struggles. I sympathize with your—"

"That's great, Jack," one of Margie's supporters called out. "But what's your plan for runnin' this town?"

A ruckus arose, with questions being fired from both sides of the room. I about got whiplash trying to keep up with who was saying what. Up front, Mayor Marshall began banging his fist on the podium, trying to regain control of the crowd, while Frances scurried about taking photos. I looked toward Maudy, expecting her to intervene at any second, but she wasn't paying any attention to the rising unrest in the room. Instead, she had her cell phone to her ear and seemed to be deep in conversation with someone. I watched her nod, say something and nod some more. Then, even as she continued to speak into the phone, her eyes shot upward, landing on me with a wicked gleam. Her mouth curled into a knowing sneer. Finishing her conversation, she turned to her deputy and whispered something in his ear and headed toward the back door, seemingly impervious to the uproar that'd broken out in the room.

Then it dawned on me. Turning to Hattie, I quickly excused myself and made a beeline for the exit. Because if I knew Maudy, there was only one thing that could tear her away from an opportunity to exude her authority over this rowdy gathering—the chance to nab a Harper.

Chapter 11

Southern Girl Secret #080: Truly strong women are the ones who fight the battles no one knows about.

I made it outside just in time to see Maudy roaring down the road in her sheriff's cruiser. I jogged across the road and hopped in my own vehicle, catching up to her fifteen minutes later at our farm. She'd turned her car sideways in our drive, blocking Ray's SUV from leaving. As I got closer, I saw that both she and Ray were standing outside their cars, animatedly discussing something.

I parked and ran over. "What's going on?"

Ray looked angrier than I've ever seen him. "We're trying to get to the hospital, but the sheriff won't let us leave."

"The hospital? Why?"

He thumbed toward his car. "It's Daddy. He's not feeling well. I'm taking him into the emergency room to get checked out."

I ran to the SUV and flung open the door. My parents

were sitting in the back, Mama holding Daddy's hand while he sat slumped against the seat. His ashen face was covered with a sheen of sweat. "What is it, Daddy?"

He mustered a small smile. "Just a little indigestion, darlin'. Nothing for you to go worryin' about."

Mama shot me a look and I knew this was a lot more serious than indigestion. I drew in my breath and stomped back to Maudy and Ray. "He needs to get to the hospital now," I said, my fists clenched.

"I don't think he's sick at all," Maudy said, thrusting out her jaw. "I think Nola here saw me leave the town meetin' and tipped y'all off. Now let me at him. I've got a warrant."

I sidestepped, blocking her way. "This is crazy," I spat, standing toe-to-toe with her. "He's going to the hospital, Maudy, and if you try to stop us, I'll—"

Ray pulled me back and stepped in with a little lawyerly diplomacy. "Let's all be reasonable," he started smoothly. "I'll take personal responsibility for making sure my father stays within county limits. And as soon as the doctor clears him, I'll bring him into your office myself. You have my word." He paused, giving her time to consider his proposal.

"He doesn't look good," I jumped back in, this time, taking a cue from Ray and nixing my hostility. Instead, I tried to appeal to the sheriff's softer side. Assuming she had one. "Despite what you think about the rest of us Harpers, my daddy's always been fair to you, Maudy. You know that. And I'm sure you don't want to see anything bad happen to him." Her features seemed to relax a little. "And when have you ever known my father to run from something? He's not a coward. And he's not running now."

"This could be something serious," Ray added. "We really need to get him to the hospital. Now."

Maudy removed her Stetson and swiped the back of her hand along her brow. "Okay, fine. But I'm going with y'all. Follow me."

So we did. We followed behind Maudy's cruiser to the county hospital, where Daddy was immediately taken back for tests. Mama went with him, while the rest of us stayed behind in the waiting room.

"I'm going to head down the hall to the vending machine and grab a quick cup of coffee," Ray said. "Can I get you something, Sheriff?"

"No, thanks." She adjusted her utility belt and flopped into one of the waiting room chairs, picking up a nearby magazine.

With a lift of his chin, Ray indicated for me to follow him. As soon as we were down the hall, he turned to me and whispered, "What exactly is going on around here? Maudy was saying she went out to the house this afternoon and got a set of prints from Daddy. And a DNA swab from Mama?"

"She did? I didn't know that."

"What were they thinking, agreeing to those tests? Why didn't they call me first?"

I thought back to how I hadn't been able to get ahold of Ray all day. "I don't know, Ray. Maybe they tried. And maybe they didn't understand that they could refuse."

"This is bad, Nola. And now these problems with Daddy's heart." He folded his arms across his chest and lowered his head. I noticed the tendons in his neck stood out, visibly pulsing. Ray was scared. And that scared me.

I tried to remain calm and not let my emotions take

over. How many times during my career as an aid worker had I faced the impossible? I'd always relied on ingenuity and my resourcefulness to find a solution. Maybe this issue seemed more difficult because it cut so close and personal, but no matter how I looked at this situation, I could only see one way out of our problems. I placed my hand on Ray's shoulder. "Our only chance to relieve some of this stress is to find Clem's murderer." Then I went on to explain my plan had been to stay at the Sunny Side Up for a few days. "Only, I'm not sure I should leave Mama now that all this is going on with Daddy."

"Stay at the inn?" Ray ran his hands through his hair. "I'm not sure that's a good idea. What if Whitaker is the killer? You could be putting yourself in danger."

"I'll be careful. Besides, Hawk's staying there, re-member?"

He shook his head. "I'm not sure if that makes me feel better or worse."

I wanted to ask what he meant by that, but Mama was coming down the hall, a strained look on her face. "He's resting," she explained. "They don't know what's going on yet. It takes an hour or so for some enzyme test they took to get back, and then they have to rerun it later, too. But either way it turns out, the doctor wants to run more tests. They're going to keep him overnight." She looked over her shoulder toward the waiting area. "The sheriff's left. Said she'd be back tomorrow."

I felt a little relief, mixed with a lot of apprehension. Enzyme tests I'd heard could prove—or rule out—a heart attack. But what other tests after that?

"He's awfully upset, though," Mama continued. "All this stuff with the murder. And it just keeps getting worse.

The sheriff came out earlier today, demanding all sorts of things. Then when she came back this evening with a warrant . . . well, your father became so upset. Then those pains started up. I'm so worried that maybe it was a small heart attack."

Ray shifted uncomfortably and glanced my way. "It's okay, Mama. He'll be all right. And don't worry about things at the farm. I'm going to stick around for a few days and help out."

Mama's face instantly brightened upon hearing that news. "Thank you, Bud. Your daddy will be so relieved to hear that. I think I'll stay here tonight with your father. But you two should head on home. Get some rest. And, Bud, don't forget to let Roscoe out tonight. And he does love a little bacon for breakfast."

After much discussion back and forth, and a lot more doggy care advice, we finally agreed on a plan of action. Ray was going to head back to the house and pack up a few things that Mama needed for a couple days at hospital. She wanted us to keep things going at both the farm and the shop, so as not to worry Daddy any further. Since we operated on such a narrow margin, a few days' lapse on either end would cut into our profits. And Daddy hated losing money. No matter the reason.

After all the details were worked out, Mama returned to my father's bedside, and Ray and I made one additional plan. After hearing how the stress of this murder investigation was affecting Daddy, Ray decided that my staying a couple nights at the inn wasn't such a bad idea after all. So, while Mama was going to be at the hospital taking care of Daddy, I'd be at the Sunny Side Up, taking care of him in my own way—chasing down a murderer.

Only as I left the hospital I found that I was the one being chased down. Frances Simms, our relentless newspaperwoman, practically accosted me in the parking lot. "What's going on, Nola?" she asked, suddenly popping out from behind a parked car. "Is someone sick?"

"They're running some tests on my father," I started to explain, then stopped myself. This was Frances Simms doing the asking. She wasn't concerned about my daddy's well-being. She was digging for information. "He'll be fine, though. But thanks for your concern. Excuse me," I said, pushing past her and starting toward my truck.

"The sheriff's got something big on your daddy, doesn't she?" she asked, keeping stride with me. "Don't try to deny it, Nola. I got suspicious when I saw y'all leave the town meeting in such a hurry. I asked around and someone told me they overheard the deputy say something about a warrant. Is that an arrest warrant?"

"No."

"It's not an arrest warrant?"

"No, I mean no comment." I shook my head and picked up my pace. "How'd you know where to find us? Did you follow us out here?"

She patted her pocket. "I carry a scanner. Sheriff called in to dispatch to let them all know she was heading out this way with the suspect."

Suspect. The word made me bristle, and Frances must have caught it. She narrowed her eyes. "Heard they searched Clem's house again. Sheriff must've found something that points directly to your daddy."

Don't talk! Don't say a word! I bit my lip and started digging around in my bag for my keys. We'd reached the truck. I fumbled with the keys in the dim light, finally connecting to the keyhole. This was one of those times I'd do about anything for automatic locks and a key fob.

"You know what I think," Frances was saying, "I think this all has something to do with the rumors going around town about your mama and Clem. About some hot affair they had way back when."

Hot affair! "Those are nothing more than nasty rumors, Frances!" I snapped, my hand frozen on the door handle. Of all the—she'd write anything for her blasted headlines condemning my family. "There's not a shred of printable facts. Besides, my daddy isn't the only suspect the sheriff has."

Her thin brows arched. "Yes, but he's the only one she's got a warrant for, right?"

"Well, that's just because she doesn't have all the facts yet." I held my head up, glaring at the woman.

"So she *does* have a warrant for your daddy?"

"I didn't mean that. I meant—" I started, then clamped my mouth shut and started opening my door, but Frances pushed against it.

"Are you saying you have information about another suspect? That your daddy didn't kill Clem? Do you have proof that someone else killed him?"

"Yes! I mean, no, Daddy didn't kill anyone and I—"

"And you *do* have proof? What type of proof? Who is it?" Even in the dimly lit parking lot, I could see the hunger in her eyes. "Margie Price?"

"No. That's not what—"

"That new fellow in town? John Whitaker?"

I shook my head, trying to calm myself, not to tangle myself further in her snares. "I'm afraid I'm not at liberty to say."

"So you *do* have proof. Where is it?" She darted a

glance at my truck, my purse. "Locked up somewhere safe? When are you going to reveal this evidence? In time for the Tuesday edition of the paper?"

Despite my suddenly weak knees, I managed to pull open the door to slide past her and climb into the truck. "You're making too much of all this," I said. "Twisting my words." I turned the key and pumped the gas pedal. With a couple *pop*s, the old truck engine roared to life.

"Wait!" She wedged herself in front of the door before I could shut it. "You haven't taken this proof to the sheriff yet, or she wouldn't still be going after your daddy. Why are you keeping it to yourself?"

"I'm not!"

"Then who else knows about it?"

"No one! I don't . . . Oh, for crying out loud! Just forget I said anything, okay?" But one look at her gloating face told me a new headline was already churning in her mind. What had I done? All the way to Sunny Side Up, I cursed myself for yet again falling into one of her traps.

"I appreciate you being here," Margie said. "Especially considering everything your family is going through right now." She sighed. "I'm sure the stress of being so vehemently pursued by our local sheriff has contributed to your father's illness. I know how stressful it is to be the accused."

I'd just finished filling her in on my father's sudden illness and Maudy's intent to arrest him as soon as he recovered. It was almost midnight and we were standing in a beautifully appointed room on the second floor of Sunny Side Up. Hawk was still out doing heaven only knew what and John Whitaker was in his room for the night.

Except for our hushed conversation and the ticking of a grandfather clock in the hall, the house was morguelike quiet.

"Yes," I replied. "I do think all the stress of the investigation is attributing to his condition. But now that the sheriff is convinced she's found her killer, you're off the hook. I guess that's good news for you." While I unpacked a small duffel bag, Margie moved to a large antique armoire and opened a drawer for me. I placed my jeans and tees into the drawer, glancing up at her to respond, to say something, anything that might help me learn more about this woman who might be behind a murder. But Margie's attention was elsewhere as her fingers ran over the carved corners of the armoire, admiring its craftsmanship.

"A gift from my ex," she explained. "The only thing I've saved from our time together."

"I didn't realize you were married before."

"Oh yes. I married young. Too young." She waved it off as nothing, but I had to wonder if her previous marriage might have had something to do with the secret she'd been guarding so closely. "But, that's all in the past," she continued. She perched herself on the edge of a pretty floral wing chair by the fireplace and addressed me with a serious look. "I want you to know that I don't believe for a second that your father had anything to do with Clem's murder. When Deputy Travis hushed the shouting at the meeting, he explained that our intrepid sheriff had gone off to make an arrest, leaving him to hold the peace. It was obviously an arrest of someone not at the meeting, and I realized your poor father was next on her list. I'm just so sorry that you and your family are going through this."

Her sincerity and words brought a little lump to my

throat. How could I be here investigating her when she was being so sweet to me?

"And I must warn you, Frances Simms must have been thinking along the same lines as me. She immediately started poking around, asking people all sorts of questions about who the sheriff might be arresting."

That lump in my throat slid all the way down to my stomach and settled in like a rock. *And after that disastrous conversation in the parking lot she believes that I have proof that someone else is guilty. Heaven help me!*

Before I could even wrap my mind around this current dilemma, Margie continued in a brighter tone, "Anyway, since I do seem to be off the hook, I'm wondering if I shouldn't consider letting Mr. Hawkins go. It's true that I do feel safer with him here, especially with the snoopy Mr. Whitaker around, but his investigative services are quite costly. I don't really see the need to keep paying an investigator, now that I'm not under suspicion."

Since Hawk and I had sort of agreed on sharing information, the news that he wouldn't be working on the case was just one more strike against my getting help for Daddy. Another small part of me wondered if Margie wasn't getting off the hook a little too easily. And in the back of my mind—the dark recesses where I hated to linger—there were still questions that needed to be answered about Margie. Her secret that Clem had threatened to expose, for one, which gave her more than plenty of motive. Then there was the fact that no one could account for her whereabouts during the time of the murder. But if I was going to make any progress at all during my stay, Margie needed to believe that I was simply here as a friend. "What about Mr. Whitaker? I thought you felt more comfortable with Hawk around."

I pretended to shiver. "Especially at night, when the house is dark and it's just you two."

She started worrying her hands. A little part of me felt bad for laying it on so thick, but then again I really did need Hawk around to help with the investigation. "Yes, I've been thinking about that, too. I know it's not right to suspect Mr. Whitaker just because he's not from here, but . . ." She took a deep breath. "It pains me to do so, but truthfully, I just don't feel comfortable with him here, and I simply can't expect you and Mr. Hawkins to stay on forever. So, I thought perhaps I'd ask him to go midweek. After the election."

"Midweek?"

"Yes, and I would have asked him to leave instantly but I didn't want to upset him, considering I couldn't trust what his reaction might be. I simply made up some excuse about new guests coming in and told him he'd have to find different accommodations. But you can stay until then, can't you, Nola?" she asked. "I hate to intrude on your time, but—"

"I'll do my best," I said. "I can't make any promises though, since my father is sick. Mama may need me at home."

"Of course. And thank you."

I forced a smile and said, "I'm happy that you'll be able to move past all this and focus on the election. How did the rest of the debate go?"

Her expression changed to an emotion I didn't quite recognize. Anger? Bitterness? And once again, I had to ask myself just how well I really knew Margie. "Well, Jack Snyder certainly is the hometown hero," she said. "He'll be hard to beat."

"I suppose so," I agreed. "Jack has roots here and people

tend to trust someone they've known all their lives. Even if that doesn't necessarily mean he's the best person to run the town."

"Yes, but my revenue-raising ideas didn't go over very well with tonight's crowd. Seems no one wants to sacrifice any more than they already have. Which I can understand, considering the town's just barely starting to fight its way back from the economic downturn of the past few years. But Cays Mill needs to invest in its future now. Otherwise, it may not survive the next financial slump. In truth, this town's only a couple bad harvest seasons away from real decline. And I think I'm the person for the job. Just look at all I've achieved here."

I glanced around the gracious room, taking in the four-poster bed covered in a pretty percale duvet, the white-mantel fireplace flanked by full bookshelves and a cozy seating arrangement. Breezy curtains framed double French doors, which opened onto a second-story veranda that wrapped around all four sides of the home. "You don't have to convince me. You've done such a wonderful job with this place. It's just magnificent," I told her.

"Yes, and to think I almost lost it."

I paused and turned her way. "You mean because the sheriff initially had you pegged for Clem's murder?" Or did she think that if the secret Clem threatened to expose came to light, she'd lose her standing in the community?

She exhaled and smiled tightly. "Well, it certainly would be difficult to run a bed-and-breakfast from prison. Why, what else would I have meant?"

I checked myself. "Oh, nothing. I just . . . well, I'm so glad things have worked out for you. Even your secret seems safe now."

She stiffened. "I suppose you're right. There's no chance of it getting out now."

Yes, especially since Clem is dead and Maudy Payne is off your back. How very convenient.

She stood and adjusted her skirt. "Well, I'll let you finish getting settled. I'm off to bed. It's been a very long day."

"Yes, it has," I agreed.

Chapter 12

Southern Girl Secret #122: Dating a man is like
making iced tea: boil his ego, filter his issues,
add oodles of sugar and enjoy.

And it was a long night, too. After calling Cade and letting
him know everything that'd happened, I climbed wearily
into bed but hardly slept a wink. Instead, I tossed and
turned with worries about Daddy and moments of panic
about whether or not I'd be able to find Clem's killer, all
topped off with runaway thoughts of Tuesday's newspaper
headlines: "Local Peach Farmer Ripe for Arrest"; or "Local
Peach Farmer Stuck in a Murderous Jam"; or, just as bad,
"Peach Farmer's Daughter Digs Up Murder Evidence" . . .
Heaven only knew what that woman might come up with!
Then, sometime during the wee hours, the telltale sound
of Hawk's heavy boots on the main staircase propelled me
into an anger-fueled state of wakefulness. No doubt he was
returning from a late-night rendezvous with Laney Burns.
If that man put half as much effort into his investigative

work as he did that woman, he'd have the case solved by now and I wouldn't be worrying about headlines!

Then, certainly only seconds after I actually fell asleep, slivers of sunlight crept over the room and the slightly bitter smell of coffee mixed with the yeasty smell of fresh baking bread pulled me from my bed. After a quick shower, I checked in with Mama at the hospital. They were just waking themselves, so she didn't have any news to share. Daddy was scheduled for more tests and she promised to call me as soon as she knew something. She also asked me to make sure Reverend Jones offered up a prayer at church this morning. I told her I'd see to it.

After giving the preacher a quick call—no need for Mama to know I didn't actually plan on attending services this morning—I made my way down to the dining room. Margie didn't have a specific breakfast time but instead accommodated her guests' schedules by setting out a hot buffet every morning, chafing dishes keeping everything warm until her guests had their fill. This morning, the side bar was set with a large urn of coffee, steaming trays of eggs and bacon, fresh fruit and a basket of warm biscuits. I gladly filled my plate with a little of everything, taking an extra biscuit and a healthy dollop of Harper Peach Preserves which, I was glad to note, were nicely displayed next to the bread basket.

A few minutes later, Margie wandered in wearing an apron over a flowered dress. "Good morning, Nola. You're the first guest up this morning."

"Well, you know what they say about early risers. Great breakfast, by the way," I said, munching on a slice of bacon while she checked over the food, giving the scrambled eggs a quick stir.

"Are you heading to church?" I asked, noticing how nicely she was dressed.

"Yes, and I'll be leaving a little early. I'm on the committee for the Founder's Day Parade, and we're planning a quick meeting at the church before services start. Are you going? We could ride together."

"Oh—no, thanks. I have some errands to do for Mama today. Which reminds me, would you happen to have paper and a pen I could borrow? I need to make out a list."

"Oh, no problem." She disappeared into the butler's pantry and emerged a second later with several pieces of paper and a couple pens. "The pantry doubles as my office. People seem to call for reservations when I'm busy in the kitchen," she explained. Her eyes focused on something over my shoulder. "Oh, hello, Mr. Whitaker. Heading out for your morning run?"

"Good morning, Ms. Price. Yes. Just going to grab a sip of coffee before I go." He crossed the room to the breakfast bar, pouring himself a cup of coffee before regarding me with a tight smile. I smiled back, noticing that what I'd first thought were handsome features suddenly seemed sinister to me: his strong chin now looked brutish; his black hair just a little too slick and why-oh-why did he have his nylon running suit unzipped to reveal all that curly black hair on his chest? Ick!

"Oh, excuse my manners," Margie said. "Mr. Whitaker, this is Nola Harper. She'll be staying here a few days while her . . . uh . . ."

"While some remodeling work's being done at my house," I said, rising from my seat and extending my hand. "The drywall dust really gets to me, you know?"

He shuffled his coffee cup and offered a quick shake.

"Anyway," I continued, "it's nice to meet you." I paused for a second, then added, "Whitaker? Do you have family in the area?"

"Uh, no, I don't."

"Just vacationing, then? Or are you here on business?"

He took a quick sip, eyeing me over the rim of his cup, before setting it back down on the table. "Vacationing." He adjusted the zipper on his Windbreaker—thank goodness!—and turned to head for the door. "Excuse me," he said over his shoulder. "But, I'd better hit the road." His jogging suit made little swishing noises as he left.

I didn't like this fellow. Not one bit.

There wasn't much time to spare, so as soon as Margie left for her meeting, I bolted upstairs and headed straight for Whitaker's room. After a quick check of the door, which was locked, I scurried back downstairs toward the butler's pantry. If Margie used this area as her office, perhaps she kept other innkeeper essentials there, like copies of room keys.

Inside the little room, I looked over a few glass-front cabinets filled with serving plates and stacks of china. Then my eyes moved to the computer, which occupied the center of one of the countertops. There was a bank of drawers underneath. I started there.

The first drawer was chock-full of miscellaneous items: a minihammer, picture-hanging brackets, a pack of gum, pencils and pens . . . at home, we would call this our catch-all drawer. I pulled open the next, however, and was thrilled to find a large binder. Margie's reservation book! I quickly paged through until I came to the entry with John Whitaker's reservation. I noticed he listed his home address as

Mobile, Alabama. Strange. His accent didn't sound a bit like Alabama. He must've paid in cash, because there wasn't a credit card number, but there was a license plate number listed. Grabbing a pen and piece of scratch paper, I scribbled down his address and the license number for his rental car, hoping to goodness that I didn't get caught at what appeared to be identity theft.

"Need a little help, darlin'?"

I jumped and grabbed at my heart. "Hawk! You, you . . ." The phrase "scared me pitless" suddenly popped to mind.

He moseyed over and peered over my shoulder. "Whatcha lookin' at?" I tried to shut the reservation book, but he clasped his hand over mine and leaned in even closer. His touch and that all-so-familiar scent of fresh soap mixed with the smell of the wind and motorcycle exhaust aroused unwanted feelings. "John Whitaker, huh? You must be trying to get more proof that someone other than your daddy killed Clem."

"More proof? What do you mean?" Although, even as I asked, a sick feeling crept over me.

"Well, I was at the diner this morning . . ."

I squeezed my eyes shut as he continued on about how everyone in town had heard that I had proof of who killed Clem. The general consensus was that I was keeping this so-called proof to myself so I could one-up the sheriff . . . just like last time there was a murder in town, and the time before that. Apparently I was developing a bit of a reputation for solving crimes.

I shook my head. "I don't actually have any proof," I explained. "I only said yes to Daddy not being guilty but she'd also asked if I had proof that someone else was guilty and . . . well, you know how she is."

He chuckled and backed away. "Sounds like you've worked yourself into a big problem."

I could blame it on Frances misunderstanding what I'd said, but I should have known better than to open my mouth around that woman at all. I peeled my moist palm from the page and shut the book, returning it to the drawer. "Guess you're right. That's why I'm doing a little more investigating of my own. I figured someone should be doing that," I added with a pointed look. Then, I pocketed the scrap paper with Whitaker's information and started tearing through the other drawers. "I need the spare key to his room. Do you know where it is?"

Hawk reached up and opened one of the cabinets, revealing a narrow pegboard of keys. He selected one and dangled it in the air.

"Oh. Thanks," I said, reaching out.

He jerked his hand away at the last second. "I'm comin' with you. Just in case."

I hesitated, considering my options. There weren't any. Besides, arguing would only waste precious time, because Hawk was, among other things, bullheaded. "Fine. But hurry. We don't have much time."

I could see why Margie chose this room for Whitaker. Its natural brick fireplace and dark wood accents were decidedly more masculine than my light and pretty room down the hall. I moved directly to the nightstand next to the bed, while Hawk crossed to the closet.

"Found his computer," he said, pulling a satchel from the closet floor.

The nightstand drawer didn't reveal anything, so I

moved to the dresser. "I wonder if Whitaker is even his
real name." I was looking for a wallet or anything that
might have some sort of picture ID.

Hawk sighed. "The computer needs a password." He
flipped it shut and ran his hand through the other compartments in the satchel.

I was rifling through the top drawer of the dresser.
"Ew!" I said, holding up slick red briefs. "This guy wears
silk briefs."

"What's wrong with that?"

I shot him a strange look and turned back to the dresser.
After another pass, my hand hit on something. I pushed a
stack of socks aside and pulled out a folded piece of paper.
"Got something."

Hawk replaced the computer and joined me as I laid it
out on top of the dresser. It was a crude but detailed sketch
of Sunny Side Up and its grounds. "Look," I pointed out.
"He's checked off certain things. And here's that shed outside. It has a checkmark too."

"Looks like he's been systematically searching the place."

"But, what for?"

Hawk shrugged, running his finger along the map and
taking note of each location, stopping when he got to the
storage shed. He bent forward and squinted. "Look at this."

I leaned in, our heads touching. Once again, my pulse
quickened in reaction to his closeness, a tingle at the back
of my neck. Silently chiding myself, I fought to stay in
control of my hormones. "What is that?" I asked, looking
at the depiction of the storage shed. There was a lightly
drawn line leading from the floor of the shed to the edge
of the map.

"And here. What's this?" He was pointing toward the

corner of one of the back rooms on the main floor, where
Whitaker had drawn what appeared to be a built-in bookcase.

I wonder if—

My thought was cut short by the sound of the front door
slamming shut. Both Hawk and I bolted upright, the look
of fear on his face certainly mirroring my own.

"Crap!" he said, refolding the paper and holding it over
the drawer. "Where'd you get this from?"

"Here." I snatched it from his hand, placed it back where
I'd found it, and slid the drawer shut. We both started for
the door, Hawk putting out his hand to stop me. Footsteps
sounded on the main staircase.

"Too late," he said, his eyes frantically scanning the
room. He started pulling me toward the closet, but I yanked
him away at the last second, heading for the veranda instead.
We slipped through the French doors just as the doorknob
started to turn. At the last second, I glanced back through
a crack in the curtains to see that I'd left a pair of Whitaker's sleazy briefs on top of the dresser.

Still holding Hawk's hand, I pulled him across the veranda
and around the corner toward the back side of the home.
"Hold up," he said, yanking on my hand. We'd stopped in
front of one of the side windows. "My door's locked, but
we can sneak back in this way." He slid the window open
and stepped through, one leg at a time. Then he held out
his hands to help me do the same.

After a less than graceful maneuver, I landed inside his
room and threw myself into one of his chairs, sucking in
my breath and willing my heart to slow down. "That was
too close! But at least now we have some proof that he's
up to something. We need to let Maudy know what we've

found." Hopefully, our discovery would take some of the heat off my father.

"And what exactly is that?" Hawk had flopped casually on top of his bed which was unmade and covered with dirty clothing. Despite our close encounter, he seemed quite calm.

"The map."

He shrugged. "What about it?"

"It shows that he's up to something. Something under-handed."

"But not necessarily illegal."

I rubbed the back of my neck, rotating it a bit to loosen some tension. "You're right. All it really shows is that he's been snooping around."

"Not that, even. Only that he's drawn a map of this place."

I nodded. Again, he was right.

"So what's going on, darlin'?"

"I think he's looking for something in—"

"Not with Whitaker. With you. Why are you here at the inn? If it's to investigate Whitaker, I don't get it. That's what I'm here for. Besides, I can't be worryin' about your safety all the time."

"Like you were so worried about Margie's safety? Margie your own client? Who you leave alone at night in the same house as a possible murderer? As for me, I think I'm doing just fine, but thank you."

"As long as I'm around to save your butt, you mean."

What! Me? He's the one who headed for the closet, for crying out loud. I shook my head. Hawk had an ego that just never quit.

"You didn't answer my question," he continued. "Why are you here? And who's taking care of my dog?"

"To investigate Whitaker." And Margie, but I didn't say that. Since he thought he was still being paid by her. "And don't worry about your precious dog—my brother's watching him. And FYI, Margie is thinking about taking you off the case. My daddy's being arrested for Clem's murder. And since she's off the hook, she doesn't feel the need to keep you on anymore."

He sat upright. "Your daddy's in jail?"

"Well, not yet. Actually, he's in the hospital right now. But Maudy has a warrant. She just hasn't booked him yet."

Hawk's expression quickly changed from irritation to concern, the look on his face so sincere, it made my heart stop. We sat there, quietly regarding each other until he finally he said, "I'm sorry, darlin'. I'll do everything I can to help you. Whether Margie keeps me on or not."

I swallowed hard. "Thank you."

"Is your daddy okay?"

"I think so. They're running more tests today. I'm going to head over after lunch."

He blew out his breath and rubbed at the stubble on his chin. "Okay then. Let's discuss this. First, the map. Looks like this house has a lot of secret hiding places."

"It was a stop on the Underground Railroad, places where they hid runaway slaves." I quickly filled him in on everything I'd found at the library. "And that line leading from under the shed is probably an escape tunnel."

"So, Whitaker's searching those spots for something. Or"—he shrugged—"he's just a history buff."

I shook my head. "Whitaker would have just asked Margie about the house and not been sneaking around in that

case." Hawk agreed. I took out the information I'd copied
from Margie's reservation book and showed it to him. "It
says he's from Alabama. But I don't believe that for a second.
Everything about him says—"

"He's a Yank."

I cringed. I did almost say that, didn't I? Guess I wasn't
much better than some of the town folk I'd deemed narrow-
minded and judgmental. "Well, definitely not from Alabama. He paid cash, so there wasn't a credit card number.
But Margie did list his car rental information and license
number."

"Wonder if he paid cash for his rental, too?"

"I don't know. How would we find that out?"

He grinned and held out his hand. "Let me have that.
I'll see what I can find."

I knew Hawk had worked as a cop. Maybe he still had
connections and could find out that sort of information. I
handed it over, but almost snatched it back at the last second.
Maybe I should copy down the information, just in case.
But in the best interest of our newly formed alliance, I
instead handed it over, albeit somewhat reluctantly. "If you
find something, you'll let me know, right?"

He shoved it into his pocket. "Yes. You'll be the first to
know. Now tell me who else is on your list, and I'll tell you
what I've been able to find."

For the next twenty minutes or so, we exchanged information. I relayed not only my suspicions about Whitaker,
but about Lucas Graham and Jack Snyder, too. I left Margie
off the list. Although, any smart investigator would realize
that she belonged there as much as any other suspect. She
had motive and lacked an alibi. But until he heard otherwise, Hawk was still officially working for her.

Hawk also added a couple pieces to the puzzle, telling me that he'd been looking into Lucas Graham and found that he'd been in trouble with the law. Not just once, but several times. Minor things, like vandalism and a couple possession charges. Those were in the past, though. And as far as everyone knew, he'd been on the straight and narrow since working for Clem. He'd also been able to find, through his former cop connections, that Clem had paid a substantial amount of money, a few months back, to an investigative firm up in Detroit. Presumably to look into Margie's past. Apparently, Clem got his money's worth. Or, he'd paid dearly for his own death, depending how a person looked at it.

All that was interesting, for sure. But the next thing Hawk told me was a game changer. Apparently, Laney, his nail tech girlfriend, was putting a set of acrylic tips on Candace yesterday, and Candace mentioned that she had been in to see Doc Harris that very morning. Which wasn't surprising, since Candace spent more time at the doctor's office than anywhere else. Anyway, while she was at the doctor's, she happened to run into Jack Snyder. He was there seeking treatment for an infection on his arm. A nasty infection, which had festered from an untreated wound—a burn wound.

After Hawk and I finished rehashing the case, I snuck back to my room to retrieve my bag and truck keys. There were still a couple of hours to spare before I needed to head over to the hospital. I planned to use them wisely.

Cade had other plans, however. I found him sitting on the front porch, waiting for me. He popped out of his chair the second he saw me. "Nola."

"Cade! What a nice surprise."

His jaw tightened. *Uh-oh.* He was ticked about something. I didn't want to linger on the porch and possibly run into Whitaker, so I motioned for Cade to follow me to the side of the house. "Is something wrong?" I asked, once we'd reached my truck.

"I just thought I'd come by and see how you were doing. See if maybe I could give you a lift to the hospital. How's your daddy?"

"He's okay. And it's so sweet of you to come by." I leaned in with a hug, expecting our usual warm embrace, but Cade stiffened. I backed up and searched his face. "What's the matter?"

He pointed across the street to a smaller white clapboard home. An older woman was sitting on the front porch, enjoying the morning sun while she worked on some sewing. She tossed us a friendly wave. Suddenly I recognized the face. "Oh, I know who that is. That's Mrs. Busby. She does alterations at Hattie's shop."

"Yes. I know who she is. And she definitely remembers you."

"I bet she does," I said, enthusiastically returning her wave. Mrs. Busby and I had met under horrific circumstances last spring. And as I'd quickly learned during my time as an aid worker, such traumas had a peculiar way of bonding people together.

"In fact," Cade continued, "she called me just a little while ago to tell me just how well she remembered you. Something about your short hair making you recognizable even from a distance."

I fingered a piece of my closely cropped brown hair. I'd been trying to grow it, but just last week, grew impatient and took to it with Mama's fabric scissors. Again.

"It looks fine, Nola," Cade bit out. "But what Mrs. Busby couldn't understand, and what I definitely don't understand, is why you were holding some guy's hand up on the veranda? And let me guess. Dane Hawkins."

Uh-oh.

Chapter 13

Southern Girl Secret #040: A Southern gal doesn't wish for it to happen; she makes it happen.

"It's not what it looked like," I started to explain. But judging by his folded arms and steely glare, Cade wasn't going to buy the short explanation. I squinted Mrs. Busby's way and wondered just how long it was going to take this current bit of scuttlebutt to travel the Cays Mill rumor lines. And what if John Whitaker caught wind of it? Would he put two and two together and figure out that we were snooping in his room?

"Nola?"

I turned back to Cade, who was impatiently staring at me. "I've got a couple things I need to do," I said. "Come with me, so I can explain everything to you." His lips pressed into a thin line as he stood firm in his stance. "Oh come on, Cade. You know me better than that. Get in and I'll tell you all about it. Please."

He finally relented and climbed into the passenger side.

I drove straight for my shop, where I planned to pick up the shopping list Carla had made after taking inventory. Mama had asked me to pick up a few items, so I might as well get a little of my shopping out of the way, too. Kill two birds with one stone, so to say. Actually, three birds. Because, even though it was a long shot, I was hoping Lucas Graham would be working at the Pack & Carry this morning. I had a few questions for him.

Along the way, I filled Cade in on my sleuthing adventure. "So, you see. I wasn't holding Hawk's hand. Nor would I ever *want* to hold his hand," I quickly added. "I just grabbed ahold of him to get him out of the room before Whitaker caught us."

Cade seemed to relax a bit.

I went on, "But wait until you hear what I found." I filled him in on the map and what I thought it meant. I also told him about the new information I'd garnered about Lucas's past brushes with the law and Clem hiring the investigative firm in Detroit to dig up dirt on Margie. Finally, I told him about Jack Snyder's wound. "Candace said it was a burn. It could be just a coincidence, but—"

"But it could be from starting a barn fire," he finished.

"Exactly. There's so much to consider. Maybe you were right when you suggested that Clem was killed by two people."

"Could be. If that's the case, you just have to figure out which two of your suspects are connected."

He was right, of course. And the first pair that jumped to mind was Tessa and Lucas. Had Tessa wanted the farm all along and put Lucas up to killing her uncle? Of course, maybe Margie and Whitaker were really connected somehow. Pretending to be a guest at the inn would be the perfect cover. They could act like strangers and yet still easily plot a murder together. Or maybe Jack and Lucas . . . or Margie and Jack . . . or was there someone else out there who I'd completely missed? I mulled over the possibilities for the remainder of the ride, and by the time we arrived at the Pack & Carry, the only thing I'd concluded was that I really didn't have any conclusions.

There were only a few cars parked in the Pack & Carry lot—most of the good citizens in town were probably at Sunday services, not doing their grocery shopping—so, I easily spied what I thought was Clem's old pickup truck and parked next to it, getting out to take a closer look. "This was Clem's truck," I told Cade, recognizing its custom chrome accents and vanity plates that read "GA FRMR." "Lucas must be driving it now."

"Lucky kid. This is a nice truck."

"Yeah. Tell me about it." Just one more way Lucas benefitted from Clem's death—fancy new wheels to drive.

As I moved past, something in the back of the truck caught my eye. "Hey, Cade. Come here." I reached into the bed and pulled out a small metal tube. "What's this, I wonder?"

He took it, holding it up and squinting. "I don't . . . oh, I *do* know what this is." He looked at me, his brows coming together. "It's called a quick connector."

"A quick connector," I repeated. "What's that used for?"

"It's a type of fitting used on air-conditioning units."

My eyes grew wide. "Oh really?" I cast another quick glance at the truck of the bed. "A person sure could haul a lot of scrap metal in this truck."

"That's what I'm thinking," Cade said. "What do you say we head inside. Maybe have a little talk with Lucas."

"Actually," I said, looking over Cade's shoulder and

quickly pocketing the air-conditioning part. "Here he comes now."

Lucas lumbered toward us, the tail of his work shirt hanging out of his pants. "Hey! What are you people doing— oh, Ms. Harper. Hello."

"Hey, Lucas. How's it going?" I asked.

"Okay, I guess. Just came out for a smoke break." He used a key fob to open the door of the truck, reached in and pulled out a pack of cigarettes and a lighter.

"We were just heading in to get some shopping done," I started. "My friend Cade saw this truck and wanted to check it out."

Cade offered his hand. "Hey, buddy. Cade McKenna. Nice truck."

Lucas shook his hand and then lit up and blew out a stream of smoke. He was an awkward smoker. Made me wonder if it wasn't a new thing for him. "Thanks. It really belongs to my girlfriend."

"Oh, that's right," I said. "This used to be Clem's truck, didn't it?"

Lucas nodded and took another drag from his cig, using his free hand to move a long flop of hair out of his face. "Yeah. He just got it last year. Let me drive it for farm work and stuff. I'm just borrowing it now since Clem . . . well, you know. My truck's in the shop. It needs an alignment job."

Cade ran his hand along the tailgate. "V6?" he wanted to know.

Lucas's face lit up. "Yeah—285 horsepower, turbo diesel. This baby can tow three tons."

"Cool." Cade worked his way around the truck, eyeing me pointedly. I realized he was waiting for me to take the lead in questioning Lucas. I briefly considered my options.

I could show him what we'd found, point an accusing finger and demand some answers. But the only thing I had was a little connector thingy, not exactly solid proof. And even if it was, it only indicated that Lucas was somehow involved in the recent rash of scrap metal thefts, not murder. I wanted to stay focused on the murder.

I finally decided to take an indirect approach. "How's Tessa doing?"

He shrugged. "Okay, I guess. We had a big party for her last night out at the farm. Seemed to cheer her up a little."

"I'm sure she misses her uncle. Can't be easy for her. How about you? Were you close to Clem? I mean, I noticed that you and Tessa seem serious."

"Yup. We're talking about get married."

"Hey, that's great," Cade threw out. "I bet Clem was pleased when you told him."

Lucas's expression turned dark. "Well, I hadn't yet. I was going to, but . . ." He shrugged and took another drag on his cigarette, throwing it down and crushing it under the toe of his cowboy boot.

"Clem could be difficult," I offered. "A lot of folks didn't get along with him."

"True," he agreed. "But, he'd always been good to me. Gave me a job out at the farm. Made me crew manager the second year."

"Sounds like he was happy with your work," I said.

He shrugged, but didn't answer. His eyes darted toward the store. I sensed he was getting ready to bolt. "Well, Tessa sure is lucky to have you during this difficult time," I quickly added. "She was in my shop yesterday, singing your praises." Out of the corner of my eye, I noticed Cade smiling encouragingly. Lucas seemed to relax a little.

I continued, "Will you be able to go to the funeral?" I tipped my head toward the store. "I mean, were you able to get time off work? Tessa was telling me it's in the morning, and I know how much it would mean to her."

"Yeah. I worked it out with my boss. I've been on the six to two shift all month, but I'll stay a little later tomorrow. Make sure all the stocking is done to make up for the time off." He opened the truck door and tossed his cigs and lighter inside. "Well, I gotta get back to work. Good meeting you, Cade."

As I watched him walk across the lot, something niggled at my mind. Something Lucas had said. What was it?

"Should we head in and get the shopping done?" Cade asked.

What was it Lucas said? What was . . . ? Then it hit me. I looked up at Cade and smiled. "Think I'll hold off on grocery shopping for now. There's something else I need to do. It's a bit of an adventure, though. Care to join me?"

Cade's dark eyes gleamed mischievously. "Ms. Harper, I'd join you on any adventure."

"Well, I certainly didn't expect this," he said a little while later. We were parked on the road outside Clem's farm. "Hope you know what you're doing. The shortcut you're planning could tear the heck out of your truck." After talking to Lucas, something clicked in my mind. He'd claimed that he worked until two o'clock every day, but I remembered Tessa saying that he showed up at the courthouse at about the same time she received the phone call about the fire. So, I called Carla and asked her to get ahold of Tessa to find out exactly what time she got that phone call. Tessa

checked her cell log and said it was at 5:12. That left a
narrow time window. Was it possible that Lucas had been
at the farm, seen my daddy argue with Clem, killed Clem,
and then got back to town in time for Tessa to get that call? I
knew it took me almost twenty minutes to get to town, but
that was on the usual roads, without rushing. By everyone's
estimates, the fire was started sometime between four
thirty and five o'clock. But I knew that Daddy left Clem,
still alive, at about a quarter to five. It would have taken the
killer at least another ten minutes to kill Clem and get the
fire started. Give or take a few minutes. What I needed to find
out was if Lucas could get from the farm to the courthouse
in less than twenty minutes. If so, he not only had motive,
but means.

"I'll try to be careful," I said. Although I did recall
Lucas saying something about his own truck being in bad
shape. Perhaps he tore it up racing back to town after killing Clem? I drew in my breath. Guess I was about to find
out. "Ready?" I asked, glancing across the seat to where
Cade's thumb hovered over the start button of his cell
phone's stopwatch.

"Ready."

I gunned it and tore off down the gravel road, leaning
slightly forward over the wheel. I squinted through the
gravel dust, on the lookout for my turn.

"Up there," Cade said, indicating a small break in the
trees.

Slowing only slightly, I took the turn at breakneck
speed. "Time?"

"Just under two minutes."

I tightened my grip on the steering wheel, trying to keep
the truck steady. We were racing down an old logging trail

that ran between two main roads and, by my estimate, would shave at least five minutes off the trek into town. I'd taken the road before when I was in a hurry, but never at this speed. Trees zoomed by, their branches whipping the sides of the truck, each new scrape making me cringe. A loud pop sounded as the front tire hit a pothole.

"Whoa! Easy!"

"Time?"

"Not quite three minutes," he responded, his free hand reaching for the dash. "You're making good time."

We were just about to the main road and nearing Candace's place. I spotted her out by her mailbox, and honked twice as we approached. She leaped back, eyes round with shock. I dared a quick glance in the rearview mirror as we zoomed past. She had hands on her hips and was glaring my way.

The back end of the truck slid as I cranked the wheel and turned onto the main road. I punched it again, hoping to make even better time now that we were on pavement.

"Cop!" Cade suddenly shouted. I slammed on my breaks, but it was too late. I whizzed past the sheriff's cruiser going about twenty miles an hour over the speed limit. A siren sounded behind us.

"Crap!" I said, pulling over to the side of the road. I put the gear in park and buried my face in my hands. "Please don't let it be Maudy, please . . ."

I could hear Cade turning in his seat. "You're in luck. It looks like Travis."

Breathing a little easier, I cranked down the window and offered my best smile. "Hey, Travis."

"Nola? Thought this was your truck." He removed his Stetson and leaned into the window. "Hey there, Cade."

Cade nodded and Travis looked back at me. "What's the all-fire hurry? You could get hurt drivin' like that."

"I'm sorry, Travis. We were . . . uh." Telling him that we were investigating Clem's murder probably wouldn't go over too well.

"We were in a hurry to get out to the hospital," Cade interjected.

Travis's eyes registered concern. "Oh, that's right," he said to me. "Your daddy's up there with heart problems, isn't he? Sheriff's been keepin' me informed of his progress."

I bet she has. I smiled tightly. "Please tell the sheriff that I said thank you for her concern. And I promise I'll drive more carefully from here on out."

He shook his head and stood upright, his hand slowly moving toward his shirt vest pocket where I knew he kept a ticket pad. My mind quickly calculated what exactly twenty miles over the speed limit might net me: a fifty-dollar fine? Seventy-five? "I have some information for you," I blurted.

Cade flinched. "Nola," he hissed. "Do you really want to . . . ?"

"Information?" Travis dropped his hand and leaned forward again. "About Clem's murder?"

"No, about the rash of scrap metal thefts going on around here," I explained.

Travis's eyebrows came together. "Scrap metal thefts? Now what exactly do you know about that?"

I shrugged. "Just that a lot's gone missing lately: the bleachers, downspouts at the library, some air-conditioning units from businesses downtown . . ." I thumbed toward Cade. "And some copper wiring from his construction site."

Travis turned his attention to Cade. "Is that right? I don't recall any reports on wiring missing from your site."

Cade bobbed his head in agreement and mumbled something under his breath.

"Yup. That's right," I reiterated for him. "Just odd things here and there, but it all seems to add up to scrap metal theft. Did you know a person can get quite a bit for stuff like that? Especially copper. Recyclers pay good money for it."

"So, what type of information do you have?" Travis wanted to know.

I glanced over to Cade, who turned over his palms and shrugged. Just a little too late, I realized that I'd jumped into this before thinking it through. After all, what evidence did I really have? The connector thing I'd found in the back of Lucas's truck? That could have come from anywhere.

"Well, I didn't actually mean substantial information," I backtracked.

Travis raised his brows over the rims of his mirrored sunglasses, his hand inching back toward his pocket.

I straightened my legs and reached into the side pocket of my cargo pants. I handed him the metal piece I'd found. "We were at the Pack and Carry earlier this morning and I found this thing in the back of a truck."

Travis turned it around in his fingers. "What is this?"

I looked to Cade for help. He sighed. "A quick connector."

"Yes. A quick connector," I echoed. "They're used on air conditioners. And I heard a couple of those were stolen earlier this week."

Travis nodded. "That's right. A couple of units have gone missing. Whose truck are we talking about?"

I hesitated.

Travis leaned forward and looked at both Cade and I. "Did y'all recognize the truck, or not?"

"It belonged to Lucas Graham," I admitted.

Travis straightened and took a swipe at his brow. "Damn, kid," he mumbled, shifting his feet a couple times before leaning back into my truck. "Okay. Thanks, Nola. I'll look into it."

"Maybe it doesn't really mean what I think it does," I halfheartedly added. But despite all the good things Ginny had told me about Lucas, I had disliked him from the moment I met him. Actually, scrap metal theft was probably the least of his crimes. Judging from the time I'd been making—before being pulled over by Deputy Travis, that is—Lucas could have easily murdered Clem, started that barn fire and made it back to town in time for Tessa's phone call. There was no doubt in my mind. "You won't tell him it was me who pointed the finger, will you?" I asked Travis.

"Nope. I'll just keep that little tidbit between us. In fact, maybe you'd best not mention anything to the sheriff, neither. I'll take care of that. That way if it doesn't pan out, you won't be to blame for sending her on a wild-goose chase." He raised one eyebrow, and we both understood.

Travis was right. If I went to Maudy with this information, she'd just assume I was trying to throw her off Daddy's case. And heaven knew, I didn't need to give Maudy one more reason to dislike our family. I let out a long sigh. "Good idea, Travis. I won't say a thing to her."

"Good to hear. Especially since you'll probably run into her at the hospital. She happened to mention that she'd be poppin' in to pay your daddy a visit today."

. . .

Cade stayed behind in the waiting room while I went in to see Daddy. Both Ray and Ida were already there, along with Mama, who was perched next to Daddy on the bed. "Mama," I said, "why don't you head home and get some rest. I can stay here with Daddy for a while."

Ida waved her hand through the air. "Don't even bother. I told her the same thing. But she won't leave his side."

Daddy smiled up at Mama and patted her hand. Just a small gesture, but for some reason tears pricked my eyes. All these years they'd been together: raising children, raising peaches, seeing each other through the good and the bad. Like two pieces of a whole. I quickly looked away, unable to bear the thought of one without the other.

"Everything okay, darlin'?" Daddy asked.

I swallowed hard and turned back with a brave face. "Sure, everything's fine. What did the doctors have to say?"

"Sorry to disappoint y'all, but they said I'm nothin' but a stubborn old mule and that I'll be around for more years than y'all can count."

"Raymond!" Mama chided. "That's not what they said and you know it."

We all looked expectantly at Mama. I was holding my breath, waiting for the other shoe to drop. Was it worse than we all thought?

"Your father needs to have a couple stents put in his arteries," she said. We must have all looked horror-stricken, because she quickly added, "The doctor says it's a common procedure. He's recommending a specialist up in Atlanta. We'll be heading up there soon."

"And once that's done, I'll be as good as new," Daddy added.

I breathed a little easier.

Mama pursed her lips and shook her head. "That's not exactly all he said, Raymond."

"What else did he say?" Ray wanted to know.

Ida was standing a few feet away; she clenched her arms around her middle as if trying to hold herself together. I went to her, wrapping my arm around her shoulders. I could feel her trembling.

We all waited and watched while Daddy fidgeted, his mouth opening and closing a few times as he struggled to find the right words. "Maybe we ought to wait," he finally said to Mama.

"No, Raymond. We've waited long enough. I'm not going to take any more chances with your health. I'm just not." She turned to us, a resolute look on her face. "The doctor told him he needs to give up the cigars and Peach Jack. For good, this time. And he'll have to make some dietary changes, too. I'll need to change the way I've been cookin'." I could feel my shoulders relax. *This isn't so bad.* I could stand to lay off all the fried food and gravy myself.

But then she dropped a bombshell. "And he'll have to give up peach farmin'."

Chapter 14

Southern Girl Secret #030: Always wear your pain with a smile, like a pair of high-heeled shoes—no matter how much it hurts, all they'll see is how nice you look.

As I keyed into the side door of the inn later that evening, I felt not only exhausted, but my stomach rumbled with indigestion: a combination of bad hospital food and stress over the latest turn of events. As if finding out Daddy needed surgery wasn't bad enough, Maudy Payne showed up with her usual air of pundit authority, demanding to know when Daddy would be released. She wasn't happy to learn he was going to go straight from our local hospital to Atlanta for his operation. And her presence at the hospital only served to add to our family's upset. Luckily, Ray was able to spout some legalese and expedite her departure.

Perhaps just as disconcerting as Daddy facing surgery was the realization that, as a family, we faced another tough problem—what to do with the farm. While no one came right out and said anything, I knew there were really only two choices: we sell the farm, or I take over the day-to-day operations. Since Ray was already working long hours at his legal firm over in Perry, and Ida had the twins and a new baby, the responsibility naturally fell to me. I could tell that Daddy hoped I would step forward and offer to take over things. I could see it in his eyes, although he insisted he didn't want to talk about it right now. I appreciated not being backed into a corner with direct discussion about it. But something made me hold back from jumping to answer the unspoken question. I'm not sure what. Maybe it was because I knew running the farm was such a huge undertaking. Then there was my shop, which had barely been in business for a year and was growing daily. I'd come to really love my little business and hated to give that up. But how could I possibly manage both the farm and the shop?

It was late and the interior of Sunny Side Up was as dark and broody as my mood as I bumbled through the screened porch, juggling both my bag and my laptop case, flipping on a few lights as I headed into the kitchen. Margie kept drinks and other snacks on hand for her guests. I was hoping a soda might settle my stomach. Bending over the fridge shelves, my hand had just connected with a can of ginger ale when I sensed a presence. I wheeled around to find John Whitaker hovering just inches away.

My free hand flew to my chest. "Mr. Whitaker, you scared me!"

He stood his ground, a lock of his slick black hair falling over his wide forehead as his intimidating eyes bore into me. "Were you in my bedroom this morning?"

"In your bedroom?" I tried really hard not to think about that pair of silky red briefs. "No. Of course not! Why would I be in your bedroom?" I quickly popped the top on the can and took a swig of ginger ale, only to have it go down the wrong tube and send me into a coughing fit. Whitaker still didn't budge. I thumped on my chest and cleared my throat. "Excuse me. I swallowed wrong. Where is everyone, anyway?" I tried to slide around him, but he moved in even closer, blocking my escape.

"Someone's been in my room," he hissed, his face only inches from mine. "And I don't think it's just a coincidence that you show up here at the same time my room gets searched. What are you up to?"

"I'm not up to anything. Now if you'll excuse me, it's been a busy day and I'm tired." I started to push around him, but he snatched my arm. Could this be the same hand that killed Clem and then set his barn afire? I felt my pulse pounding against his tight grip.

"What's your game, lady?" His hot breath assaulted my nostrils.

I stepped back and yanked my arm away. "I'm not playing any games. Now get out of my way!"

Surprisingly, he stepped aside. I quickly reached over and grabbed my bags off the counter and stormed past him, breaking into a jog as soon as I rounded the kitchen corner and checking over my shoulder a couple times as I scurried up the staircase.

Safely inside my room, I double-checked the door lock and flopped onto the bed, trying to catch my breath. Adrenaline coursed through my veins, making my heart beat double-time. A couple seconds later, I heard the thud of another door shutting followed by the clicking of a lock. I shuddered, realizing that the ugly son of a gun was sleeping just a few feet away. Paranoid, I slid from the bed and crossed to the veranda door, double-checking that lock and pulling the drapes tight.

Then I paced nervously back and forth for a few seconds before stopping to take a deep breath. Panic wasn't going to solve anything. I needed to get a grip on myself.

After a quick teeth brushing—and, no, I didn't dare look into the mirror—and pulling on my oversized Bulldogs T-shirt, I propped up in bed with my laptop. Determined to organize my thoughts, I opened a fresh page and listed everything I'd discovered over the last few days, including suspects and their motives and opportunities. When I finished, it looked like a jumbled mess.

Still, as I read over my notes, I realized Margie was the one wild card in all this. It certainly seemed too coincidental that Clem was killed the very same day he threatened to reveal something about her past. I switched over to an Internet search engine and began searching her name. Turns out the name "Margie Price" was popular. I found Dr. Margie Price, head of obstetrics at Tulane Medical Center, and a few social network pages for Margie Price, a boy crazy senior at Rosemont High School, but nothing for *my* Margie. Next, I tried Margaret Price. Still nothing promising. Remembering that she moved here from Detroit, and Clem had hired a firm up there to investigate her, I cross-referenced her name with Detroit and got a few listings for the family name "Price." I was about to click on one of them when a soft knock on my door made me jump.

"Nola. Are you in there? It's me, Hawk."

I scrambled into my jeans and padded across the floor to let him inside, glancing down the hall toward Whitaker's room before shutting the door. "Glad you're here," I said.

"Why? What's up? You look . . . hey, what's this?" His hand gently pulled at my arm. "Looks like you've got the start of a nasty bruise." His brows furrowed as he studied the angry red marks on my biceps. My skin was bruised in a couple spots where Whitaker's nails had dug into me. Hawk's own arm muscles twitched as his blazing eyes met mine. "Who did this to you?"

I stepped back, reclaiming my arm. "Whitaker. About an hour ago down in the kitchen. He suspected that I'd gone through his things and was ticked off."

Hawk whipped around and reached for the doorknob. I jumped in front of him, my back pressed against the door. "I can handle Whitaker. Besides, if you charge in there and threaten him, he'll pack up and leave. I need to get more information first."

The corner of Hawk's mouth twitched. "Threaten him?" He shook his head. "Darlin', I'm not gonna threaten him. I'm going to beat the crap out of him."

"Please calm down, Hawk. I need to find out a little more first. It's important to me. For my family. And I can't do that if you go in there and kill him."

My choice of words seemed to bring a little comic relief to the situation. Hawk backed up and blew out a long breath. "He needs to be dealt with." He rubbed at the back of his neck, a swatch of dark hair falling over his brooding eyes. "Obviously I've misjudged the guy."

"I understand if you're concerned for Margie, but I'll be okay. I can handle Whitaker. And he's already leaving in a couple days. Which doesn't give me much time to figure out what he's up to. Like you said before, if he was going to harm one of us, he would have already done it. Think about it. Whitaker has no detectable motive. Besides, there's nothing to tie him to this community. So if he had killed Clem, he would have just left by now. No, I really don't think Whitaker is a killer."

"If he's not your killer, then why do you care if he stays or not?"

Touché. "Because he's up to something, and I'd like to know what. It could still be related." I didn't dare tell him it was to see if, like Cade suggested, he was in cahoots with someone like Margie. After all, Margie was still Hawk's client.

A low growl sounded from the back of Hawk's throat, but he didn't comment one way or the other. Instead, he pulled a folded piece of paper out of his back pocket. "I've got some information. Whitaker's car rental was paid for with a credit card belonging to a guy named Felix Ganassi. Could be Whitaker's real name. I'm having a friend track it down for me. I'll probably have more information soon. I also did some checking on Jack Snyder. You know those signs Snyder has plastered all over town?"

"Yeah?"

"Well, I checked with the local print shop. He put in the order a few days before Clem was killed."

"No way."

"Yeah. I went out to his farm and asked him about it. He admitted to it. Said that he'd made the decision to run for office just a few days before Clem was killed."

"That's not what he's been telling people. He said he thought the farmers needed a representative after Clem was killed."

"Yeah. He claims he was getting ready to make the announcement, but then Clem was murdered, and he saw a good opportunity to play on people's sentiments. You know, carry on Clem's cause, and so on."

"Or he killed Clem in order to create the opportunity for himself." Either way, the guy had lost my vote.

"I asked him about the burn, too," Hawk said. "He claims he's been burning off pruned wood from his trees. He said he got a little close to his burn pile." While I mulled that over, Hawk moved on to a more personal subject. "How's your father doing?" he asked.

I filled him in on the latest news, leaving out the part about Daddy quitting the peach farming business. I hadn't been able to wrap my own mind around it, let alone explain it to Hawk. I also prattled on with my other revelations regarding the investigation, all to which he occasionally nodded in agreement, but had nothing more to add. Finally, after a little more rehashing of the case, and a few well-meaning warnings concerning Whitaker, Hawk left to go back to his room. As soon as I'd locked the door behind him, I went back to my computer and began searching the name Felix Ganassi.

After trying quite a few searches, I found a Felix Ganassi with a Whitepages listing for the Detroit metro area—where Margie was from. Was Whitaker really Felix Ganassi and were Margie and Ganassi somehow connected? I sighed and rubbed my eyes. The day's events had left me so exhausted, nothing was making sense anymore.

I shut down my computer and stowed it under the bed. But as I lay awake in the dark, my thoughts kept returning to the case. It just seemed too coincidental that both Margie and Whitaker were from Detroit. Could they have been working together all along? I shook my head and mumbled to myself, "No, that can't be right." All that sneaking around her place when she was gone would have been unnecessary. And Margie would have to be some actress

to have played such a part at the diner the other night when
she talked to Cade and me about her worries over Whitaker. Besides, the map, the threatening way he approached
me in the kitchen . . . Whitaker, or Ganassi—*or whatever
the creep's real name is*—was up to something sinister.
And my gut told me that Margie just wasn't the sinister
type.

   Of course, my instincts had been off before.

J. B. Cain & Sons funeral parlor was housed in a Federal-
style home, located just down the street from Sunny Side
Up. For as long as I could remember, old man Cain had
been working hard to send our town folk off to their maker
with a final flourish. The "& Sons" weren't much to talk
about, though. As Mama always said, J. B.'s sons were
about as useful as a screen door on a submarine. Rumors
were that one of them had smoked himself stupid on cigarettes dipped in embalming fluid, while the other fancied
himself a volunteer video game tester and spent all his
time living in a virtual haze. I wasn't much for rumors, but
I did know that I hadn't seen either boy since my return to
Cays Mill. But, maybe they'd come out of hiding today.
After all, something as big as the murder of one of the
town's most prominent citizens—a mayoral hopeful nonetheless!—was sure to draw a few snakes out from under
the rocks.

   Speaking of which, Frances Simms was the first person
I saw as I slipped into the nearly filled parlor designated
for Clem's service this Monday morning. She eyed me with
one of her pompous know-it-all looks. I sighed. Obviously,
she'd finally gathered enough dirt on my daddy to craft a

sell-out headline for tomorrow's issue of the *Cays Mill Reporter*. I could hardly wait.

Feeling self-conscious, I slunk into an empty seat in the back of the room. After a somewhat sleepless night, I'd awakened late, then spent most of my morning routine catching up with Mama on the latest news about Daddy. Then I made a last-minute decision to attend the funeral, not that I knew Clem all that well—and what I did know of him, I didn't particularly like—but after a little consid-eration, I decided it would be a nice gesture toward Tessa—and, in a roundabout way, Carla—if I came and offered my formal condolences. But my split-second decision meant I had to wear what I had on hand: my usual cargo pants and Peachy Keen T-shirt. Although, I'd buttoned a navy blue sweater over my work T-shirt, in an effort to look a little more respectful and to cover the nasty bruises Whita-ker had put on my arm. I thought back with a tiny thrill to Hawk's reaction when he discovered the bruises. I was surprised he even cared enough to be concerned, let alone so protective. Then again, Hawk's reactions always sur-prised me. Which made me think maybe I'd made a mis-take all those years ago by not telling him about the baby. Maybe he'd have stood beside me, maybe even after the miscarriage, and then I'd have never left town and . . . I sighed. That was all in the past. And like Mama always said, "It's best to let sleeping dogs lie."

Looking past the crowd, my eyes settled on the room's focal point: a dark urn set on a small marble pedestal and surrounded by floral arrangements. For some reason, the sight of the urn surprised me. Did they simply scoop up his ashes from the murder site, or did they cremate his remains further? I shook my head, wishing away the morbid thoughts and focusing instead on the crowd, my eyes bouncing from one suspect to another. First, Lucas and Tessa, who sat together in the front row, his arm resting on the back of the pew behind her, ready to offer quick comfort when needed.

Next, Jack Snyder, who also sat near the front of the room, straight-backed and alert, wearing the same suit he had worn for the town meeting. Jack intrigued me. Running for any office was hard work and expensive, a tough go even once. But twice? And this idea that he'd decided to run just a couple days before Clem's murder didn't add up—at that point he knew he'd be running against two strong candidates. Why set himself up for failure again? But Clem's death narrowed the field to only one other candidate, one who just happened to be under suspicion of murder, no less. Making Jack's win a given. Could Snyder really be that power crazed to murder Clem just to be called "Mr. Mayor"? Could having cousins in the offices of mayor and sheriff benefit the mayor in some way? I could see a mayor maybe granting more perks to the sheriff's department. I couldn't see it going the other way around, but I wasn't all that up on politics. Or . . . were there other benefits to being mayor that I hadn't considered yet? Could it help his business somehow, like making some tax exemptions or something? Could being mayor in Cays Mill give him any clout for expanding his fruit stands into other counties? Not that I could figure out. But even if I could, was it enough to kill for? None of it made sense. And that made him very suspicious to me.

A couple rows behind him, Margie was shifting uncomfortably in her own seat, dabbing at her face with a handkerchief. Which brought my mind around to my mother's handkerchief and the fact that it was found tangled up in

Clem's sheets. Just how did it end up there? I glanced back at Margie. Mama did say that she'd gone to Sunny Side Up for a campaign tea the day before the murder. Was it possible that she'd left one of her handkerchiefs there? Of course, she could have left one of her hankies anywhere. And then how and when could Margie—or anyone, for that matter—get it into Clem's bedroom? Still . . . I narrowed my eyes and focused Margie's way. I'd intentionally avoided her at breakfast time this morning, just coming down to grab a cup of coffee and plate of muffins to take to my room. I was closer to figuring out her secret and was afraid I'd tip my hand before I had all the pieces in place. Hopefully Hawk would have some more information soon, but I did place a call to Ida on my way to the funeral parlor, asking her to check with Hollis about Margie's financial history. After all, Hollis was president of the only bank in town, and he did owe me one. Or two. And in my experience, most secrets worth dying for, or murdering for, had to do with love or money. So, to cover that base, it would be prudent to follow the money trail. I only hoped Margie had left behind a few crumbs for me to follow.

As for Mr. Whitaker/Ganassi, he wasn't in attendance. Not that I expected him to be here. He was probably taking this opportunity to search through a few more spots at Sunny Side Up. What he was looking for, heaven only knew. But I couldn't help but feel as if I were on the brink . . .

A tap on my shoulder interrupted my thoughts. I turned to see Candace from the bank had slid into the seat next to me. "These straight chairs are so hard on my back," she started with a dramatic sigh. "Why, I can already feel my sciatica starting to act up. Doc Harris always tells me not to—" She stopped herself midcomplaint and furrowed her brow. "That was your truck that sped past my house yes-terday, wasn't it? You about ran me off the road, you know. What in the world got into you, Nola Mae?"

"I'm sorry, Candace. I didn't mean to scare you. I was just doing a little experiment, that's all."

She waggled her shoulders. "An experiment? On what? How to kill people?"

A few heads swiveled around; I shrank back in my chair. Then I thought of something. Maybe Candace saw someone drive by the afternoon Clem was killed. It would have been about the time she was arriving home from working at the bank. It was such a quiet road, any traffic would certainly draw attention. I leaned forward and qui-etly asked, "Candace, do you remember seeing anyone drive past your house last Tuesday? It would have been late afternoon."

"Last Tuesday? Why, no. Don't you remember me tellin' you about my bursitis?"

"Your bursitis?" I did sort of remember her saying something about bursitis the other day at the bakery. Of course, every time I saw her she had one complaint or another and, admittedly, it all blurred together for me after a while. Besides, what did that have to do with anything?

"Yes, my bursitis. I swear I told you about this. But anyway, my bursitis has been actin' up somethin' awful. And well, bless his heart, but Doc Harris didn't know what to do for me. So he sent me to that specialist over in Colum-bus . . ." She paused for a breath.

"That was on Tuesday? Are you sure?"

"Yes, I'm sure. I remember because I drove past Clem's place on my way home and saw all the emergency vehicles."

She shook her head and raised her eyes to the urn up front. "Poor Clem. Such an awful way to go."

Tuesday? Something about that didn't seem right. The low tone of an organ suddenly cut through the room's chatter, drawing our attention up front where Mrs. Betty Lou Nix, who was held in high esteem by the local Baptists for her musical talents, had begun the opening hymn. But I barely listened to the slow, melancholy tune, because my own thoughts were unfolding at a frantic tempo, jumping from one conclusion to another. And by the time Mrs. Nix finished the stirring melody, I'd discovered yet another discrepancy in Clem's murder case.

Chapter 15

Southern Girl Secret #089: The reason we Southern gals like diamonds is because they're a lot like us: beautiful, shiny and unbreakable.

Either the rest of the service was super short or I blanked out. Probably the latter. I was so preoccupied with my own thoughts—of hidden treasure and murder—that I didn't tune back in until I heard Reverend Jones announcing that the Baptist Ladies' Altar Society would be providing refreshments in the church basement directly following the service. Everyone was invited to head over and offer support for the bereaved. Unfortunately, I needed to get to work, but I did track down Carla and let her know that there was no hurry for her to get to the shop. I could handle things there and it was important for her to stay with Tessa awhile longer.

Since I'd walked to the funeral home that morning—it was just down the street from Sunny Side Up—I still needed to swing by my room for my laptop and keys before heading to Peachy Keen. I started off at a brisk walking pace, enjoying the crisp breeze in the air and several bright displays of potted chrysanthemums lining the front porches of the stately homes I passed by, when all of a sudden I spied a red nylon running suit jogging my way. Whitaker! My mind flashed back to the underwear I'd discovered in his dresser drawer. This guy must have a penchant for silky red things. Ick.

I froze in my tracks, watching as he drew closer, a cruel smile creeping over his face. Then to my horror, he clenched his fists and picked up his pace, moving to the center of the walk. *What's he doing?* He was running straight toward me! At the last minute, I jumped aside. My foot landed on the uneven edge of the walk, causing my ankle to bend and sending me spiraling downward. I hit the ground hard, grass and pebbles digging into my palms. I stayed that way for a second, momentarily dazed, before I felt a hand on my shoulder. "Nola, are you okay?"

It was Hattie. "Yeah. I think so."

"I was just coming from the funeral home and I saw some man knock you off the walk." She shielded her eyes from the sun and squinted. "Wasn't that the guy Ginny thinks is so mysteriously handsome? What's his name?"

I slowly stood, testing my ankle. It was a little sore, but nothing serious. I brushed my hands together. "John Whitaker."

"Yeah. What's his problem?"

"He's a jerk, that's what." I could have told her more, but it would take a lot of time to catch her up on everything that'd happened over the course of the week.

"Sure you're okay?" She was looking down at my foot.

"Yeah. I'm okay." In order to prove my point, I took a

few steps back and forth. "See. It's fine." It was probably a good thing I was wearing my usual lace-up field boots. The extra ankle support had come in handy.

We both turned at the sound of a car horn tooting. Hattie had stopped in the middle of the lane and a couple of cars had come up behind her, waiting for her to move. "I'm blocking traffic. Here, hop in. I'll give you a lift."

I crossed over to her car and got into the passenger side, drawing my sweater tighter, trying to smother a sudden chill. If Whitaker was trying to intimidate me, he was doing a good job. "I've been staying at the Sunny Side Up if you could drop me there," I told her, not sure if she knew or not. I hadn't seen her since the town hall meeting, and I'd rushed out before telling her much of anything.

She reached over and flipped on the car's heater, the diamond in her engagement ring sparkling with the movement. "I heard all about it from Cade. You're looking into Clem's murder. I also heard you'd found some sort of proof—"

"That's not true," I blurted. "Just some crazy rumor floating around town."

"I didn't think it was." She tilted her head and cocked a brow. "I mean, if you had proof, you'd take it straight to the sheriff, right?"

"Of course," I assured her. "I only wish I did have something. Maudy Payne's up to her usual tactics—hassling my family."

"I wish you would have told me what was going on. Maybe I could be of some help." She let out a long sigh. "And now I hear that your daddy's in the hospital."

I nodded and started filling her in on Daddy's condition and his pending surgery as we drove down the street and parked outside the inn. "But he's going to be fine," I finished. "The doctors say it's a routine procedure. He'll just have to make some lifestyle changes afterward, that's all." Some *really* big lifestyle changes, considering his health was forcing him to give up his livelihood. I swallowed hard, wondering once again about the fate of the farm. But all that was too overwhelming to think of at this point. Hattie was my best friend, maybe the only one who could fully grasp all the ramifications that such a change in my life might mean, but I just couldn't deal with it right now. I vowed to plan a time when we could talk about it.

"And how's your mama holding up?" she asked.

"She's doing okay. She's strong."

"You're a lot like her in that way." She smiled faintly and touched my arm. "I'm so sorry, Nola. I haven't been much of a friend to you this week. Guess I've been so wrapped up in my own thing."

"Your own thing? Hattie, you're trying to plan your wedding. That's a huge deal. I don't expect you to keep up with what I've got going on. Besides, I feel I've let you down, too, all wrapped up, as you say, in my own thing. I should be here for you, since your wedding should be one of the happiest times in your life." I watched as her face fell and shoulders slumped. "But it's not, is it?" I whispered.

"No. I'm trying, but . . ." Her lower lip began to quiver.

"But you're missing your mother. That's what this is all about, isn't it?"

She let out a jagged breath and began twisting the ring on her finger as she talked. "Yes. All these things I want to share with her: my dress, picking out flowers—she loved flowers, you know? Especially daisies. Oh, how she loved daisies! And then there's Daddy. He's so ill and his memory isn't . . ." She swallowed and continued, "It's like he's gone, too. And I feel so lost. And . . . and Pete never knew my mama. I wish more than anything that he'd had a chance to meet her. It's like every time I look at him, I see someone who can't share something so important to me, someone who can never share it."

"And if he could share it," I said, "he could understand just how much you miss her. Especially now."

She took a deep cleansing breath, shook her head and attempted a smile. "I'm such a mess. I'm so sorry for unloading like this. Especially since you have so much—"

"Stop it, Hattie. I'm your best friend. And besides, you've kept this bottled up for far too long. Everyone knows you're miserable. Half the town thinks it's because you don't really want to get married."

She turned square to me, her eyes wide. "They do?"

"Yes. Sorry to be the one to tell you, but you've been almost unbearable the past month or so."

"I have not!"

"Let me ask you something. When you start talking about wedding stuff, what do people do? What does Pete do?"

She looked out the window for a second, then back at me. "He gets all nervous and tries to change the subject. But he's a guy. You know how guys are?"

I lowered my chin and raised my brows.

"Well, I guess a few of my friends have been doing the same thing." She smiled halfheartedly. "I have been pretty witchy lately, huh?"

"Ya think?" I patted her hand. "You and Pete will be happy together. You know that, right?"

She heaved a sigh. "Yes. I know that. I can't wait to be his wife."

"Then focus on the *marriage*, not the wedding. The wedding is just the opening act. Your marriage is the main event. And you and Pete . . . well, you two have a lifetime of happiness ahead of you."

She cleared her throat. "You're right, I guess." She drew back and looked out the window.

It seemed my advice wasn't making her feel much better. I reached up and tugged her arm, drawing her focus back to me. "Listen, Hattie. I wish more than anything that your mama could be here now. But she's gone. And I'm so sorry that she can't be here to share your special day, but in so many ways, she's still with you. She still lives in your heart and in your mind. And all those things she taught you over the years have made you who you are—the woman Pete's going to marry. So, in a way, Pete *has* met her. He's met her through you. And in the years to come, you can share all the special memories about her—the ones that make you laugh and the ones that make you cry. And through your stories, he'll grow to love her as much as you do." We were both crying now. "And you know what?"

She sniffed. "What?"

"Your father, Cade and me; we'll all be there at your wedding. And Ginny and Sam. All the people who love you. We'll all be there to watch you and Pete start your new life together. It'll be such a happy day, Hattie. A beautiful beginning."

Her blue gray eyes glistened as she choked back a couple sobs and asked, "Do you . . . do you think Mama will be there, too? Do you believe in that sort of thing? Like

maybe she could be lookin' down, watchin' over me." She
swiped away a tear. "Listen to me. I must sound crazy."

I shook my head. "No, Hattie. It doesn't sound crazy.
Not a bit. I have no doubt your mama will be there. And
she'll be so proud of you. I know she will."

Chapter 16

Southern Girl Secret #068: A good woman knows her place. A strong woman knows enough not to stay there.

After leaving Hattie, I popped into Sunny Side Up to grab my laptop and keys. On a whim, I knocked on Hawk's door, hoping he'd have some more information for me, but there was no answer. So, I hightailed it out of there. I definitely didn't want to run into Whitaker again. I shivered at the memory of him bearing down on me out on the sidewalk. Hard telling what he might try next.

It was well after eleven by the time I unlocked the door to Peachy Keen. Fortunately, the town seemed deserted—probably everyone was still at the funeral luncheon—so it was doubtful anyone had even missed me. I whipped through my opening chores: counting out the bills in the cash register, checking and straightening the displays, restocking bags and packaging tissue, a quick dusting . . . all the while, my thoughts wandering back to Clem's murder. Now, more than ever, I needed to get it figured out. Daddy didn't need to have the idea of another appearance in front of Maudy hanging over his head when he was trying to heal up from heart surgery! I felt as if I was so close to figuring out Clem's murder. But how many times before had I jumped to conclusions? Certainly Hawk's friend would have had a chance to dig up some more information by now. If Hawk and I could just compare notes, maybe that would clear up a few of the loose ends. Because I wanted to be sure, really sure, before I took this any further.

Deciding to try to reach Hawk by phone, I placed a call to the Clip & Curl Salon. I didn't have Hawk's cell, but certainly Laney would. "Hello, Doris. Hi, this is Nola Harper. . . . Yes, my daddy is doing better. Thank you. . . . No, I don't need my hair done. . . . No, that's quite okay, Doris, maybe some other time. . . ." I sighed. "Is Laney there? Yes, Laney . . . what? She doesn't have time to talk to me?" *That's weird. How busy could they be on a Monday morning? Especially since half the town was at Clem's luncheon.* "Could you tell her that this is important? . . . Please, try again, Doris. . . . I really need to talk to her."

Doris must have put her hand over the mouthpiece, because there was a long stint of garbled talk before Laney finally came to the phone. "What do you want?" she grumbled.

"Hi, Laney. Sorry if I caught you at a bad time. But do you know where Hawk is? I need to—"

"'Course I know where he is. He is *my* boyfriend."

"I know that. I just need to talk to him about something. It's important."

"I'm sure it is."

Huh? I scrunched my face at the phone. "Uh . . . could you give me his cell phone number, please?"

"Give you his cell phone number?" There was a little pause in the conversation where I heard her call out to whomever was in the room, "Did y'all hear that? Now she wants his cell phone number." Laughter broke out in the background as Laney came back on the line. "Sure," she said sweetly. "I'll give you my boyfriend's cell phone number." *Finally we're getting somewhere,* I thought. I reached for pen and paper, just to hear Laney yell over the line, "When hell freezes over!"

I stared down at the phone. She'd hung up. *What in the world? Oh shoot!* Laney must have heard the rumor about Hawk and me holding hands on Sunny Side Up's veranda. And judging by her curt phone conversation, had jumped to the wrong conclusion. I shrugged it off and dialed Ray's number instead. He'd used Hawk's investigative services before; maybe he'd know his cell phone number. Only I couldn't reach Ray. Nothing new there. To his credit, though, he was probably at the hospital, where he planned to spend most of the day. Cell reception was lousy out there. Then, I remembered I'd promised to swing by the house and let Roscoe out for a yard break sometime after lunch. Maybe I could find the number there. I recalled that he kept an address book with his contacts mixed in with the briefcase full of work stuff he usually carried around with him.

The bells above my door jingled, drawing my attention upward. I expected to see Carla coming in for her shift, but it was a couple of young ladies from town. "Hi there!" I greeted them. "Welcome to Peachy Keen! Just holler if you have any questions." They smiled and made a beeline for my candle display. I'd just added the new line of home-made peach-scented, soy-based candles. A while back, I'd happened upon a local woman peddling them at a nearby festival and convinced her to sell some on consignment in my shop. Packaged in tiny mason jars with rustic lids and taffeta labels, they were as cute as could be and smelled absolutely divine. They'd become wildly popular. A great deal for both of us.

While the candle ladies were sniffing away, another customer came in for a quick purchase. She was having company this week and wanted to treat her guests to some homemade peach preserves. We exchanged some pleasant chitchat while I quickly wrapped her purchase. Then, just as I started ringing up the candle ladies, the bells over my door announced another customer. Or two customers, that is. The Crawford sisters shuffled in, a strange-smelling cloud wafting behind them. I sniffed the air. *Burned popcorn?* "Are you ladies just coming from the luncheon over at the church?"

"No, we couldn't make it to the luncheon on account of our hair appointments this mornin'." I glanced upward at their matching heads of slightly damp poodlelike curls.

"Perms," the older sister explained, patting her head.

"That's right," the other said. "We want to look good for tomorrow's parade."

"And for the dance," her sister added with a gleam in her eye.

I put the finishing touches on the gift bags for the candle ladies and handed it over. They seemed pleased. "Enjoy the candles, ladies," I told them. "And come back again soon."

As soon as they left, the Crawford sisters came up to the counter with their merchandise and started up again. "We're so sorry to hear of the trouble your daddy's havin' with his heart."

"You should know that we prayed for him at church yesterday," the other sister added with a nod. Then, she leaned forward and, even though we were the only ones in the shop, added in a hushed tone, "Of course, all the added stress he's been under, with the sheriff houndin' him like she is, well, that can't be good for his ticker."

I turned my focus back to the jars of pepper jelly they'd brought to the counter and changed the subject. "So, you ladies are planning on attending the dance?"

"Why, of course, dear," one of them answered. "We were quite the dancers in our day, weren't we, sister?"

The younger sister's cheeks flushed. "Yes, we were. Though can't quite keep up with the fast songs like we used to back in the day."

"Speak for yourself," her sister countered. "Besides, the slow songs are much more satisfyin', especially if there are a few young studs around."

They both giggled. I fumbled with the second jar of pepper jelly, finally getting it wrapped and tucked safely into a paper bag along with the first.

"But you don't need any help in that department, do you dear? You've got your hands full with two hunky men. How *do* you do it?"

"Two? What do you mean?" I started tallying their purchase.

The older sister pulled out her pocketbook and shook her head. "No need to play coy, Nola Mae. We completely understand. Cade McKenna is a handsome man, but that

Dane Hawkins, well, that man is hot enough to make the house paint peel."

"You got that right, sister," the younger one agreed, cheeks practically blazing now. "You should hear some of the things Laney says about him. Makes me wish I was thirty years younger."

Aw . . . so that's it. My eyes darted from their devilish grins to their all-so-tight curls. The Crawford sisters had been at the salon when my call came in for Laney. Laney, no doubt, had not only jumped to the wrong conclusions, but had embellished it as she related my call to the patrons. Heaven only knew what the story had grown into by now. Or how far it'd spread. Maybe that was part of the reason for Whitaker's little stunt this morning. Perhaps he'd heard about Hawk and I roaming the veranda, put two and two together, and deduced that we really were snooping around in his room. One thing for sure: I would not be staying another night at Sunny Side Up.

The older sister leaned forward and continued, "Is that why you're staying at Margie's place? Because no one can figure that out. At first I told sister here that you were probably staying there to help Margie with her campaign, being that you seemed to have crossed over to the other side. But now we're all wonderin' if Hunky Hawk isn't the reason you're stayin' at the inn. Laney Burns sure seems to think so."

"Or maybe it has something to do with your sleuthing," the other sister added. "Heard you got some sort of proof—"

I waved my hand through the air. "That's just some silly rumor going around town. Not a speck of truth to it."

They didn't look convinced. It was time to steer this conversation in another direction. "No, no ladies. I'm just staying at the inn to help Margie." Not exactly with her campaign, but they didn't need to know that. "She's had to step up her game ever since Jack Snyder decided to run for mayor."

"Bet that's the truth." The older Crawford sister handed the bag of peach pepper jelly to her sister so she could put the change in her pocketbook. "Jack ran a hard campaign last time. He'll be hard to beat this time around."

"That's right," I said, glad for the topic change. "He ran against Wade Marshall, didn't he? And I heard it was a close race."

"Yes. Jack was fit to be tied when he lost," she said. "He had the votes recounted, you know."

"Twice," the other sister added. "But it turned out that Wade Marshall won it fair and square."

The younger sister shook her head. "Although Mayor Marshall never got a chance to celebrate properly. Poor man."

I tilted my head. "He didn't? Why's that?"

"Had a terrible accident that evening. Guess he was makin' his way to the inauguration dance and wrecked his car out on that twisty road that leads to McManamy Draw. Bad breaks, if I remember. He was darn lucky to survive."

I hadn't heard that story before. Could it be that it wasn't an accident? Perhaps the übercompetitive Jack Snyder had tampered with Wade's brakes way back then. I shook my head. *Talking about jumping to conclusions.* But before I could think too much more about it, the door burst open and Carla flew inside. "Sorry, I'm running so late," she said, shooting the ladies a quick smile. She'd reverted back to her all-black garb, which was appropriate considering she really had come from a funeral today.

"That's okay. How was the luncheon?" I asked.

She rolled her eyes and shook her head. "Poor Tessa. It didn't go quite as planned."

"How's that?"

"Well, you know how the town hall had to borrow chairs from the church because so many people went to the debate?" I nodded, remembering that I'd seen the bus from the Baptist church unloading chairs at the courthouse the other day. Carla continued, "Seems they're all missing."

The sisters gasped.

"The chairs are missing?" I asked.

Carla nodded. "Yup. The church custodian went to unload the bus this morning, getting ready for the luncheon, and all of them were missing. Someone broke in to the van and took them during the night. Crazy, huh?"

The Crawford sisters exchanged a look. "We'd best get over to the diner and see what's goin' on," the older one said. I suppressed a roll of my eyes—from beauty shop gossip to diner rumors—these ladies were out to get their fill today. Instead, I tossed them my usual friendly shopkeeper's wave, but they were already on their way and too busy chewing over the latest news to even notice.

Carla moved behind the counter and booted up the laptop to check for online orders. "Did anyone report the theft to the sheriff?" I asked, because this was obviously the work of our local scrap metal thieves. I briefly thought of Lucas and the air-conditioner connector I'd discovered in his truck.

"Yeah," Carla answered. "Well, not the sheriff exactly. But her deputy was there at the luncheon. I saw him talking to Reverend Jones about it." She paused to type in the password and then changed the topic. "I'm looking forward to tonight."

"Tonight?"

She glanced my way and chuckled. "Did you forget? It's Monday." I must have had a blank look on my face, because she went on to clarify, "Monday. Our usual cooking night."

"Oh, that's right. I did forget. We'd better plan on it, too, because we're running low on preserves."

Carla nodded. "Yeah, and tomorrow's the election and the parade. I bet we get a few extra customers. If there's time tonight, I might try a new chocolate recipe I found online. The peach molds haven't come in yet, but I could figure out something else to use. Just for testing. Half the trick is going to be finding the perfect recipe."

"That sounds good," I said, hoping I sounded enthusiastic. My mind was still stuck on the missing chairs and now all the things I needed to get done before our cooking session. Plus, I'd just added talking to Lucas to my long checklist. And I really did want to get ahold of Hawk. "You know, Carla, I need to run out to the farm and take care of a couple things for my mama. Do you mind being in charge for a while?"

Her face brightened at the prospect. "Sure thing, boss. I can handle things, no problem."

I reached out and touched her arm. "Great. Thanks, Carla. I'll be back by four." I glanced up at the clock. It was already a little after noon. And If I hurried, I might be able to get everything done and still go by the Pack & Carry by the time Lucas finished his shift. He and I had some serious talking to do.

I had the strangest feeling as I pulled in front of our home. Something seemed off. Putting the truck in park, I sat behind the wheel staring at the house and trying to figure out what had me spooked. It wasn't like anything was out of place. The house looked the same as it always did. Except for the peeling paint along the roofline. When did that happen? I sighed. Just one more thing to add to my list of things to do.

My eyes roamed the area directly around the house, then out to the barn and the orchards beyond. Even from here, I could see we'd fallen behind on the pruning. It was a huge job. Too much for just one person. Daddy usually hired a crew to come in and help. Looked like I'd have to see to it now. Pruning was one job that couldn't be ignored. By removing the thinner limbs and damaged branches, we could prevent weak spots, which would eventually cause breakage, invite disease and lead to the tree's early death. Was I ready to take all this on? More to the point, was I even willing to take it on? No wonder I had a strange feeling when I pulled up: I was seeing it for the first time from a new perspective, one where every bit of the burden and responsibility could weigh on my shoulders. I blew out my breath and hopped out of the truck. I had to tread carefully with this new decision.

I was about to open the front door when out of nowhere, Roscoe came scurrying up the porch steps, his claws making little *click-clack* noises on the weathered boards. Bending down, I ruffled the fur between his ears. "Hey, fellow. What are you doing out here? Did Ray leave you out?" He whimpered and began pawing at the screen door. I pulled it open and unlocked the storm door, holding it as he shot under my feet. *The poor thing must be dying of thirst!* Sure enough, he went straight to his water bowl and started lapping water. "Sorry, Roscoe. I should have known better than to leave

Ray in charge of you." *Or this house,* I thought, throwing my bag on the hall table and turning for the kitchen.

I froze.

Prickles of fear raced up my spine as I turned my gaze back to the living room. Davenport cushions were all cattywampus, drawers left partially open . . . even Mom's favorite potted philodendron lay on its side . . .

But this wasn't Ray's lazy housekeeping—this was the mess left by someone in a hurry searching for something. Who? John Whitaker, no doubt! Was he still here? I strained my ears, trying to hear something other than my own frantic heartbeat. Nothing, except the sound of Roscoe crunching on kibble. Still, I slowly started backtracking toward the door, my eyes darting about, scanning every nook and cranny in the room. Then suddenly, a sharp yap from Roscoe pierced the air and sent me running helter-skelter. I nearly put my hand through the screen as I burst through the front door.

Out on the front lawn, I stopped, my stomach lurching as I realized I'd left my bag, and keys, inside. I was standing there, suspended between fear and confusion, when I heard the telltale rumble of Hawk's Harley coming down the drive. I turned and ran toward him.

"Whitaker's been in the house!" I hollered, as he parked his bike. "He may still be in there. I think he knows we were looking through his stuff and—"

Hawk threw down his helmet and started for the door. "Where's my dog?"

"Your dog? Roscoe's inside." I followed behind Hawk, too freaked-out to stand outside by myself.

On the porch, he turned and grabbed my arm. "Does your daddy have a gun?"

I swallowed hard and nodded. "In the den. There's a closet behind his desk. It's on the shelf."

"What type is it? Do you know?"

"A shotgun. The shells should be next to it."

He lowered his face, looking me directly in the eyes. "Go back and lock yourself in your truck. Don't come out, you hear?"

"I can't. I—"

"Just do what I say," he bit out, giving me a tiny shove toward my truck before turning and heading inside. Normally, I would have shoved back, but in this case, I made an exception. Besides, there was no arguing with stupidity. If he wanted to run in there and play hero, then more power to him.

So, I nervously paced on the porch until he finally came back outside, shotgun cradled in the crook of his arm and Roscoe at his feet. "Thought I told you to lock yourself in your truck."

"The keys are in my bag, which I left in the house."

"Oh." He propped the gun against the railing and plopped into one of our cane rockers. "It's all clear. No sign of a forced entry. Looks like he just walked through the back door. Seems it was left unlocked."

Well, of course, nearly all the farmers in these parts left their doors unlocked under usual circumstances. But with Daddy and Mama out of town . . . well, I'd be talking to Ray about that, first thing. "What made you come out here anyway?" I asked Hawk, as I took the chair next to him. "I've been trying to reach you all day."

"Yeah, tell me about it. Laney said you called the salon looking for my number. She's all bent out of shape over it, too. Some busybody told her that you and I were getting it on—"

"Getting it on?" I rolled my eyes. *Disgusting.* "Mrs. Busby lives across the street from Sunny Side Up," I explained. "She apparently saw us slip out of Whitaker's room and sneak around the veranda. And you know how this town is."

"Yeah, word travels fast 'round here. Anyway, I figured it was important, so I stopped in at your shop and Carla told me you were headin' out this way." He bent down and scooped an excited Roscoe onto his lap. "And I really wanted to see my little fellow," he added, burying his face between the pooch's ears and making kissy noises. *Definitely a side of Hawk I'd never seen before!*

I watched until he finally came up for air and said, "So you think Whitaker was here?"

"Yeah. He must think I found whatever it is he's searching for."

"Well, I know what that is," Hawk said, pulling his shoulders back. "Diamonds."

I leaned forward. "Diamonds? What?"

He nodded and gently set Roscoe down on the porch. Slumping back in his chair, he began to explain, "My contact came through with some information. John Whitaker, or Felix Ganassi, rather, was working as an armored truck driver back nearly twenty years ago. He was part of a team, with two other guys, making a large delivery for a diamond brokerage firm out of Chicago. Ganassi was driving. Somewhere en route between Chicago and Detroit, their truck experienced mechanical issues and they were forced to pull off on the side of the interstate. Two men, last names Turner and Gray, pulled up behind them in a white van. They shot one of the guards immediately and held Ganassi and one other guard at gunpoint."

"And made off with the diamonds," I added.

"Uh-huh. About four million dollars' worth. But some-one tipped off the authorities and they eventually tracked down Turner and Gray. They were holed up in some sleazy hotel. They didn't go down without a fight, though. Gray was shot and killed during the arrest. The other guy's still in the pen."

"And you're thinking that Turner and Gray had inside help from Ganassi. Because how else would they have known that the armored truck was going to have mechani-cal issues and be pulled over at that particular spot on the interstate?"

"Exactly," Hawk agreed. He rocked back and forth a few times, gathering his thoughts. "Thing is, Gray's half of the take was never found."

"And Ganassi wants it," I said. "Let me guess. Margie was married to one of them?" I recalled her saying something about her ex-husband, and I knew she was from Detroit.

"Gray," Hawk responded. "Price is her maiden name. She must have changed it back, left Detroit and started a new life for herself."

"So maybe she was involved with the robbery. That's hard to imagine, but I've always wondered how she funded the renovations for Sunny Side Up." Hopefully Ida would get back to me with Margie's financial information soon. If Margie took out a loan to buy and renovate the inn, it would go a long way in proving her innocence in the dia-mond heist. After all, two million dollars in diamonds would pay for a lot of renovations.

Hawk shook his head. "I thought the same thing at first. If that were the case, though, she should have recognized Ganassi. On the other hand, even if she wasn't in on the heist, it could be that somewhere down the line she found the diamonds and kept them. Clem might have suspected the same thing. I'm thinking he found out about Margie's past and put the facts together. And if she did build her business on stolen money, then she's in big trouble." He shifted in his seat and sighed. "Can't believe I misjudged the woman. Could be that I've been working for a killer."

I didn't have anything to add to that. It was possible, I guessed. And here I thought I'd started to figure things out. Now I was confused again. I needed to get some more information to make sense out of it all, starting with talking to Lucas. I began getting out of my chair when something else occurred to me. "Ganassi must be feeling pretty desperate if he broke in here and searched the place. He knows we're onto him, Hawk. So far all he's done is nose around. But things are heating up, and if he thinks there's even the slightest chance that Margie knows where the diamonds are, then he might try to force it out of her. If that's the case, she could be in danger." I stood, heading inside to get my purse. I turned back. "You go find Margie," I told him. "Make sure she's okay. Then swing by the sheriff's office and let Maudy know what we've discovered about Whitaker. I'll try to meet you there a little later. Right now, I've got something else I have to do."

"What's that?" He stood, his expression full of concern.

"Just an errand I need to run," I said, but he stood firm, folding his arms and lowering his chin. I sighed. It was probably getting close to two. I desperately needed to talk to Lucas and didn't have time to explain everything to Hawk. "Go on and take care of this thing with Margie," I said. "If I'm not able to meet you there before you're done, come by the diner tonight around six. I should be done cooking by that time, and I'll probably be able to explain more then."

I caught Lucas just as he was making his way through the Pack & Carry parking lot. I pulled up next to him and rolled down my window. "Hey, Lucas. Hop in, will ya? I need to talk to you for a sec."

"Me?" He shuffled his feet and glanced around. "What about?"

I pointed to the passenger door. "It's important. Come on, and I'll buy you a burger." My own stomach was grumbling. I hadn't eaten since breakfast.

He shuffled a little more and then finally agreed, climbing into the passenger side. We were barely out of the lot when he asked, "So what do you want to talk about? Something with Tessa?"

I made a right hand turn and headed for the Tasty Freeze. "Sort of. I'm going to be up front with you about something, Lucas. And I need to know the truth."

He fidgeted, drumming his fingers on his knee. Probably wanting a cigarette. "Sounds serious."

"It is."

I was stalling, preferring to wait until we were parked and eating our burgers. But Lucas seemed anxious to get on with the conversation. "Am I in trouble for something?" he asked.

"Should you be?"

He turned slightly in his seat, staring out the window. "I forgot. There's something important I'm supposed to do. Can you pull over? I can walk back to my truck."

"The Tasty Freeze is just up ahead. Let me at least get you a burger."

"I'm not really hungry."

I sighed. "You're in trouble, aren't you? I can help."

His hand hovered over the door handle. "I don't need your help. Just pull over."

"My friend Ginny speaks so highly of you. Says you're a good kid. I guess you and her son, Jake, used to be friends."

"Used to. That was a long time ago."

"Good kids sometimes find themselves in bad situations. I know, Lucas. I've been there. I understand what you're going through. I want to help you."

"You don't understand crap." He sounded panicked.

"Do you know who killed Clem?"

He yanked on the handle, opening the door. "Pull over. I want out."

Afraid he was going to jump, I whipped into the Tasty Freeze lot and came to a screeching halt. He pushed the door open the rest of the way and jumped out. I spoke quickly, "I know what you've been doing and I have proof. Help me now, or I'll go straight to the sheriff." He was striding away. "Okay, I'm going to the sheriff now, Lucas." I put the truck in gear.

That stopped him.

He turned back to me, defiance in his voice. "What exactly is it that you think you know?"

"I know that you've been stealing scrap metal all over town." His mouth dropped open and he seemed to sink into himself. I added quickly, "But if you help me, I'll make sure you get a fair break. My brother's an attorney. He'll help us." The kid stood still, and I knew I had him. "Come back in the truck."

When he got back in, I said, "I think Clem knew about the thefts, too. He threatened to expose you, didn't he?"

"I didn't kill him."

"Maybe not. But you weren't working alone, were you?"

He didn't answer. I blew out my breath and tried another approach. "You told me you've been working the six to two shift all month at the Pack and Carry."

"Yeah, so?"

"Well, Tessa told me that you worked until five o'clock the day of the murder. Is that true?"

He looked down at his hands.

"Where were you between two and five that day, Lucas?"

"I already told you that I didn't kill Clem."

"And I believe you. But were you out at the farm? Did you see who did?"

He shook his head. "No, I was . . . running an errand."

"An errand?" I remembered Cade telling me there was a big recycling plant over in Perry. "You were in Perry, weren't you?"

His head slowly bobbed up and down. That whole back road thing I did, about destroying my truck, was in vain. Lucas was never at the farm. He was hauling stolen scrap metal to the recycler.

I took a deep breath and tried to gather my thoughts. There was so much at play here. Greed, power, and so many loose elements that just didn't fit together: past secrets, old scores to settle, scrap metal thefts and now a decades-old diamond heist with two million dollars in diamonds still missing. Not to mention all the clues that just didn't seem to fit: Mama's handkerchief, the gas can with Daddy's prints, Jack Snyder's burned arm, Wade Marshall's car accident way back when . . . I'd been thinking that all these things were tied together into one overall set of crimes, and that two people were involved. Now I wasn't sure. Maybe they were separate, completely unrelated crimes. Which only complicated figuring any of them out. I glanced across the seat at Lucas, knowing that he held the answers to so many of my questions. I decided to lay it on thick. "Do you really love Tessa," I asked, "or are you just using her for a cool truck to drive? Or maybe it's the farm you're after."

His whipped his head around, his eyes dark and angry. "That's not true! I love Tessa."

"Then how can you stand by and watch her suffer when you might know who killed her uncle? Think of the closure she'd feel if his killer was brought to justice." His facial muscles tightened with anger. I tempered my tone, but kept up the pressure. "You should hear how she talks about you, Lucas. She trusts you. How's she going to feel when she finds out that you allowed her uncle's killer to get off scot-free?"

He suddenly slammed his fist on my dashboard, causing me to startle. "Shut up!" he yelled, sitting back and folding his arms, his chest heaving as he seethed.

But he didn't bolt, and I knew I had to jump back in. "Listen, Lucas," I said, struggling to keep my voice calm. "I think you're in over your head. I think you're being manipulated and you don't know how to get out of this mess. I'm offering you a chance to help yourself and bring down Clem's killer. You'd be Tessa's hero."

After a long pause, he pushed open the car door and stepped out. He turned back at the last minute. "I can't go to the cops about this. I just can't."

"I understand. I really do. But let me try to help you, Lucas," I pleaded again. "Come by the diner tonight around six. I'll ask my brother to meet us there. We can figure something out."

"I don't know. Okay? I just don't know."

Just before he slammed the door shut, our eyes connected. What I saw in his expression made me feel sorry for the kid. Because his eyes weren't full of anger, or defiance, but fear.

Chapter 17

Southern Girl Secret #077: When lookin' for Mr. Right, always pick a man who'll spend his life mussing up your lipstick . . . not your mascara.

After Lucas left, I placed a couple phone calls. The first to Ray. We talked a bit about Daddy's condition, the plans for his surgery, how Mama was holding up, and so on. Then, I filled him in on a few things I'd discovered about John Whitaker. The rest I wanted to tell him in person, so I asked him to stop by the diner so we could discuss it tonight. I also wanted him to talk to Lucas—if he showed up, that is—to see if there was anything he could do to help the kid. Then I called Ida to find out if she'd talked to Hollis yet. She had. And he told her that Margie had indeed taken out a substantial loan to purchase and renovate the inn. Some of the best news I'd heard all day. Because if Margie knew where two million dollars in diamonds were stashed, she probably wouldn't need a bank loan.

I'd decided the best way to celebrate this tidbit of good news and satisfy my grumbling stomach was with a Tasty

Freeze special double cheeseburger, onion rings and an icy Coke. But I never did get that burger. Because just as I was putting my truck in gear for the drive-through, my cell rang. It was Hawk. He was at Sunny Side Up and he wanted me to come by right away.

"Sheriff's not happy about Ganassi," he said. "She's worked into a tizzy and is takin' it out on Margie."

"I'm on my way," I told him, mindful of the time. If I was quick about it, there was still enough time to do this and make it to the diner for tonight's cooking session.

Arriving at the inn, I found Maudy in the front, her county-issued shoes leaving little scuff marks on Margie's highly polished wood floors as she paced back and forth, berating Margie in a blustery voice, "Guess you really did have a secret to hide, Ms. Price. You were once married to a thief and a murderer." She shook her head and chuckled. "Boy, some women sure know how to pick 'em."

"I didn't know anything about Kevin's plans to rob the armored truck," Margie shot back. She was crumpled up in one of the wing chairs by the fireplace, pale-faced and trembling slightly. Hawk was standing behind her. "I swear. I was shocked when I found out."

"Oh, I see." Maudy stopped pacing and scowled down at Margie. "You were married to the man, but had no idea he picked off an armored truck and made off with over two million dollars in diamonds. Frankly, Ms. Price, I'm havin' a hard time believin' that you were ever that stupid."

"I was young, Sheriff. Young and naive. I'd lived such a sheltered life, always the good girl, doing exactly what I was told. And then along came Kevin." She sighed. "He was so good-looking and dangerous. The classic bad boy."

She looked my way. "You understand what I'm saying, don't you, Nola?"

My eyes grew wide and darted toward Hawk. He caught my look, his full lips slowly turning upward. I blinked double time and quickly turned back to Margie, who continued in a dreamy tone, "It was always something new and exciting with Kevin. Even the way we got married. He simply swept me off to Vegas one night where we took our vows in one of the cheesy little white chapels." She chuckled lightly at the memory. "Oh, I know it all sounds so cliché. But to me, every day with Kevin was an adventure." Her face drooped. "At least for the first year or so. Then things started to change. He never finished his degree, choosing to go into business with his roommates instead. Some sort of real estate investment venture. Such a sure thing, he'd said. But it didn't pan out, and when money got tight, Kevin started to change. We drifted apart. So, I really had no idea." Her tone was pleading. "You have to believe me. For all real purposes, my relationship was over when Kevin planned all this. We weren't even living together at the time. I'd moved back home."

"And you had no idea who Ganassi was?" Maudy wanted to know.

"No. None."

"Then how'd he track you down?"

"I think I can answer that, Sheriff," I said.

The sheriff's eyes slid my way with a sneer. "Oh, I'm sure you can. Y'all probably think you have this whole case figured out already. Probably Clem's murder, too. In fact, rumor is that you have some sort of proof pertaining to my murder case." She folded her arms across her chest.

"Not that I'd believe for one second that you were able to come up with any proof—"

I shook my head. "You're right. It's just a rumor. Honest," I added, continuing on before she could think too much about it. "Like I was saying, I think Ganassi was able to track down Margie the same way Clem was able to track down her true identity—through an investigative firm."

The sheriff smirked. "What are you talking about, Nola Mae?"

"Clem was so intent on winning this election that he hired an investigative firm to run a background check on Margie. He was hoping to turn up some dirt to use against her in the election."

"And he did stir up dirt," Margie said. "He took great delight in telling me what he'd discovered about my past. Marched right over here the day before our debate and threatened me with it. Said if I didn't pull out of the race, he'd tell the whole town about my secret. He would have, too. If someone hadn't . . ." She stopped, her eyes widening.

"If someone hadn't killed him," the sheriff finished. "Someone like you, maybe?"

"No!" She frantically shook her head. "I didn't kill Clem. There's no way I could ever do something like that!"

"But you had so much to lose, Ms. Price. Your reputation, your business." She hooked her thumbs in her utility belt and puffed out her chest. "Here's what I think. I think you knew all about your ex's shenanigans. Heck, maybe you even helped him plan it. Then when he got busted, you played all dumb-like."

Margie shook her head, discreetly swiping a finger under her eye. But her wet mascara left a telltale black smudge. "No, that's not what happened. There was an investigation. I was exonerate—"

Maudy held up her hand and silenced her. "You waited until things cooled down, then changed your name and moved down here to start a new life. Always wondered why you chose to come down here in the first place, bein' that you're a Northerner, and all." She said the word "Northerner" like she had a mouth full of mud. "And this place." She waved her hand around the room. "I remember what it looked like before. It was a dump. Must've cost a fortune to fix it up. Maybe you used those diamonds to—"

"I don't think so," I interrupted. Of course, although I knew from Ida that Margie had taken out a huge loan from the Cays Mill Bank & Trust, saying so might land Hollis in trouble. Hollis had already had enough trouble to last a lifetime. "But Ganassi might have thought so. Otherwise, he wouldn't have gone to so much trouble looking for them. He practically searched every inch of this house." *And mine.* "But Margie couldn't have stashed them here, because she didn't have them and she'd left behind everything of her old life when—" My breath caught. Then it hit me! "Except there's one spot I bet he didn't consider."

I hurried down the hall to my room, stopping in front of the large armoire. The others had followed me, and I turned to see Margie's puzzled face. "The other day you told me this was the only possession you kept from your first marriage. Why?"

She shrugged. "I don't know. It was a gift from Kevin . . . the last gift he gave me. He'd said he wanted to start things over for us, sent it to me where I was staying at my parents and . . . I liked to think he'd meant it."

The armoire had a large top section for hanging clothes and three drawers on the bottom. I opened the double doors on the top section and started knocking on the interior wood.

"You're looking for a secret compartment," Hawk said, joining me. He started running his fingers along the joints of the wood and then on the outside of the cabinet, where ornately scrolled pilasters flanked either side. I, in turn, started pulling out the drawers and dumping their contents on the bed, so I could closely examine each one.

Margie joined in, knocking on the outside panels of wood, listening for a hollow sound. The sheriff stood off to the side, shaking her head. "Y'all are wastin' my time with this hogwash. Hidden compartments? I've never heard anything so stupid."

"Whoa! I think I've got somethin'," Hawk said. He was halfway inside the cabinet, pushing against the lower back corner. "This corner piece feels different. . . . Oh hey, look at this." Suddenly, a little piece along the bottom of the cabinet popped out, leaving a small hole. Hawk hooked his finger in and lifted up a large portion of the wood, revealing a false bottom.

"Move out of the way," Maudy ordered, elbowing her way in closer. "Well, I'll be!" she exclaimed. "Look at what I found." She turned around, grinning like the Cheshire cat and holding a diamond between her thumb and forefinger. She slid her eyes toward Margie. "You best come with me, Ms. Price. You've got some explainin' to do."

"Explaining? What's there to explain?" Hawk's mouth twisted in anger. "She didn't know the diamonds were hidden here."

"That's right," I agreed. "Why would she have kept

them hidden here all these years? She could've cashed them in a long time ago."

Maudy pulled out an evidence bag and started scooping up the remaining gems. "Who's to say she *didn't* sell off a few? Now step aside. I'm takin' her in until I can get ahold of someone in Detroit and get some answers."

"This is crazy." Margie shook her head. "I honestly had no idea they were hidden here, Sheriff. And I can't go in for more questioning. I have obligations this evening. Tomorrow's Election Day!"

Maudy clutched the bag of diamonds in one of her meaty hands while she wrapped the other around Margie's arm. "Well, your 'obligations' will just have to wait." She turned a nasty glare at me, saying, "Seems everyone has other issues to deal with when I end up on their doorstep," as if my daddy's surgery was just a ploy to avoid her. "But it's just a matter of time and I'll 'get my man,' if you get my drift."

Oh, I got her drift, all right: she still wanted to take down a Harper. Other crimes and suspects took a backseat to that personal vendetta of hers. I swallowed my anger and fear and tried to appeal to her ego, if not her reason. "We understand you're just doing your job, Sheriff. It can't be easy, what with several crimes at once, from murder and high-value thefts to all those church chairs missing and—"

"Chairs gone missing? Nola, don't you think for one second that you can distract me into forgetting about your daddy. He's not off the hook, that's for darn sure. Until I get to the bottom of *this*," she shook the evidence bag full of diamonds, "he's still top on my list for Clem's murder." She jerked Margie's arm. "Come on, let's go."

Hawk started to protest, but the sheriff elbowed past him, escorting Margie toward the door. Margie turned to me in a panic. "Can you lock up for me, Nola? Just in case . . ."

"I sure will. And don't worry, Margie. One way or another, this will be cleared up soon. I promise." But she didn't look reassured.

"You sounded awfully sure of yourself, darlin'." We were on the front porch of Sunny Side Up. I'd packed my belongings and was double-checking the front lock before leaving.

"How's that?"

"When you told Margie that things would be cleared up soon."

I told him about how I thought Lucas knew who killed Clem. "I tried to convince him to come by the diner tonight and meet with Ray." I shook my head. "But I don't know. He's scared. You see, I've been looking at things all wrong, thinking that there were two people working together. I mean, how else could someone have killed Clem just minutes after my father met with him? And then worked so hard to frame Daddy with the handkerchief in Clem's sheets, the gas can . . . well, it all seemed like it would be a two-person job. And then for a while, I thought for sure it all had something to do with Whitaker, I mean Ganassi. But now, I'm not so sure. I think Clem's murder is tied in with the scrap metal thefts. At least I'm pretty sure. I just need to prove it."

He was smirking. "And how do you plan to do that?"

"It's not going to be easy," I was about to tell him my plan, but we were suddenly interrupted by a loud rumbling sound. I looked over to see someone pulling up on a Harley.

Hawk tensed. "Oh crap."

"Is that Laney?" I asked. But I didn't have to wonder for long. She slid off the bike and slowly removed her helmet, shaking her long, highly processed tresses over her shoulders. Then she bent down, generous cleavage in full view beneath her half-zipped black leather jacket, peered in the handlebar mirror and fluffed up her teased out bangs. Satisfied that she was properly tidied up, she headed up the walk, the silver studs on her knee-high leather boots scraping together as she sashayed toward us, heavily lined eyes trained on Hawk.

"Hey, babe," he said, his tone a pitch higher than normal.

"Don't *hey, babe* me. I've been lookin' all over town for you." She briefly slid her eyes my way. "Where've ya been?"

Hawk shifted uncomfortably. "Nowhere. I mean, here. Margie Price just got taken away by the sheriff and I was here to help her." He looked hopeful, like a little boy hoping a wilted dandelion would make up for a poor report card.

"Really?" Laney looked around at the locked house and empty street. "And so it's just the two of you here now, is it?"

"Well, yeah, but I was just . . . uh, talking to Nola here."

"Great bike, Laney," I said, attempting to bring this fiasco around to some semblance of normalcy. But the look she shot me made me squirm. I swallowed hard. "Hawk was just helping me with some investigating stuff. You know, to help Margie. Really," I added.

"Investigating stuff? Is that what y'all call it?"

"Easy, babe," Hawk said. "No need to get all worked up over nothin'."

"Nothin'? That's not what I've been hearin'." The fringe on her leather jacket swung back and forth as she waggled her shoulders. "And now you've stood me up."

"Stood you up?" Hawk's mouth fell open. "Oh, I completely forgot."

"Forgot!" she shrieked. "You said we were goin' out to lunch and then for a ride. And after I took the afternoon off from work and everything! Well, maybe you've been so forgetful because your mind's been somewhere else." She gave me a nasty up-and-down. "Or on someone else."

Hawk's Adam's apple bobbed. "No. 'Course not, darlin'." He grabbed her hand and started leading her down the porch steps. "Come on, let me make it up to you. I'll take you to that nice restaurant over in Perry. The one you've always wanted to try."

"But what about the case?" I yelled after him.

He turned back briefly. "I'll come by the diner later. Until then, don't do anything stupid, okay?"

Chapter 18

Southern Girl Secret #057: Strong Southern gals are made up of ninety percent good-heartedness and ten percent badass.

"You're late," Ginny said the moment I walked into the diner's kitchen. She was helping Carla stir something on the stove.

"That's because—"

Ginny continued before I could get a single word out about the diamonds, "We've been worried sick that something might be going on with your daddy. How is he?"

"He's doing okay." I suddenly felt a twinge of remorse for not visiting the hospital today. But when I'd called earlier Mama's voice had told me as much as her words: that Daddy was resting well and seemed to be doing fine. Which had further set me on resolving Maudy Payne and her dogged determination to stick it to my family. I knew that tracking down Clem's real killer was the best thing I could do for my daddy right now, even though I'd have rather been at his bedside. "Actually, I was working on the case.

And have I got a story for you!" Both of them looked up, eager for more. "You remember John Whitaker?"

Carla giggled. "Does she remember him? She talks about him all the time."

"I do not!" Ginny's cheeks flushed. "Well, not like that, anyway. I'm just curious about the man, that's all. He . . ." She briefly stopped stirring and looked my way. "He's just so mysterious, don't y'all think?"

"Not anymore, he's not," I said with a slight grin, leaving them hanging while I checked on a large container of frozen peaches that Ginny had already set out to thaw. They were just about ready. I started assembling the other ingredients for peach preserves, including ginger root. Just a pinch of ginger added so much to the flavor of the jam.

"What do you mean?" Ginny anxiously demanded.

"His real name is Felix Ganassi. And—"

"Felix Ganassi?" Ginny blurted. "That doesn't sound right! He doesn't even look like a Felix." She leaned over and squinted at a thermometer clipped to the top portion of a large double boiler and looked over at Carla. "I think this chocolate is ready to pour." Carla eagerly slid a lined cookie sheet her way. I stopped what I was doing and joined them at the counter. Oh, the lure of chocolate!

With mitted hands, Ginny tipped the bowl and poured the dark, smooth liquid onto the tray. A sweet chocolate aroma filled the room. "I think this is one of the best ideas y'all have had yet," Ginny said, reaching for a spoon. She scraped it along the side of the bowl, lifting it to her lips and blowing over it lightly before taking a taste. Carla did the same thing. I shrugged and did the same, deciding my story could wait for a second.

For a second, no one spoke. We were too busy rolling our tongues and moaning. "Good, really good," Ginny said.

"Excellent," I added, reaching for another spoonful. It was so smooth, with undertones of just enough sweetness to not overpower the depth of the rich chocolate taste.

"It's okay," Carla said. "But it needs something. Something to make it extraordinary. Something that makes it stand out from the regular stuff you can buy at the grocery store." She started running a knife over the poured chocolate, smoothing it to the edges of the pan. "At least it looks like it'll firm up okay."

Ginny caught my eye and smiled, both of us delighted to see both Carla's enthusiasm and her thoughtful analysis. "Keep working at it," Ginny said. "You'll get it." She turned to me. "So what's this big story on John?"

"Felix, you mean. Felix Ganassi. He's from Detroit, actually."

Ginny moved over to my counter and began grating the ginger root. "Detroit? That's not where I pictured him living."

"Where'd you think he was from?"

"Oh, I don't know. Guess I'd imagined he was from New York City."

Carla sniggered.

"Well, hate to break it to you, my friend, but he is definitely from Detroit. And there's more." While we continued to chop and grate, measure and mix, I told them everything I'd learned about Felix Ganassi, rounding off the story with the diamonds we'd found at Sunny Side Up.

"Diamonds!" Ginny exclaimed. Carla was all ears, too.

"Yup. About two million dollars' worth."

Carla let out a whistle. "Whoa. And they were hidden in that armoire all this time?"

I nodded. "Yeah. Felix has been looking for them this whole time. Now it seems he's disappeared. Must've figured we were onto him."

Ginny shook her head. "I sure as heck misjudged that guy."

"Don't feel bad. We all did." While we waited for the peach liquid to boil, I rummaged around in the fridge for some leftovers to heat up. My eyes lit on a container of Sam's chili. "Mind if I have some of this?" I asked Ginny. I hadn't eaten since breakfast and was half-starved.

"Help yourself." She was placing jars in the sterilizer while Carla took the dirty dishes back to the sink. "Do you suppose Ganassi is responsible for Clem's murder, then? I always did think it was an outsider. Nobody from 'round here could be that evil."

Really? I thought to myself. Had she forgotten about the last two murders, both committed by local people? I started to remind her of the fact when there was a knock at the back door. Carla left the water running and went to answer it. "Hi, Ray. I mean, Mr. Harper. Come on in."

"Hey, Ray," Ginny said. "What brings you here?"

"I asked him to come by," I said casting a glance toward Carla. "Do you think you can handle the rest of this?" I asked her. "There's a few things I need to talk over with my brother and Mrs. Wiggins." Ginny's eyebrows crept up her forehead, but she didn't ask any questions.

Carla, on the other hand, suddenly became nervous, a dish in her jittery hands slipping and splashing back into the sink. She glanced my way. "Does this have something to do with Lucas?"

"Why do you ask?" I wanted to know.

"Because I saw him earlier. He was all worked up about something. It looked like he was going to leave town. Is he . . . is he in trouble?"

I sighed. "I know Lucas is your friend, Carla. And I'm going to do everything I can to help him. Okay?"

She looked at Ray and nodded, probably recalling how much he'd helped her last year when she found herself in a heap of trouble with the law. I only hoped this time around things would turn out as well for Lucas.

"What's this about Lucas?" Ginny asked, before we'd even settled at one of the diner's tables.

I explained everything to her, including my talk with Lucas outside the Tasty Freeze. "I know he's been stealing scrap metal. He admitted it. And I think he knows something about Clem's murder. I was hoping he'd show up here tonight." I looked to Ray. "I sort of told him that if he came clean and told us everything he knew about the murder, you'd be willing to help him."

Ray's expression tightened. "Where is he? I can only help him if he's willing to help himself."

"Please do what you can," Ginny pleaded. "I've known Lucas since he was just a baby. He's a good kid, Ray. Really he is. He's just mixed-up, that's all. You know how kids get."

Ray blew out his breath. "I'll do what I can for him. Y'all know that." He shifted in his seat. "But if he's not going to bother showing up tonight, then I'm going to head back up to the hospital and see about Daddy."

"Hold on," I said, touching his arm. "I've been thinking. Lucas may not want to talk, but there might still be something we can do to bring Clem's murderer to justice."

Ray leaned forward. "I'm listening."

"Me, too," Ginny echoed.

"You know those rumors around town about me having some sort of proof about Clem's murder?"

They nodded in unison. Ginny said, "The whole town's been talking about it. I hear it 'bout every morning. People are chewin' up that rumor faster than Sam's breakfast hash."

"Good," I said.

Ray squinted. "Good?"

I nodded. "Uh-huh. We're going to use it to draw out Clem's murderer." I leaned forward and drew in my breath. "I've got a plan."

Ray and I rehashed the entire plan the next morning over coffee and toast. Ray was on board to help in any way he could. Ginny, of course, was willing to help in any way she could, too. I figured, since everyone in town thought I had some sort of proof about Clem's murder secreted away somewhere, it should be easy to lure the real killer into believing the same thing. Or maybe he or she already did believe the rumor. Because the more I thought about it, the more I realized that maybe I was wrong about whoever had ransacked our house. I'd assumed it was Ganassi searching for the diamonds. But now, looking back on it, I realized it could have been the real killer looking for that suspected proof that everyone was talking about. Which meant, in reality, that any one of the diner regulars could be our killer. Of course, I knew Jack Snyder was a regular—just one more strike against him.

"So, everyone knows their part, right?" Ray asked.

Roscoe was under the table, sound asleep, his big hound ears flopped over his face. The temperature had dropped overnight, so I slid my bare feet under his curled-up body for warmth. "Yup. I called Cade last night, and he's on board, too." I would have preferred to have Hawk on board also, but of course, he never did show up at the diner. Guess he couldn't peel himself away from Laney.

"And I got ahold of Hawk," Ray said, making me think he could read my mind. "After you told me about your conversation with Lucas, I got a bit worried about the kid. I sent Hawk out looking for him. He caught up to the girl-friend, Tessa, who said Lucas had left town. She wouldn't say where he'd gone, but Hawk was going to keep working on it."

I sighed. "Yeah. He's sure scared of something. He's the key to all this. If only we could convince him to talk." I shook my head and thought back to the way he had practi-cally bolted from my truck earlier. *He could be anywhere by now. We may never find him.* "Anyway," I continued, "Cade will go into the diner first thing this morning and strike up a conversation with Ginny. Maybe something about how awful it is that our house was broken into yes-terday and how fortunate it is that my proof had been stored in that old storage shed in the south orchard and not in the house."

Ray nodded. "Perfect. And I've got the camera all ready to record." The old shed backed up to some treed acreage on the southern edge of our property, so we planned to use the thick forest as a hiding place while we used a video camera to record the killer in action. That way we'd have irrefutable proof of his or her identity. We'd gotten the idea from listening to Sally Jo talk about the security cameras she'd installed at the Mercantile. We didn't have time for something so elaborate, but my family did have an old video recorder that we could use to capture the evidence we needed.

"So, this plan will only work if the killer happens to come in for breakfast this morning," Ray was saying.

"True, but I'm thinking that since today's the election, he wouldn't want to miss all the scuttlebutt." I pointed to an untouched piece of toast on his plate. "Aren't you going to eat that?"

"Nope, go ahead."

I snatched it up. It was going to be a busy day; I needed to fuel up. "I know there are holes in my plan, but it's better than no plan, right? Anyway, Cade is supposed to be at the diner by eight. That's when he and Ginny will strike up a conversation about the proof being in our shed. Cade will also mention that I'm expecting a really busy day at the shop and that you're tied up at the hospital with Daddy. That way, the killer will be sure to strike while he thinks we're both away from the house." I spooned some jam onto the toast.

"How can we be sure the killer will overhear them talking about all this?" Ray asked.

"This is Ginny we're talking about, remember?"

He chuckled. "You're right. She's very loud. Once she starts talking, everyone at the diner will be tuned into the conversation."

"Exactly." I took a quick bite and swallowed. "And the killer will see his opportunity to get that evidence and we'll be ready to capture it all on film. It'll be easy as pie." I'd already asked Carla to open the shop for me, so everything was set on that front. I'd found Daddy's old lockbox, filled it with a couple rocks for weight and placed it inside the shed. All Ray and I had to do was get to the hiding spot and be ready with the camera.

"Yeah, well, maybe getting the evidence will be easy, but after that, good luck with the sheriff. Nothing is ever easy with Maudy Payne, especially asking her to believe that she was wrong all along. Plus, she's still hell-bent on arresting Daddy. She was up at the hospital again yesterday. So was Frances Simms."

"Frances Simms? Dear heavens, does that woman ever give up?" My outburst startled Roscoe. He jumped up, made a *woo-woo* sound and began sniffing around under the table.

"I was able to keep Frances away," Ray said as he began rummaging in the fridge for something. "But not Maudy. She kept harassing Mama and Daddy with all sorts of questions. I swear that woman's spent half her career trying to put away a Harper. It's like she thrives on it."

"Meanness is what it is. Meanness and stupidity."

Ray pulled out a block of cheese out of the fridge and then fetched one of Mama's paring knives. "No. Revenge is what it is. And we have our sister, Ida, to blame. I'm not sure what prompted her to beat the tar out of Maudy all those years ago, but I hope it was worth it. We've been paying for it ever since." He peeled off a sliver of cheese and popped it in his mouth. After swallowing, he added, "Daddy's surgery is all set up, by the way. It's scheduled for Friday morning, at Emory in Atlanta. I've convinced the doctors that he needs to remain at the hospital until his surgery. Once I told them about the stress he's under, they agreed. But we'd better make sure he doesn't see a copy of today's *Cays Mill Reporter*. Judging by the questions Frances was asking yesterday at the hospital, the headline will be scandalous."

I gasped. "Did she act like she knew about Mama's handkerchief? The one they found—"

"Oh yeah. She knows. And the gas can, too. Plus, she's been gathering all sorts of rumors about Mama's past with Clem. Not that she can substantiate any of them, but you know Frances. Confirming sources isn't one of her strong points. She was also sniffing around about this supposed proof that you have. Asking me if I knew why you were withholding evidence in a murder case." His shoulders drooped. "Today's issue is sure to be a doozy."

"As if we don't already have enough to worry about! We'd better give Mama a call on our way out to the site and make sure that she knows to intercept today's paper. It wouldn't do to have Daddy reading his name in the head-lines." I could hardly wait for this whole murder mess to be resolved so all Daddy had to do was focus on getting better.

"Good idea," Ray said, peeling more cheese off the block. Roscoe caught a sniff and started thumping his tail and whining. Ray tossed him a piece.

"Ray! You know how he gets when he eats people food."

"Oh, lighten up," he said, tossing another piece. Roscoe practically snatched it from midair. "See, he likes it."

I sighed and changed the subject. "So, do you really think you'll be able to help Lucas?"

"If it was his first time in trouble, then I'd say he has a good chance, but with his record and now that he's taken off somewhere . . ." Ray shrugged off the rest.

"I know you'll do everything you can," I assured him. "Thank you." And I meant that. Over the past year or so, Ray had stepped in and helped out several friends, even Hollis, our somewhat disreputable brother-in-law, without asking for anything in return. My brother was that way, though. Family and friends meant everything to him.

Which is exactly why I should have seen his next comment coming.

"And I know you'll do everything you can to help put Daddy's mind at ease about this farm. I don't want to tell you what to do, but he's got his mind set on you taking it over, keeping it in the family for the next generation. That type of stuff is important to him."

I hadn't seen that comment coming. Suddenly it felt as if I had a pallet of bricks on my shoulders. Was it just what Daddy expected . . . or did everyone feel the same way? "And what about you, Ray? Is it important to you, too?"

He leaned back against the counter and rolled his eyes toward the ceiling, choosing his words carefully. After a few seconds, he looked my way again. "I'm not sure what to say, sis. I'd be lying if I said it wasn't important to me. And not just for Daddy's sake. This is our home. But I feel guilty for saying it. Makes me feel like a hypocrite. Especially since there's no way I would ever take on this farm. It's a hard life and frankly, I don't much care for farm life. Still, it's my home. Our home." His eyes roamed around the room. "There're so many memories."

I started to tell him that I understood, but he cut me off. "Just make sure you really understand what you're getting into if you say yes. This place needs a lot of work. It runs on such a narrow profit margin that one mistake or one bad harvest could wipe us out. And I'm so busy with my practice, I wouldn't be here much. Of course, there's Ida, but . . . well, she's got the kids. Hollis would be no help." He sighed. "You'd pretty much be running it by yourself. And there's the shop to think about. Honestly, I don't know how you'd do it."

Me either. But it was all too much to think about at the

moment. One stress at a time, as Mama always said. "Wonder if the sheriff's tracked down Felix Ganassi yet," I said, jumping to a whole new topic.

Ray didn't seem to mind. "Hope so. A guy like that could be dangerous." I'd filled him in on all the details after we finished talking with Lucas the night before. We'd both agreed that everyone involved would be better off with Ganassi behind bars.

"He hasn't shown up again, and he left his stuff in his room, so I'm guessing he saw the sheriff's car or something and has hightailed it out of here. But Margie's going to keep Hawk on for a few more days. Just to keep a watch out. I think she's scared Ganassi will come back looking for the diamonds."

"Can't blame her. Of course, once the story's out that the diamonds were found, it won't take long for it to spread all over town." He let out a nervous chuckle. "Actually, this is one time I hope the gossip spreads quickly. And it'd be great if the media picked it up. The sooner Ganassi hears that the diamonds have been confiscated, the better."

"At least one thing's for sure. After news gets out about the diamonds and we turn over Clem's real killer, Frances Simms will have her fill of legitimate headlines. And they won't have anything to do with a Harper."

Chapter 19

Southern Girl Secret #043: We peach farmers
don't judge our lives by the harvest we reap, but
by the saplings we plant.

"Was it really necessary for us to get here so early?" Ray
asked, swatting at mosquitos. "I'm getting chewed alive out
here." Just to be on the safe side, we'd arrived at the site
extra early and found our position. Now we were crouched
in the thicket, waiting for our man to show up. Ray had
been whining practically the whole time.

"Suck it up, Ray. You didn't want to risk being spotted,
did you?"

"Yeah, well, it stinks to high heaven back here," Ray
continued complaining. We'd positioned ourselves in the
woods behind a row of port-a-potties we kept in the area
for the workers who came during harvest season. The
chemicals used to deodorize the toilets smelled nearly as
bad as the smell it failed to cover. "Wonder how long it'll
take for him to get out here? This is horrible."

I rolled my eyes. "Maybe if you hold your breath long

enough, you'll pass out." We were bickering like grade school kids, but honestly, who knew Ray would be so averse to a little stench and a few mosquitos? Of course, during my days as a humanitarian worker, I'd traversed some rough terrain: not only bug-infested jungles, but sharp concrete rubble that cut my skin as I frantically searched for survivors in the wake of massive earthquakes, and even barren deserts where sand-filled air whipped at my body like a thousand hot knives . . . so, a few swarming mosquitos didn't bother me too much. I glanced back over at Ray, taking note of his red-tinged face and perspiration-stained shirt, and felt a little sorry for him. Because then again, maybe my take on the whole adventure was different from Ray's, who'd been working behind a desk all these years. "It shouldn't be much longer," I said in a nicer tone this time.

As if on cue, my phone vibrated. It was a text from Cade. "Looks like everything's in place," I told Ray. "We'd better get set."

So we waited, squatting in the knee-high weeds along the back side of the port-a-potties. After a while, my nose finally grew numb to the smell, but my patience began to wear thin. Ray was driving me nuts. He'd gone from complaining to being overly enthusiastic: fidgeting with the camera, checking and double-checking the settings, and jabbering on and on about how relieved Daddy was going to be to have this burden lifted from his shoulders . . . blah, blah, blah. Then, he switched back to complaining. How long was it going to take? And maybe the killer wasn't even at the diner this morning, we should've thought the plan through more, and on and on.

Then, just as I was about to throw in the towel, we heard

the distant sound of a truck approaching. We jumped up and got into position, Ray flipping on the camera and lifting it to his eye. "I'm recording," he whispered.

I held my breath, watching as a truck bounced along the bumpy orchard terrain. But as it came closer, my heart fell. I recognized the truck. And it didn't belong to our killer. It was Deputy Travis's truck. He must have overheard the conversation at the diner and come out to get the evidence for himself. Who could blame him? He probably had visions of using the "evidence" to crack the case wide open and prove himself to the sheriff.

We both stayed hidden though, watching as Travis jogged over to the shed and disappeared inside, only to emerge a second later with the locked box under his arm. Probably intending to take it back to the sheriff's department and gloat over his successful conquest.

"Well, that was a bust," Ray said as soon as Travis drove off.

"Sure was," I agreed, watching the shiny bumper of Travis's new truck disappear among the peach rows. Something struck me as odd, but I didn't have time to think about it too much, because the snapping of a twig behind us diverted my attention. I scanned the tree line, my eyes catching a familiar flash of red darting between the trees. "Did you see that?" I hissed.

"What?"

The hairs on my arms stood up. I recognized that flash of red. As quickly as I could, I shot a text off to Cade—*Ganassi is here. Help.* Sliding the phone into my pocket, I grabbed Ray's arm and started pulling him toward the orchard, hoping we could make a run for it. But it was too late. Felix Ganassi popped out of the woods, his signature red nylon running suit gleaming in the sun and his hairy knuckles gripping the handle of a pistol. "Stop right there," he said, aiming the gun at us.

He slowly walked our way, the butt of the gun bobbing up and down with each step. His greasy black hair hung low over his forehead, partially concealing his wild eyes. The man Ginny had found so handsome and mysterious was now sweaty and unkempt. "Don't know what you're up to, lady, but I'm betting it has something to do with my diamonds."

Ray shuffled back a step. "We don't have your dia—"

"Shut up!" Ganassi yelled, then turned to me. "Been hiding out in these woods since I heard the cops were onto me." He rotated his neck, eliciting a loud popping sound. "Sleeping in some crummy shack for the last couple nights. I can't wait to get the heck out of this Podunk town and back to the city." Then he raised his chin and screwed up his face. He began sniffing the air, his eyes sliding toward the port-a-johns. "Smells like crap out here." With a wave of his gun, he ordered, "Move over there, by the house."

My fear-laden legs shuffled through the weeds as my mind reeled in despair. What had always been one of my favorite spots in the orchard now seemed creepy and all too isolated and it occurred to me that even if Cade had received my text, he wouldn't be able to get help to us in time. Ganassi was going to shoot us, then what? Dump our bodies in the woods? I shuddered with horror at the thought of someone discovering our corpses and our poor parents receiving the news of our deaths. An image of the headline flashed in my head: "Siblings' Corpses Found Planted in Peach Orchard"—it would surely kill Daddy. And Mama, too. The thought of that scared me more than my own looming death. I had to do something.

"Right here will do," Ganassi said. "Now turn around and face me."

I turned, staring down the steel barrel of his pistol. A circle of sweat had soaked through the red nylon under his raised arm, but his eyes remained menacingly cold. I could feel Ray next to me, but I didn't dare risk a glance his way, afraid of what I might see. My big brother Ray had always been my rock, my stronghold. I couldn't stand it if his expression mirrored my own fear.

"Who's this guy?" Ganassi asked. "Your boyfriend?"

Ray spoke up. "I'm her brother. And she doesn't have your dia—"

"Brother, huh? Perfect." Ganassi stepped closer, raised the gun, placing it directly on Ray's forehead.

I started to tremble, my eyes darting about desperately for something, anything. They landed briefly on a nearby pile of tree trimmings.

"Bet she loves you, doesn't she?" Ganassi was saying. "Let's just find out if she loves you more than a couple million in diamonds. Turn around and kneel down."

"What?" Ray whispered. "No."

"I said, turn around and kneel down!"

Ray turned and bent one knee at a time until he was kneeling in the dirt, arms limp at his sides.

I began pleading, "Please don't do this. We don't know where your diamonds are."

Ganassi ignored me, placing the barrel of the gun against the back of Ray's skull as he turned his evil eyes my way. "I knew you were on to me as soon as you showed up at that dump of an inn. Then when I saw someone had gone through my stuff, I figured you'd put it together and knew who I was. What'd you think? That you could simply move in on my score?"

My eyes glued to his finger as it hovered over the trigger of the gun. I had to do something. Something to convince him . . . "You're right. I've got them."

Ray started to protest. "I told you to shut up," Ganassi yelled, whipping Ray on the side of the head with the pistol.

Ray doubled over, clutching his head in pain. I wanted to go to him, but couldn't. And suddenly, an anger sparked inside me, growing and building until it overtook my fear. No way was I going to allow this man to take my brother from me. To destroy my family. "He doesn't know anything about it," I said. "I didn't tell him. I found the diamonds in the old armoire in the room I was staying in. I kept it a secret, because I wanted to keep the money for myself. You think I like living in this backwoods town? Peaches, peaches, peaches. That's all anyone ever talks about around here. I'm planning on using the money to get out of here. Go up North. Buy me a nice place up in the mountains somewhere I never have to think about peaches again."

"Oh yeah? Then where are they?"

"I'll take you to them, but only if you let my brother go free."

He shook his head. "No games, lady. Tell me now, or I'll blow his head off." He straightened his arm, once again pointing the gun directly at Ray's head.

"They're back at the house," I blurted. "In a safe in my daddy's den. If you kill him, I won't give you the combination."

He narrowed his eyes at me, probably considering his options. Finally, he indicated toward the orchard. "Get him up and let's go. But you'd better not be lying to me, or I'll shoot him on the spot."

I bent down to help Ray, but as I lifted him, he lost his balance and stumbled forward, falling to the ground again. "Ray!" I knelt down and lifted his face to mine. His eyes were dazed, and blood trickled from a gash on his temple. "Ray," I whispered. "Get up. You've got to get up." He moaned, his eyes rolling back before his body went limp. He was out cold.

"Leave him!" Ganassi barked.

"He's injured. He needs help."

Ganassi tilted his head back and let out an evil laugh. "Help?" He laughed some more, then turned eerily serious. "I'll be glad to help him."

To my horror, he steeled his stance and aimed the gun at Ray's head. I moved in front of my brother, holding out my hands. Ganassi swung out his free arm to push me aside, and just then, the sound of an approaching siren cut through the air. Ganassi's head snapped upward, and in that split second, I lunged for the nearby scrap pile and snatched up a large branch.

In one fluid movement, I jumped forward and swung with all my might, connecting to Ganassi's head with a loud *thunk*. He dropped the gun and screamed out in pain. Gritting my teeth, I raised the branch high in the air and whacked him again. This time he went all the way down.

I dropped the branch and scurried back to Ray just as the sheriff's cruiser pulled into the site. Right behind her came Cade's truck.

Maudy was the first out of her vehicle. She rushed over, immediately secured the gun, and then started placing a call for medical transports.

Cade rushed over and began tending to Ray. "Hey, buddy," he said, lightly slapping his cheeks. "Can you hear me, Ray?" To my relief, a low moan escaped from the back of Ray's throat as he began to move his body. "He'll be fine," Cade said. "But he needs to be seen right away. What happened to him?"

"Ganassi hit him with the back of the gun."

"And who hit Ganassi?" he asked.

I looked over at Ganassi's limp body and swallowed hard. He looked dead. I rolled my hands over and stared at my palms. Did I do that? Did I kill him?

Cade leaned over and placed two fingers alongside Ganassi's neck. "His pulse is weak, but he's still alive."

I breathed a little easier. *Not that I wouldn't have killed him. I'm just glad I didn't.*

The sound of Maudy's voice distracted us. "Darn deputy's been good for nothin' lately." She crammed her phone into her pocket and came over to join us. "Ambulances are on their way," she said. "Now how 'bout someone tells me what happened here?" When we didn't respond right away, she folded her arms and rocked back on her heels. "Well? I'm waitin'!"

Cade and I exchanged a look. Explaining all this to Maudy wasn't going to be easy.

Boy, was I ever right. "Of all the stupid things!" Maudy yelled, slapping her hand down on her desk. Papers went flying, but she made no move to pick them up. Then she pushed away from her desk and started pacing the floor. "I should throw you both in a cell right now. Interfering with my case like this. Of all the idiotic things. Someone could have gotten killed because of you two."

Cade and I solemnly nodded. She was right. We were ever so lucky that Ray wasn't more seriously hurt. As it turned out, both Ganassi and Ray had been transported to County Hospital—Ray checked over and admitted for a concussion and Ganassi admitted for much more serious injuries, for which I still had no regrets. Cade and I were at the sheriff's trying to explain ourselves.

"It's just that it seemed like such a good idea at the time," I said. "The rumor that we had proof of Clem's murder had already spread all over town, so it seemed logical that we could use it to draw out the killer."

"Yeah. Frances Simms even managed to work it into today's paper," Cade added, reaching across the sheriff's desk and picking up a folded copy of the *Cays Mill Reporter.* "It's all right here," he said, holding it up for us to see and pointing to the front page headline: "Local Storekeeper Stashes Evidence of Father's Innocence." Which was just the top headline. Right below it was the real kicker. "Past Love Affairs Motive for Murder?"

My jaw clenched with rage. *The nerve of that woman!*

The sheriff shifted in her chair. "Is that so? I haven't had a chance to read that yet. It's been a little busy 'round here."

Cade nodded and tossed the paper aside. I resisted the urge to snatch it up and see for myself what lies Frances had printed this time. Instead, I refocused on the conversation at hand. "Only, our plan didn't work," I continued telling the sheriff. "It was your deputy that showed up instead of the killer. He probably overheard Cade's conversation with Ginny at the diner this morning and hoped to get the evidence for himself."

Maudy frowned. "Which just goes to prove that you two aren't the only ones with mush for brains. Travis knows better. He should have come to me if he thought there was evidence hidden out at your place. Not gone traipsin' off by himself to play hero."

"That's true," I said, thinking that Travis probably couldn't help himself. Being fairly new to the department, he probably wanted to prove himself to the sheriff. After all, pleasing someone like Maudy would be no easy feat, even if she did seem to favor the boy. Then, something else came to mind. Something that didn't quite add up: Travis had been out at the farm, taking that lockbox full of false evidence, and left just minutes before Ganassi showed up. Then, I sent my emergency text to Cade. He'd told me that he put in a call to the sheriff the second he received it. So Travis should have still been nearby. He could have simply doubled back and come to our aid immediately. He should have been the first on the scene.

"Why didn't Travis respond to our emergency call first?" I asked. "He'd only left the farm minutes before Ganassi showed up. He would have been the closest responder."

The sheriff frowned. "Couldn't reach him, that's why. I swear, that boy's been good for nothin' lately. Half the time he's got his head in the clouds." She shook her head. "I reckon it's a girl who's got him so distracted."

Next to me, Cade chuckled. "That would explain that new truck he bought. The thing must have cost as much as a small house." While Cade and Maudy went on about the truck's leather upholstery, supercharged hemi engine and chrome wheels, the wheels in my own head started turning. That new truck was expensive. Much too expensive for a deputy's salary. Unless he had another source of income. Like maybe from scrap metal? That would explain why Lucas was so afraid to come clean. I remembered Carla saying that he and some of the other kids had been caught with alcohol a while back, but no charges were pressed. That didn't seem like the sheriff, but maybe the sheriff didn't know anything about it. Maybe it was Deputy Travis who broke up the party that night. And Lucas, with a prior record and all, well, he'd be easy to manipulate.

There were other things, too, but before I could put it all together, the front door opened and Deputy Travis sauntered inside, whistling a tune as he juggled a red-and-white boat of vinegar fries—probably from one of the food trucks parked outside the courthouse—and hung his Stetson on a metal tree rack by the front door. Upon seeing us, he stopped whistling, his brows shooting upward. "What's wrong? Y'all look like your dog's died."

I shifted uncomfortably, thinking of Roscoe. Now that I sort of had a dog in my life, I hated that expression.

"Where ya been, Travis?" Maudy asked. "We had a call a little while ago."

Travis seemed surprised. "A call?" He glanced down at the two-way radio clipped to his belt. "Sorry, Sheriff. Must not have heard it come in. I was patrollin' the parade like you asked. Darn noisy with those bands and all. Sorry about that. Just bad timing, I guess."

Timing? That's why my daddy was in so much trouble in the first place. Timing. There was only a short amount of time between when Daddy left Clem's farm and the barn fire was spotted. Travis had admitted he was the one who called in that fire. Something about that gnawed at my mind, but what was it?

Across the room, Travis was going on about the day's events: the floats, the high school band, the Jaycees' tent, and on and on. He finally paused and lifted another fry from the container. He pointed it our way. "And good news. The polls are 'bout closed and it looks like Jack Snyder's goin' to be our next mayor."

Maudy sighed and shook her head.

Travis squinted with confusion. "You don't seem too happy 'bout it. Thought you'd be thrilled, considerin' y'all are kin."

"That's because I'm not wonderin' about the election. I'm wonderin' what my deputy was doing hiding evidence from me."

Travis turned bright red. "Hiding evidence? I don't know what you're talkin' 'bout, boss." His eyes slid toward us as he spoke.

Cade looked between Travis and the Sheriff, his brow furrowed with confusion. "But we've got you on tape," he said, holding up the camera that Ray had been carrying earlier that morning. "Taking the lockbox from our shed."

Travis's jaw went slack. "Oh, that. I, uh . . . well, I overheard people talkin' and I thought I'd go out and see for myself." He looked at the sheriff. "I didn't want to bother you with it until I knew it was legit. Turns out it didn't amount to nothin'. Just a couple rocks in an old lockbox, that's all." He narrowed his eyes at me. "What type of game are you playin' anyway, Nola? Putting me on a wild-goose chase like that?"

"Sorry, Travis. We were just trying to draw out Clem's killer," Cade started to explain.

I held up my hand. "Wait a minute." I turned to the sheriff. "There might be a few other things Travis has been keeping from you."

The sheriff tipped back in her chair and folded her arms. "Oh yeah. Like what?"

"Earlier when I mentioned that a bunch of folding chairs had gone missing from the church, you didn't seem to know what I was talking about."

She scrunched her brow. "Folding chairs? What the heck—"

"And there's been other stuff," I continued. "The downspouts from the library? Scrap piping missing from Jack Snyder's place? The air-conditioning units?"

"Shut up, Nola," Travis said. Cade sat straighter in his chair.

Maudy glanced at Travis and held up her hand. Looking back at me, she asked, "I knew about some of it. Just what are you saying, exactly?"

"Have you been looking into any of those thefts personally?" I asked her.

"No, I put Travis on it."

"Did he tell you about the evidence we found in the back of Lucas Graham's truck? A piece off of an air-conditioning unit? I reported it to Travis."

The sheriff shook her head. "In Lucas Graham's truck?" She stared with disbelief at Travis. "The kid has a record, doesn't he? Why didn't you mention this to me?"

"I talked to Lucas," I told her. "He pretty much admitted to being involved in the scrap metal thefts, but he wasn't working alone. He's afraid of something . . . or someone," I said, looking directly at Travis.

Cade leaned in and asked, "What exactly are you saying, Nola?"

I looked his way. *Saying.* It was something someone said . . . Then it came to me. My eyes grew wide as I then glanced across the room. "I'm saying that we know Travis had called in that fire. And he would have had to have been close by to spot it so quickly. He'd said to me that he was out that way responding to a call from Candace. But when I saw her at the funeral the other day, Candace had told me that she was away at a doctor's appointment the day of the murder. I'd dismissed it as some sort of mix-up. But now . . . I don't think our plan failed. I think we *did* draw out Clem's killer."

The sheriff slapped her hand on the table. "That's a lie! No deputy of mine would do such a thing." She stood and moved toward Travis. "Tell 'em, boy. Tell them that they've got it all wrong."

But instead of telling us we were wrong, Travis moved his hand toward his gun belt. Maudy reacted quickly, stepping back and drawing her own gun. "Don't move, Travis." She stood her ground, the gun bobbing slightly in her hand as she tried to make sense of it all. "What were you thinking? Stealin' from our neighbors? The folks we've sworn to protect? Why?"

Travis's expression turned dark and bitter. "Why do you think? This job doesn't pay crap. How do you expect me to make a livin' with what I get paid? Besides, plenty of folks around here have more than enough to spare. Think of everything we do for them. They owe us."

Maudy stared in disbelief, her voice hard. "Clem, too?"

Travis grew still. Tiny beads of sweat broke out on his hairline and upper lip.

"Answer me, Travis. Did you kill Clem Rogers?"

Travis's eyes darted our way. He swallowed hard. "I . . .

I didn't mean for that to happen. I swear. You've got to believe me, boss—"

"Don't ever call me 'boss' again," Maudy bit out. The vehemence in her voice scared me. It must have scared Travis, too, because he flinched and turned even redder. Maudy reached toward him. "Give me your gun belt, Travis."

I watched the scene unfold before me, holding my breath: How would Travis react?

"Come on, Travis," Maudy repeated. "Give me your gun."

Travis's right hand trembled as he reached across his body, his fingers connecting with the buckle on his belt. He started to unfasten it. His eyes, wide with fear and moist with regret, looked straight at Maudy. "I'm sorry," he whispered, jerking his hand back and drawing his gun.

"No!" Maudy screamed, raising her own gun. Shots filled the air. I ducked and covered my ears as Cade covered me with his own body, holding me so tightly I thought my bones would break. When we finally unraveled and looked up, Travis was on the ground, blood pooling around his body.

The room felt strangely still for a few seconds, until an animal-like moan sounded from Maudy. "What have I done? Oh, Lawd, what have I done?" Maudy fell to her knees, her gun still in one hand, the other reaching out, trembling, to touch the body of the young deputy.

I immediately went to her, crouched down beside her, uncertain what to do. "You did what you had to do," I said. "He drew on you. You had no choice."

I saw her shoulders shudder. "But I knew him. Should have known he wouldn't let me take him in . . . I should've been able to stop this. And . . . and I shot him," she whispered. Her broad shoulders seemed to shrivel. "How am I going to tell his family?" She shuddered once more, then stiffened, her moist eyes turning dark and flat as she looked at me in a silent plea for answers. I knew that she wanted me to say something that would make sense of all this. Something to take away her pain. But I was at a loss for words.

For a second or two, the room remained eerily still, until the sound of Cade's voice cut through the silence. "I'm at the sheriff's office in Cays Mill," he told the 911 operator. "There's been a shooting. Deputy Travis Hines is dead."

Later that evening, I went to the hospital to fill my parents in on the latest news. Ray was still there, too. He'd suffered a mild concussion, but the doctor agreed to release him to my care as long as I watched him closely for the next twenty-four hours. Which meant that I was going to miss going to the inauguration dance with Cade. Not that it really mattered. After everything that'd happened, neither of us was in the dancing mood.

"I still can't believe that young man is no longer with us," Mama was saying about Deputy Travis. "So very sad, really. How's Maudy taking it? This can't be easy on her."

"She's not taking it well at all," I said. I felt sorry for Maudy. I truly did. Learning the truth about Travis was devastating to her. Especially since she'd hired him straight out of the academy, trained him and taken him under her wing. At times, I'd thought she'd even felt somewhat motherly toward Travis.

"I never would have thought Travis was capable of thievin', let alone murder," Daddy said. "And you said he was stealin' from about everyone in town?"

Ray shook his head. "Even worse, he was blackmailing a young man into doing his dirty work for him."

Soon after the shooting, Hawk had called Ray. He'd tracked down Lucas, who was hiding out at his aunt's house in Macon. Ray had then talked to him from the hospital and gotten the whole story. And was it ever a humdinger: A while back, Travis had busted a bunch of kids, including Lucas, up at Hill Lake for underage drinking. He'd let the other kids slide, but singled out Lucas, who was already on probation for some minor offences. Then, Travis blackmailed Lucas into stealing scrap metal around town.

"At first it was just small stuff," I told my parents. "A few pieces here and there. Then when no one seemed to catch on to his scheme, Travis convinced Lucas to take bigger, more valuable items. Like the air-conditioning units. And copper wiring from Cade's construction site. And more recently, several dozen folding chairs from the Baptist church." I drew in my breath. "There were other things, too. And Travis was clever. He handled most of the complaints himself, making people think he'd written up a report and was investigating their thefts, when really he was just hiding the facts from the sheriff. Considering how few people like to chat with Maudy, it's no surprise that they never later asked her directly about it. And the things she did know about, like the high school bleachers, she just wrote off as a bunch of kids pulling a prank."

Ray nodded. "Lucas said he cashed in the stuff over at the recycler in Perry. The guy paid Travis directly. Lucas never handled any of the money."

Daddy rubbed at his chin. "So Clem found out about it and that's why Travis killed him?"

I nodded. "For the past two years, Lucas has been

working for Clem. He even managed the farm's crew last year. And as you know, he's also dating Clem's niece, Tessa." Daddy nodded, and I continued, "Well, according to Lucas, Clem caught him with a bunch of scrap metal in the back of his truck. He figured out what Lucas was doing and fired him. He also refused to let him see his niece."

"But Tessa wasn't going to have any of that," Ray added. "She knew all about what was going on with Lucas, so she told her uncle the whole story, including how Travis was blackmailing Lucas into doing the stealing for him."

"That's right," I agreed. "But Lucas panicked when he found out that Tessa had told her uncle about Travis. He figured he'd end up the scapegoat and go to jail for sure. And he didn't know who to turn to. He couldn't go to the sheriff. She'd never believe him. Who would? He was a kid who'd already been in trouble with the law on several occasions. Whereas Travis was well-thought-of not only in the community but by the sheriff, too. Lucas figured he didn't stand a chance if he came clean. So, instead, he warned Travis that Clem knew about the scrap metal thefts. He thought maybe Travis would stop what he was doing, leave town, or something. We'll never know what Travis's idea was in going out to see Clem that day. I'd like to think it was to strike some bargain or other, but things got out of hand." I recalled some of Travis's last words, how he'd sworn he hadn't meant for Clem to die. We'd never really know now.

"Either way, he killed Clem," Daddy said with a shake of his head. Then he shifted his weight and moaned a little.

I jumped up and plumped his pillow. "Are you uncomfortable, Daddy? Is there something I can get you?"

"No, no, darlin'. I'm fine. Just sick of this blasted hospital room. Can't wait to get back to my own bed."

I patted his shoulder. "Soon, Daddy. Real soon."

"Yeah, Pops. And now that the real killer's been found, you can rest easier."

Daddy's eyes filled with pride. "I sure can, Bud. Thanks to you two."

"Actually," Ray said, "it was mostly Nola. She was determined to find Clem's real killer. Even stayed a couple nights at Sunny Side Up so she could observe John Whitaker, or rather Felix Ganassi."

"I really thought Ganassi was Clem's killer," I admitted. And I still wished it were him. How much easier that would be than finding out that Travis, who we all knew and trusted, was guilty of such a heinous crime. "It really all boiled down to the timing of the crime. Since it was such a narrow opening between the time Daddy left the farm and the call came in for the barn fire, I knew whoever killed Clem had to have been in the general area. That really only left a few people who had both motive and opportunity: Jack Snyder, who lives just down the road and was desperate for a mayoral win; Whitaker/Ganassi, who was giving Joe Puckett a ride out that way near the time of the murder; and Lucas and Margie, whose whereabouts I never could quite pin down. And they both had motive. I never even considered Travis until I was at the funeral and Candace mentioned being out of town the day of the murder. Then I remembered that Travis had told me earlier in the week that he was the one who spotted the fire and called it in. He said he was in the area, answering a call from Candace. Which, at the time, made sense to me,

because . . . well, you all know how Candace can be."
Everyone nodded. "Then when I realized Candace wasn't
even in town, well, it added doubt about Travis and finally
it all started to come together."

Mama spoke up, "But what about my handkerchief?"
She stole a glance at Daddy, her cheeks turning crimson.
"The one they found in Clem's bedsheets."

"That threw me for a loop," I admitted. "I knew it was
planted. That and the gas can. The gas can wasn't as difficult to explain. Our barn is never locked, so anyone could
have snuck in and took it. I even recall Roscoe waking me
up in the middle of the night last week. He was barking at
something outside. I didn't think too much of it at the time,
but now I'm guessing that it was Travis out in our barn,
taking the gas can."

"That makes sense," Daddy said. "But what about that
handkerchief?"

"That was tricky," I answered. "At first, I thought whoever planted it must have taken it from our house or out of
your purse. Now I'm wondering if it wasn't simpler than
that. Do you remember that day at the sheriff's office, when
Daddy was being questioned about Clem's death? Ray
came over from Perry and we were all there? Daddy was
so stressed, and, well, it was hot in the sheriff's office that
day. I remember you took out your handkerchief and gave
it to Daddy so he could wipe his brow."

"That's right!" Mama exclaimed. "Things got so heated,
I don't think I remembered to get it back from him."

I bobbed my head in agreement. "I don't know for sure,
but I think that's how Travis got it. We'll never really know
now that he's . . ." I swallowed away the last of the sentence.
"Anyway, I wish it would have been Ganassi, not Travis."

Mama reached over and touched my shoulder. "At least you got the best of that fellow Ganassi. I shudder to think what might have happened if you hadn't hit him with that branch." She glanced Ray's way, her mouth drooping a bit at the corners. "Why, I'd cry forever if anything ever happened to one of you children." Then she looked back at me, her eyes blazing. "Excuse my language, but I hope you hit that jackass hard."

"Oh, she did, Mama," Ray said with a chuckle. "Heard one of the nurses say that she about knocked him into next week."

"That's my girl," Mama said, with an upward tilt of her chin.

My heart soared with pride, then sank a little. "He's going to make it, isn't he?" I asked Ray.

"Yeah, sis. Don't worry. He's going to make it."

Daddy cleared his throat to say something just as the room door swung open. Ida rushed in, bringing along a cloud of stress with her. "I just knew y'all were probably here already. I tried to get here sooner, but Junior was givin' me fits. He's in that clingy stage, you know? Won't let me out of his sight for a second. It's just drivin' me crazy. And did y'all hear? Jack Snyder's our new mayor. 'Course we all figured he'd win, didn't we?" She crossed over, oblivious to the rest of us, and inserted herself between Daddy and me. "How's my patient today?" she cooed, leaning in and kissing Daddy on the cheek. "Can I get you anything? Some water? How about some—" She stopped midsentence and scrutinized Ray's head. "Mercy. What's happened to you? The whole side of your face is black and blue."

Ray started to explain, but Daddy held up his hand. "There's going to be plenty of time to catch your sister up on all the recent happenings. But first, now that I've got all three of you here, there's something I want to discuss with y'all."

I sucked in my breath. I knew what was coming and I wasn't prepared to give an answer. "Couldn't this wait, Daddy?"

He shook his head. "No, darlin'. I'm headin' up to Atlanta tomorrow. They'll be operatin' on me before the end of the week. And I just want to have all my affairs in order, just in case."

Ida flinched. "Don't be talking like that, Daddy. Everything's gonna be fine. Just fine."

"We don't know that for sure," Daddy replied. Mama straightened her shoulders, reached out and covered his rough, work-worn hand with her own smooth, graceful fingers. Such a simple gesture, yet so full of strength.

Daddy continued, "And just in case I don't come through, I need to know that your mama's going to be taken care of properly. You see, we haven't been able to save much over the years, with peach farmin' bein' the way it is. But the house is paid for and the equipment and all."

I heard a sniffle and looked over to see that Ray had moved closer to Ida. He had his arm around her shoulders, trying to comfort her. Although we'd never spoken of it, both Ray and I understood that if something were to happen to either of our parents, Ida would be devastated. We all would. But Ida even more so.

Ray spoke up. "You know we'd make sure Mama was always taken care of, don't ya, Pops? You don't need to even worry about that."

Daddy smiled. "Yes, I know that, Ray. Your mama and I have been blessed with you kids. Truly blessed."

I looked over at my siblings and nodded. Daddy was right. We Harpers were a unique bunch—that's for sure. There was Ida, high-strung, and always the overachiever— the one we went to when something needed to get done. She adored Daddy, worshipped him even, and was so very close to Mama. After all, they had so much in common. Their love of cooking and homemaking, taking care of the family, even shopping. Boy could they ever shop! Ida was also very nurturing. She was a good mama to her own children. And when the time came, I had no doubt she'd be the one who'd lovingly nurse our parents in their old age. Ray, on the other hand, was extremely driven, deter- mined to make a name for himself. While he doted on Mama, he was also often at odds with Daddy when it came to the farm and other matters of business. Yet, I had the feel- ing that everything he did, all the decisions he'd made in his own career, were to make our father proud. And he had. I only hoped he realized it.

Me? Well, I hadn't yet figured out my role in the family. I'd always felt a bit like the odd one out. Everything I'd chosen to do was a bit unconventional, from my youthful, and often foolish, shenanigans to my years as a devoted aid worker. Now, it seemed I needed to make another choice. One that would definitely alter the rest of my life.

Daddy's next words drew me back to the conversation. "And that's why your mother and I have decided to sell the farm. Ray has his practice; Ida, you've got my beautiful grandchildren to take care of; and, well, it's not fair of us to ask Nola to take on the farm. She has the shop, her own life . . ."

Sell the farm? I'd known all along that selling the farm was the only other option, but now that I heard the words

spoken out loud, a shiver of horror spiraled up my back.
Over four generations of Harpers had worked the very land
we still lived on today. It was home—always had been—no
matter where I'd lived. I'd slept in tents on warm desert
nights and laughed with other volunteers in front of fires
in mountainous huts. I'd seen sprawling fields of rice pad-
dies and helped villagers learn new techniques to grow
squash and raise their goats. But the warm, loamy soil and
the rolling hills of peach trees, why, these were at the core
of my own family's lives. At my core. I couldn't let it go.

"It's just too much for one person," Daddy was saying.
I glanced around the room. Everyone was nodding in
agreement, seemingly resigned to the idea of letting our
family farm go to strangers.

"And how's that?" I heard myself say. "Haven't you been
running it by yourself all these years?"

Daddy looked confused. "No. Not really. Your mother's
always helped. And you kids when you were still at home."

"Mama did, sure, but she tended to us kids, never worked
the orchards all that much, right?"

Mama gave me an odd look as she nodded.

"And you hire in crews during harvest, right? Well, I
could do the same."

"But you have the shop," Mama said.

"I know. I love the shop and don't want to give it up. But
without the constant supply of peaches from the farm, I'd
have to find other suppliers. The additional costs would
probably put me out of business." I felt the words tumbling
out as the ideas flashed, clear and bright, as if I'd known
this all along, just hadn't seen it until this moment. "Besides,
I've been considering the idea of giving Carla a more active
role at Peachy Keen. She's a good worker and seems to be

interested in more responsibility. Income has been good, so there's plenty enough to support her as a full-time employee. I might also need to hire an overseer for the farm. All this will cut into our profits, but if I hire the right people, maybe we'll also increase our bottom line."

As I spoke I felt the tingle of excitement about the challenges. It was no different than tackling any of the third world projects I'd seen to completion over the years: see the problem, consider the potentials and discover the solutions. And this was the best project ever: saving our family farm. There were so many things I wanted to do both at the farm and at my shop. I'd recently read an article about popular heirloom peaches that were selling for top market price to fancy grocers and to top chefs for their exclusive restaurants in the city. I'd been meaning to approach Daddy about planting fifty or so of that variety, just to see if we could fill that specialty niche. And the shop? Well, the possibilities were endless. I thought perhaps Carla had hit on something special when she suggested selling peach-themed chocolates and candies. Something like that might really catch on around these parts and be a real boon to our online business once we could figure out a way to package and ship them.

Ida spoke up. "I could help with the farm's bookkeeping. And finding buyers and outlets for our peaches. I think I'd be good at it. And it's something I could do while the girls are in school." Her face brightened a little. "During the summer months, when the kids are home, I could possibly hire a young girl to come in and help a couple mornings a week." She looked a bit sheepish as she added, "I'd actually welcome something away from the kids for just a few hours a week."

"And I'll do whatever I can, too," Ray added. "It may not be much, though, since I'm busy with my practice. But at least you'll always have legal advice." He chuckled. "And this family sure seems to need it."

"There. You see," I told Daddy. "We're all on board with the idea. I'd like to give it a try anyway." I looked from him to Mama and shook my head. "Truth is, I can't bear the idea of the farm not being in the family anymore."

Daddy looked toward Mama, squeezed her hand and smiled. I couldn't be sure, but I thought I saw him blink away a tear or two. Mama, in turn, let out a long sigh and leaned forward, placing her head lovingly on his shoulder. And just like that, I knew I'd made the right decision. Because I'd seen this type of exchange between my parents many times over the years. Sometimes it was Daddy who was the strong one. Often, Mama. But the one steady thing was their unending support of one another. It was the same with all us Harpers. Through the many happy times and the sometimes trying, desperate times, the one thing that always held true was our love and support of one another.

Chapter 20

Southern Girl Secret #100: There's really not anything better in life than a mama who's always there for you.

"How's your daddy doin'?" Ginny asked. Ginny, Carla and I were in the diner's kitchen whipping up more stock for Peachy Keen. A couple weeks had passed since Travis's death, and things around Cays Mill had finally slipped back into a somewhat normal cadence.

"Daddy's doing just fine," I said. "He just had a follow-up appointment this morning. Those stents they put in must be doing the trick. Old Doc Harris told Daddy that his ticker sounded like the heart of a twenty-year-old."

"Oh boy," Ginny said. "Your mama better watch out. He'll be chasing her 'round the house."

We laughed. "Actually, believe it or not, Mama and Daddy are talking about spending the winters down in Florida. One of Mama's sisters is down there."

Ginny raised a brow. "Oh yeah? How do you feel about that?"

I shrugged. "A little sad. But I know it would the best thing for Daddy. I don't think he'll be able to fully rest at the farm. Already, he's talking about working on projects around the place. Not much, he says, just a little bit of this and that. But you know how he is. He can't just do something halfway. It has to be all or nothing."

Ginny snickered. "Hmm. Kind of like someone else we know, huh?" She looked at Carla, who grinned as well. I shot them a look, which Ginny waved off with another laugh. "Hey, come over and taste this."

I did a quick double check of my pressure cooker before crossing over to the stove, where she held up a spoonful of gooey chocolate from Carla's latest batch. I took a taste, rolling my eyes with delight. "Oh, Carla! This is simply your best batch yet!" For the past week, she'd been experimenting with adding peach extract and finely chopped local pecans to her chocolate. Today, she'd finally hit on just the right combination. The slight, fruity undercurrent of sweet peach, combined with the slight crunch of locally grown pecans, paired perfectly with the smooth, rich chocolate.

Her grin stretched from ear to ear. "Really? You think it's good?"

Ginny snatched up her own spoon and swirled it around the pan. She then held the spoon over her open palm and gently blew before taking a taste. Her face lit up. "Lawdy, that's good!" She tossed the spoon in the sink and shook her head. "I swear, this new candy venture of yours is going to add ten pounds to my hips." She winked my way. "You sure you want this girl working full-time for you, Nola? She's a better cook than you, any day. And if you're not careful, she might just take over the whole darn business."

I laughed. "You're right, Gin. But I'll take the risk." I patted Carla on the back. "I couldn't do it without her." My praise brought a blush to Carla's cheeks, but it was the truth. During the past two weeks, ever since Daddy's surgery and recovery and my transition to taking over the farm, Carla had been a godsend. Not only had she stepped up her hours at Peachy Keen, but she'd taken over a big part of my cooking, as well as learning how to deal with consigners and out-of-town buyers. She'd also kept up the online orders, as well as doing some of the grocery shopping for me.

Speaking of grocery shopping, word was that Lucas had put in his two-week notice at the Pack & Carry. Ray, bless his heart, was able to gently convince our grief-stricken sheriff not to pursue any charges against the kid. Lucas had taken his good fortune as an opportunity to start over fresh. He'd sworn off his wild ways and even worked up the nerve to pop the big question. He and Tessa planned to marry right after the holidays and make a go of full-time peach farming. I wished them all the luck in the world.

As for Maudy . . . well, she still hadn't recovered from the shock of losing Travis. She'd barely talked to anyone since the tragedy, bottling up her grief inside her tough exterior, not letting anyone console her. And I'm not sure who she blamed more for the travesty, herself or me. One thing for sure, she truly hated me now.

Jack Snyder was officially mayor now. I'd really had him pegged as Clem's killer: his ultra-competitiveness, that burn on his arm—which turned out to be just what he'd claimed, from burning branch trimmings—to his sneaky ways of using Clem's murder as a way to gain votes. All in all, not quite the character I'd want in a town leader.

Nonetheless, he'd won the vote by a landslide. Unfortunately, the success of his campaign had gone straight to his head. He was ruling the town like a dictator, treating everyone like an underling and enacting ordinances to benefit his circle of farming cronies. He'd already earned a nickname, Jack the Tyrant, from many of the local town folk. Hmm? Maybe an outsider like Margie Price might not have been such a bad choice for mayor, after all.

I hadn't seen much of Margie Price lately. My guess was she was still licking her wounds from her mayoral loss. Margie wasn't the type of woman who took loss easily. Which made me wonder if what'd happened with Felix Ganassi hadn't stirred up too many old memories of a different type of loss—lost love. Poor Margie. I made a mental note to stop by and pay her a visit soon.

Suddenly, the back door opened, drawing me from my thoughts. I looked up to see Hattie breeze in wearing an ankle-length coat and carrying a stack of those dreaded wedding magazines under her arm. "Cold as anything out there," she said. "Heard there's a threat of an overnight frost."

"Well, shoot!" Ginny exclaimed. "That'll probably be it for my gardenias, then. They've been just beautiful this year, too. 'Course, I could put a sheet over them, I suppose." Ginny continued blathering about gardening, but the whole time she talked, she warily eyed Hattie's bridal magazines. Finally she took a deep breath and timidly asked, "You're not still lookin' for a weddin' dress, are you?"

Her question seemed to suck the air right out of the kitchen. Carla even stopped stirring, turning from the stove with a panicked look on her face. None of us dared say another word. We'd learned our lessons. Wedding dresses were a sore topic with Hattie. Heck, even the tiniest mention of anything to do with weddings was enough to put our dear friend over the edge these days. A huge part of me just wished the crazy thing was over already. I'd do about anything to have the old, sensible Hattie back.

"No, I'm not looking for a wedding dresses anymore," Hattie stated, throwing down the magazines and reaching up to unbutton her coat. With a flare, she ripped it open, revealing a gorgeous tea-length wedding gown. "Because I've already found one!"

I squealed with delight. "Oh, Hattie! It's perfect. Absolutely perfect." And it was. The simple lines of the off-the-shoulder sheath hugged her curves perfectly, and its percale white lace created a stunning contrast to Hattie's dark hair.

"Of course it is," Hattie said. "It was my mama's dress. I don't know why I didn't think of it before. It just seems so right that I should wear it, don't y'all think?" A glisten of moisture in her smiling eyes told me all I needed to know—she'd finally found a special way to bring her mother to the wedding.

We agreed with a chorus of enthusiastic *yes*es.

"And, I've got another surprise for you," Hattie continued. "Pete and I are getting married today!"

"Today?" we echoed.

Hattie's head bobbed up and down. "Yes. Right now, actually." She slipped her coat back over her shoulders. "At the church. And y'all are invited."

"A wedding? Right now?" Ginny's hands flew to her cheeks. "I can't go looking like this."

"Yes, you can," Hattie said. "Besides, I wouldn't want you any other way. Pete says he's taken care of everything: the preacher, the flowers and the music, too. And don't

worry. He's already called Sam," she told Ginny, then
looked my way. "Cade's there, too, with our daddy. Pete
called while I was dressing and said they're ready and all
waiting for us." Her blue gray eyes twinkled. "Now, who's
coming to my wedding?"

We must've looked like quite the crew as we walked into
the church with her a few minutes later—Carla and me in
our work-stained T-shirts and Ginny still in her waitress
uniform—but any thoughts about our own appearances
melted away the second we entered the sanctuary.

   I'd assumed that they would opt to have the ceremony
in the small inner sanctuary, considering our party of not
even a dozen would be dwarfed in the main church sanctuary. But, oh no, the church's main area came alive as we
stepped through the door. There were only the handful of
us, true, but Pete and whoever had helped him had lined
both side aisles with candelabra, giving a warm, flickering
glow to the natural cedar beams and wooden pews. Even
the stained glass windows, which normally required day-
light to bring them life, glowed with the smiling faces of
angels in the candlelight. And the air! The perfume of
hundreds of flowers filled our nostrils with delight. We
gasped at the beauty of it all.

   Hattie stopped and raised her hand to her heart. "Daisies," she whispered with disbelief. "Mama's favorites."
Daisies indeed. They were everywhere: on the altar, gathered and tied with bows of tulle on the end of every pew—
there were even daisy petals scattered along the edges of
the velvet red aisle runner.

   Cade and Sam were by the door waiting for us, along

with Hattie's father, whose milky blue eyes were wide with astonishment. "What's going on?" he asked. "Did someone die?"

Cade gently gripped his arm. "No, Daddy. Hattie's getting married. You're going to walk her down the aisle. Just like we've been practicing. Remember?" He nodded to Hattie. "It'll be okay, sis. Don't worry."

Hattie leaned forward and gave her father a peck on the cheek. "Of course it will. I'm so glad you're here, Daddy." She looked at Ginny and me. "I know this isn't the wedding y'all imagined for me, but I thought about what you'd said, Nola. About how the wedding is just the opening act to a lifetime of marriage. Well, I realized you were right. All that other stuff, the dresses, the fancy reception . . . none of that really matters. All that's really important is that the people we love are here with us today." She swiped at her cheek and held out her arms for an embrace. "I just don't know what I would do without you two. Y'all are just like family to me."

Ginny and I embraced our friend, clinging to one another and giggling like schoolgirls. After a minute, we were interrupted by Pete, who'd joined us from the front of the church. "Excuse me, ladies," he said. He looked as handsome as ever in a black suit and tie, his dark eyes gleaming mischievously. "Can I cut in?" He held out a simple bouquet of daisies. "These are for you, my beautiful bride."

Hattie lifted the bouquet to her face and inhaled the sweetness of the flowers. "I can't believe you decorated with daisies."

I knew my friend was delighted, but Pete must have misunderstood. His face fell. "I'm so sorry, *amorcita*," he said, running a hand through his wavy black hair. "I ordered roses, but when the shipment came, I took one look at them and then I remembered what you said once, about your *mamacita*, about daisies. And I thought . . ." The more excited he got, the heavier his accent became. "Can you ever forgive me, *mi querida*?"

"Forgive you?" Hattie's eyes misted over. "Pete, this is the best gift you've ever given me."

Ginny looked confused. "Gift?"

Hattie looked at her friend. "Daisies were Mama's favorite flowers." She turned misty eyes at her soon-to-be-husband. "And he remembered."

At the mention Hattie's mother, Mr. McKenna became excited. "Clara? Is Clara here?" He squinted at Hattie and reached out to touch her cheek. "Clara, is that you?"

We all grew silent. My heart went out to Hattie. How difficult it must be to know her father didn't recognize her.

"No, Daddy. It's me, Hattie."

His eyes seem to clear for a moment. "Hattie, dear?"

"Yes, Daddy."

"I thought I saw your mother." He lowered his head, his shoulders folding forward. "Just my mind playing tricks on me again."

Hattie stepped forward, a single tear rolling down her cheek as she looped her arm in her father's. "No, Daddy. Your mind's not playing tricks on you." She gracefully lifted her shoulders and turned to face the aisle. "Mama is here with us, Daddy. She *is* here."

That afternoon, as I stood by Cade's side and watched my friend take her wedding vows and begin her new life with Pete, I couldn't help but reflect on how much my own life had changed since my return to Cays Mill. In many ways, I'd grown more in these past two years than I ever had in the fifteen or so that I worked as an aid worker. Sure, that work was important, but not any more important, and certainly not more rewarding, than what I'd done since returning home: from helping my family in trouble, to opening my shop and now taking over the farm and preserving our family heritage. And to think that I'd stayed away from home for so long, on the run from my past, and unable to believe that I could ever be happy living in Cays Mill. Was I ever wrong! Never before had I known such happiness as I did now, here in my childhood home, surrounded by those I cherished and loved.

As Hattie and Pete uttered their "I do's," Cade reached for my hand, squeezing it softly. I turned and looked up to see the love in his eyes and knew, without a doubt, that this was exactly where I belonged. Oh, sure, I'd always have to deal with a few gossips and troublemakers and people like Frances and Maudy with their personal agendas. I knew issues and problems would always spring up unannounced. But at this moment in time, they simply didn't matter. For today, I could write my own headline: "Local Store Owner and New Peach Farmer Finds Happiness in Cays Mill, Georgia."

Recipes

Ginny Wiggins's Perfect Peach Cake

2 cans (15 ounces each) sliced peaches in heavy syrup,
   divided
⅓ cup vegetable oil
2 eggs
2 teaspoons vanilla extract
¼ cup sour cream
1 (15.25-ounce) box yellow cake mix

Preheat oven to 325 degrees.

Lightly butter and flour a 10-inch Bundt pan. Drain 1 can of peaches and discard the syrup. Arrange peach slices evenly on the bottom of the Bundt pan and set aside. With an electric mixer, beat together oil, eggs, vanilla, sour cream and the remaining can of peaches with syrup and any left-over peaches from the first can. Add the cake mix and continue to beat the mixture until it's smooth. Pour the batter into the prepared pan and bake for approximately 1 hour, or until cooked through. Cool completely. After cooled, loosen cake from the sides of the pan and invert onto a cake plate.

*Hattie's version: For a little extra kick, Hattie likes to sub-
stitute the peach syrup in the batter with ¼ cup of Peach
Jack or dark rum.

Mrs. Purvis's Peach Drop Cookies

1 cup (2 sticks) unsalted butter, softened
½ cup granulated sugar
1 egg
1 teaspoon vanilla
1 teaspoon salt
½ teaspoon baking powder
2¼ cups all-purpose flour
1 cup peach preserves

Preheat oven to 350 degrees.

Using an electric mixer, beat together butter and sugar
in a large bowl. Add egg and vanilla and beat until smooth.
Sift together salt, baking powder and flour and slowly add
to butter and sugar mixture until a stiff dough forms. Roll
dough into 1-inch balls and place on a cookie sheet. Use
thumb or the tip of a spoon to make a small indent in the
center of each ball. Using a spoon, drop a dollop of peach
preserves in each indent. Bake cookies for 8–10 minutes or
until they are slightly brown around the edges.

Makes approximately 3 dozen cookies.

Nola Mae's Peach Hot Sauce

6 fresh peaches, peeled and pitted
4 habanero peppers—seed for a milder sauce, or leave
    in seeds for more heat (wear gloves when handling)
½ onion
4 garlic cloves
1 lime, juiced
¼ cup apple cider vinegar
½ cup water
¾ cup honey

Combine all ingredients in a blender and blend until smooth. Transfer the mix to a pot and simmer on low heat for approximately one hour. Store leftover sauce in the refrigerator for up to one week.

*Remember to wear gloves when handling peppers and refrain from touching eyes.

    This is a great sauce for spicy chicken wings. Nola coats her fully cooked chicken wings in sauce and serves them with ranch dressing and celery sticks. Yum.

FROM BESTSELLING AUTHOR
Susan Furlong

PEACHES AND SCREAM

A Georgia Peach Mystery

In the first Georgia Peach Mystery, when murder threatens her family's orchard, Nola Harper is ready to pick out the killer and preserve the farm's reputation...

To help run the family peach farm during her parents' absence, Nola Mae Harper returns to her childhood home in Georgia. But she soon discovers that things back at the farm aren't exactly peachy when she stumbles upon a local businessman murdered among the peach trees. With suspicions and family tensions heating up faster than a cobbler in the oven, this sweet Georgia peach will have to prune through a list of murder suspects—before she too becomes ripe for the killer's picking...

"Ms. Furlong's turn-of-phrase is delightful, her characters are endearing, and the mystery will keep readers guessing until the very end. Loaded with Southern charm, sassy characters, and tantalizing recipes—a pure delight!"
—Ellery Adams, *New York Times* bestselling author

"Georgia belles can handle anything—including murder—as Susan Furlong proves in this sweet and juicy series debut."
—Sheila Connolly, *New York Times* bestselling author

Includes Recipes

Available wherever books are sold
or at penguin.com

Connect with Berkley Publishing Online!

For sneak peeks into the newest releases, news on all your favorite authors, book giveaways, and a central place to connect with fellow fans—

"Like" and follow Berkley Publishing!

facebook.com/BerkleyPub
twitter.com/BerkleyPub
instagram.com/BerkleyPub

BERKLEY | Penguin Random House